THE ANIMAL GIRL

Yellow Shoe Fiction
Michael Griffith, Series Editor

THE ANIMAL GIRL

Two Novellas and Three Stories

JOHN FULTON

Louisiana State University Press Baton Rouge

Published by Louisiana State University Press

Manufactured in the United States of America

An LSU Press Paperback Original
First printing

Designer: Michelle A. Neustrom
Typeface: Whitman, Gotham
Printer and binder: Edwards Brothers, Inc.

Library of Congress Cataloging-in-Publication Data

Fulton, John, 1967–
The animal girl : two novellas and three stories / John Fulton.
p. cm. — (Yellow shoe fiction)
"An LSU Press paperback original"—T.p. verso.
ISBN-13: 978-0-8071-3294-4 (pbk. : alk. paper)
1. United States—Social life and customs—21st century—Fiction. I. Title.
PS3606.U58A55 2007
813'.6—dc22

2007015679

These stories first appeared in journals. "Hunters" was published in *The Southern Review* (Autumn 2004), reprinted in *Pushcart Prize XXX: Best of the Small Presses* (Fall 2005), and selected as a distinguished story of 2004 in *The Best American Short Stories 2005*. "Real Grief" was published in *The Greensboro Review* (Fall 2004). "The Animal Girl" appeared in *Alaska Quarterly Review* (Fall 2005) and received a special mention in *Pushcart Prize XXXI: Best of the Small Presses*. "A Small Matter" was published in *Other Voices* (Fall/Winter 2005) and "The Sleeping Woman" appeared in *The Journal* (Spring 2007).

The paper in this book meets the guidelines for permanence and durability of the Committee on Production Guidelines for Book Longevity of the Council on Library Resources. ♾

For Zoë

CONTENTS

HUNTERS

Kate answered his personal ad in late summer, soon after she'd been told for the second time that she was dying. She had always thought of herself as shy, not the type even to peruse such ads. But the news had been jolting, if not altogether unexpected, and had allowed her to act outside her old ideas of herself.

The first time her doctor told her she would die had been two years before. The cancer had started in her left breast and moved to her brain. She'd had a mastectomy and undergone a full course of chemotherapy to no effect. A divorcée, she was close to only a few people: her sixteen-year-old daughter, Melissa, her widowed mother, who was now dead, and one good woman friend, all of whom she'd told. She'd worried about what to do with Melissa, then fourteen, whose father had been out of touch since he'd left them years before. And then, after worrying, weeping, raging, and undergoing the storm of insanity that, by all reports, was supposed to end in acceptance, she learned that her cancer had mysteriously retreated and that she would live. Her doctors hesitated to use the word "cured." Cancers such as hers were rarely, if ever, cured. Yet they could find no signs of carcinoma cells in her system. She returned to work, got her hair done, went on shopping sprees, and thought about the possibility of reconstructive surgery for her left breast. Even a nipple, her plastic surgeon had informed her, could be convincingly improvised. In trying to explain her restored health to her daughter, her coworkers, her friends, she could find no other word than "cured." And now, once again, the doctors were telling her she had tumors about the size of peas in her liver and spine. She would die in a matter of months.

The news silenced Kate. This time, she told no one.

She selected his ad because of its unthreatening tone. Others had intimidated her with their loud enthusiasm and confidence: "Young vital fifty-something looking for lady with love for life." Still others sounded sleazy—"Master in need of pet"—or psychotic, even murderous: "Quiet, mysterious Lone Ranger looking for that special horse to ride into the night." By contrast, his sounded distinctly meek: "Like books and munching popcorn in front of TV." He tended toward "shyness with a goofy edge." He sought "sex, but more, too. Tenderness without attachments." That caught her eye. She wanted sex. She wanted "tenderness without attachments." In the years since her diagnosis, she'd kept her maimed body to herself. Now a feeling of bodily coldness and desolation had come over her, and she wanted to be brought back to life. She wanted to be touched—maybe for one night, one week, one month.

Kate's daughter heard his message on the answering machine first. "There's a guy on the machine for you," she said when Kate got home from work. Melissa stood next to her in the kitchen while she played it. "Kate," a heavy male voice said, "Charles here. I look forward to meeting you. Gotta say I'm just a bit nervous. I don't know about you, but I've never done this before. Not to say that I don't want to. I do. I'm going on, aren't I? Sorry. You've got other messages to hear, I'm sure." He paused, and Melissa laughed. Kate wasn't sure what to make of this halting message, though she liked the fact that he was obviously nervous; his voice was nearly trembling. "I guess I should tell you what I look like. I'm tall and have a mustache. See you on Saturday."

"A mustache?" Melissa smiled suggestively. "I didn't know you were looking for someone."

"I'm not," Kate said. Her daughter had the wrong idea. She'd assumed Kate was searching for a companion, was healing and moving on with what would be a long life. It wasn't fair to leave her with false impressions, but Kate couldn't go through all the tears again. She wanted her privacy for now. "Don't, please, get any ideas."

"No ideas," Melissa said, laughing. "I think it's great. I think it's what you should be doing."

Kate hardly expected to be afraid. She took every precaution. She'd chosen a popular coffee shop, often crowded on Saturday afternoons, which seemed the safest time to meet a stranger. Ann Arbor was hardly a dangerous town. It was clean and wealthy and civic-minded, she reminded herself. It was an especially hot September day, over ninety degrees, but the air-conditioning in the café was crisp and bracing. Kate selected a table in a sunny corner, beside two elderly women wearing pastel sweat suits and gleaming white orthopedic tennis shoes; they made Kate feel still safer. One of the silver-haired women was babysitting an infant and kept her hand on a baby carriage, now and then looking down into it with a clownish face. Students sat at other tables and read books. A toddler ran past Kate, its father in pursuit.

She heard him before she saw him. "Are you Kate?"

She stood, and he presented her so quickly with a red carnation that it startled her—the redness of it, the sudden, bright presence of it in her hand—and she giggled.

"I'm Charles," he said. He wore nice slacks, a button-up shirt, and a blazer; and was suffering—his forehead glistened—from the extremely hot day. His face was thin, his bony nose and cheekbones complex and not immediately attractive. But it was his hair that surprised her most. Thick, gray, nicely combed: it was the hair of a pleasant, not unattractive older man, a man in his fifties, as his ad had said. Kate hadn't dated for more than six years; her divorce and then her illness had made sure of that. And now, at forty-five, she was shocked to think that this middle-aged man might be her romantic prospect.

When they sat down, Kate noticed the rapid thudding of her heart. She picked up her coffee and watched it tremble in her hand before she took a sip. For some reason, the table was shuddering beneath her. "I'm sorry," Charles said, putting a hand on his knee to stop it from jiggling. "I'm terrible at handling my nerves. I'm no good at meeting people. It's not one of my skills." He took a folded white handkerchief from his back pocket and neatly wiped the sweat from his forehead.

His obvious fear assured Kate that he was harmless and maybe even kind. "I meant to say thank you for the flower." She looked down at the wilted carnation.

"It's not very original of me."

When she picked her coffee up now, her hand was steady. Clearly one of them needed to be calmer. "I liked what you said in your ad about tenderness," Kate said. "That's why I called."

"I'm not usually this adventurous." He looked over his shoulder and then at her again. "I'm still getting over a divorce. I guess that's why I'm so jittery about all this."

Things weren't going well, Kate knew. And for some reason, she wanted them to go well with this timid man, and so she continued to be brave, to say what she was thinking. "'Tenderness without attachments.' That sounded nice. None of the other ads talked about that. I thought that was original."

He wiped his forehead with his handkerchief again. "I just don't want anything serious. But I don't want it to feel, you know, like just an exchange of . . . of . . ."

"Bodies?" Kate said. He sat back in his chair, as if struck, and she felt her face deepen in color. The thought that they were here, in large part, for the prospect of sex was out on the table now. It was a bold and raw motive, for which neither of them, middle-aged and awkward, seemed well suited. But the awkwardness and shame were refreshing, too; Kate hadn't blushed in years.

"I guess," he said. He patted his mustache gently, as if drawing composure from it. "Not that we have to ever get there. We might just become friends. We might just enjoy each other's company."

"Sure," she said, though in fact she felt an unexpected pang of rejection. Was this skittish man already running from her bed?

She changed the subject then, telling him about her job as a loan officer, a serious job that had always suited her rather too serious character; her love for fresh food and cooking; her sixteen-year-old daughter, who right now was a little too absorbed in her boyfriend. "I wish my kid would fall in love," Charles said, smiling. "He's angry. His mother gave him up when she gave me up. I understand the anger. I'm angry, too. But there's something mean in him that I'd never seen before this." Ryan, Charles's son, had a mohawk that changed colors—purple, yellow, blue—at least once a month and a lizard tattoo on his forearm. Charles owned an office furniture and supply store. "It sounds boring, I know. But I actually sort of enjoy it."

It did sound boring to Kate, who was much more interested to learn that Charles enjoyed hunting. It hardly seemed like something this concerned father and furniture salesman would do. "You kill things?" Kate asked. "You enjoy it?"

He confessed that he did, though he didn't hunt large game. "Deer and elk are beautiful animals and too much of a mess. Field dressing a deer can take the better part of a morning."

"Field dressing?" she asked.

"Gutting them, removing the organs. You need to do that soon after a kill, before you cure and slaughter it. It's a real mess. I used to hunt large game as a boy with my dad. It's not for me anymore." He shook his head in a way that allowed Kate to picture this mess: the blood, the entrails, the carcass. "I just hunt upland birds now: pheasant, woodcocks, grouse. It's not so much the killing as it is the stalk, the chase. Being out in the open air, seeing the land."

"But you do kill them?"

He nodded. "I suppose you're against that sort of thing."

Kate thought about it a moment. "Not really. Though I'd say I'm not for it either. I find it odd."

Two hours later, when they walked out of the café, a hot wind was blowing down Washington Street, and the concrete beneath her felt as if it were baking through her thin-soled shoes. She felt lightheaded, buzzed from three cups of coffee, and nervous about what would happen next, how they'd say good-bye. Would they kiss? She couldn't imagine it and was relieved when he reached out with his sweaty hand and shook hers softly. "I enjoyed meeting you," he said. A train of running children shot between them, and they both took a step back. She half thought he'd turn away then and walk off, and she'd have to wonder why he put her through two hours of conversation about his divorce, his son, about slaughtering and field dressing deer. But then he asked her if he could call again, and she couldn't—hard as she tried—suppress a smile and the obvious eagerness in her voice when she said, "I'd like that."

* * *

Kate didn't feel sick yet. She'd felt healthy now for months, light of body, energetic, strong. She tried not to think of the fatigue and pain to come. But the week the heat wave lifted and the first cooler days of fall arrived, Kate succumbed to fear.

She'd been approving a loan for a pregnant couple when it happened. The woman wore a purple maternity dress that said "Mommy" at the place where her belly showed most. She carried her weight with an intimidating, ungraceful physicality, and her face glowed with acne and oil and a smile that was almost aggressive. The woman's scent of flowers and sweat filled Kate's small office, the air suddenly feeling close and tropical. She kept saying "we" in a way that left Kate feeling bereft and excluded. "*We're* looking forward to our first home. This is just what *we* need right now." The woman looked down at the roundness where she had just placed her hands. "Three more months," she said. The thoughts came to Kate before she could anticipate them. Would she be bedridden by then? Would she be gone? Could she already feel the beginning of fatigue? Would the symptoms she'd experienced last time—the headaches, the facial paralysis, the double vision—begin that very day?

Claiming illness, she left work early that afternoon only to discover Melissa and Mark in her bathroom. The shower had been on, which was no doubt why they hadn't heard Kate climbing the stairs. When she walked into her room, Kate saw steam curling out the open bathroom door before she saw her sixteen-year-old daughter, naked save for the pink strip of her Calvin Klein panties, balancing on her knees and giving pleasure with too much skill, too much expertise, to her standing boyfriend. She took it in for a moment: the bodies moving together in practiced motion, the flayed brown and white of tan lines, her daughter's breasts, mouth, and hands, the curve of her back. "Melissa," Kate said.

Melissa stopped, and Mark grabbed his crotch and turned his shuddering backside to Kate. "Mom!" Melissa's naked body lunged at the door and slammed it in Kate's face. "I can't believe you, Mom!"

"Put your clothes on now!" Kate shouted at the door.

"We can't," Melissa said. "Our clothes are all out there."

Kate turned then and noticed the storm-strewn boxer shorts, Levi's, soiled white socks, Melissa's blouse and bra, even her pink Keds. Why were Melissa's shoes on Kate's bed? She picked them up, tossed them to the floor, and then started crying. She hardly knew why, though it had something to do with the pregnant woman and the surprise of her daughter, her body so womanly, full in the hips and breasts, more beautiful than Kate had ever been, engaged, absorbed in what Kate could only think of now as an adult activity. Her loss of control left her feeling even angrier at Melissa. "I want to talk to you both downstairs in five minutes!" she shouted.

After doing her best to cover up all signs of tears, Kate sat across from Melissa and Mark in the living room. They had a messy, post-sex look about them, their hair mussed and their clothes, if secure and in place, somehow looser on their bodies. "I don't know what to say," Kate began.

"We're being careful," Melissa said. "I'm on the pill, Mom. I've had my first pelvic exam. We've both been tested. I'm doing everything I should be doing."

"You were in *my* bathroom," Kate said. These words made Mark, a tall, good-looking boy, broad in the shoulders and not usually meek, look down at the floor.

"You have the large shower," Melissa said. "We were going to clean things up. You weren't supposed to be home yet."

"Your clothes were all over *my* bed. Your shoes were on *my* bed."

Melissa smirked and flashed her blue eyes at Kate. This was her most charming and practiced gesture, and though it usually made Kate fall instantly in love with her daughter, she resisted it now. "Well," Melissa said, "we were in a hurry."

Kate felt her face go red. "You should have been studying."

"We still have time to study," Melissa said.

"You need all the time you can get. You have to apply to schools and prepare for the college boards."

"That's next year," Melissa said.

Kate took a deep breath. She was about to do something she had been afraid to do for months. "I don't think what you did was wrong. I'm more concerned about the irresponsibility of neglecting the rest of life so that you could do . . ." Kate couldn't name what they'd done, nor could she keep pretending to herself that it didn't bother her. How could her child, her teenaged daughter, take on this responsibility? How could she lie on her back in a doctor's office with her legs in stirrups so that she could, as safely as possible, give herself to a boy? A boy who made her lose so much presence of mind that she would throw her dirty shoes on her mother's bed, use her shower, and maybe even afterwards use her bed. Kate had terrifying visions of what would become of these two after she was gone. They'd end up in ten months with a baby and stuck in subsidized housing somewhere. It was possible. But what frightened Kate most was the fact that she herself was responsible for pushing these kids—and they certainly were no more than kids—into each other's arms with her own desperation, her own intensity.

Two years before, the first time Kate thought she was dying, she'd panicked. She couldn't sleep. She couldn't stand the aloneness, the waiting, the nights of insomnia. Kate clung to Melissa and made her go everywhere with her—the doctor's office, the grocery store, the post office, the accountant's. It didn't take long for Melissa to disappear. She joined the swim team, the debate club, and the school newspaper. In the meantime, Kate kept dying. She suffered from headaches, double vision, loss of balance so extreme that she'd have to lean against the nearest wall to stay upright. Kate saw Melissa only in the late evenings when she'd sit at the kitchen table, her hair stringy from chlorine, wolfing down cereal, toast, and cookies. And so when Kate woke at night and the hours alone in the dark became intolerable, she walked down the hallway to her daughter's room, gently moved aside the large stuffed bear her then fourteen-year-old child slept with, and got into her bed. She tried not to cry, but failed. Melissa said nothing, just stiffened and moved to the edge. At first light, Kate quietly got up and returned to her room.

Kate slept with her daughter as often as three times a week. She slept with her until one night she opened the door and saw in the dimness a boy next to Melissa. She had met Mark only once before then and knew that he was on the swim team and played tenor saxophone for Central High's jazz ensemble. His thick curly hair was on the pillow, his muscular back was turned to her, and his bare arm was wrapped around Melissa, protecting her from her sick mother.

After that, Kate stayed away from her daughter's room. She might have put an end to Mark's sleepovers if she hadn't been sick and, later, if Melissa and Mark hadn't cooled off soon after the cancer disappeared. Mark no longer slept over, so far as Kate knew. But her cancer was back, and she could only expect the worst when her daughter found out. So she was finally going to put her foot down, never mind that what bothered her most was not so much their having sex—she had assumed as much before this afternoon—as her having seen the sex, and having seen Melissa's dirty tennis shoes—that image returned now and made her wince—on her clean bed. Thrown, tossed with no concern whatever for her mother. "You two need to see less of each other," she said. "It would be better for both of you. You can go out on Friday and Saturday nights. But weekday afternoons and nights are off limits. Got it?"

Melissa looked at Kate with childish fury. "No," she said.

"Don't say no to me." Kate hardly recognized herself. She'd always been tolerant and open with her daughter. She'd always laid out options, pros and cons, and let her daughter make her own decisions.

Melissa shook her head. "No. I'm saying no. We're not going to do it." She stood, took Mark forcefully by the hand, and led him up to her bedroom, where she slammed the door. Kate should have done something. She should have stood at the foot of the stairs and yelled. She should have gone up there and shouted through the door. But she was too tired to go on playing the role of parent. In any case, she wouldn't be a parent much longer.

Her second meeting with Charles took place at seven in the morning at a small restaurant across from the university hospital's cancer center, where, among other procedures, she'd had her mammogram done seven times in one sitting. Kate had wanted to suggest another breakfast place, but she kept quiet. She didn't want to have to explain herself. Not yet. A line of scarlet sunrise had just begun to wipe out the last few morning stars when they stepped out of the cold. All the same, waiting to be seated, Kate felt the presence of the black glass façade across the street and couldn't help remembering the pink walls of the waiting booth where she'd spent almost eight hours with plastic pads stuck to her breasts. Only a floor above the mammogram clinic, she would lie on her back weeks later while a physician's assistant slid a needle deep between two upper lumbar vertebrae to draw out the spinal fluid in which, it turned out, carcinoma cells were actively dividing. She was told to expect double vision, speech impairment, dizziness, partial paralysis, and any number of random sensations due to the tumor that was growing in her brain. And then there was the chemotherapy, the woman named Meg who'd died in the waiting room while reading *Vogue*. It was hardly an appropriate magazine for a cancer ward, Kate had been thinking when Meg slumped over in her chair and stopped breathing. Kate was amazed at her calm as she broke Meg's fall, sat her upright, and held her in her chair until someone arrived and took her away.

Once she and Charles sat across from each other in a booth, she was able to forget the hospital. A sheet of Levolor-sliced sun fell over their table, and billows of steam rose from their coffee cups in the brightness. He was jumpy, tapping his fingers against his cup, then running them through his hair. She was already getting used to the angularity of his face and finding it vaguely attractive. His blue eyes she noticed for the first time—faint, shallow—after the waitress set their menus down. "Aren't you nervous?" he asked.

She wasn't, and she told him so.

"I am," he said, and she could hear it in his voice. "Doesn't it bother you to see a grown man afraid?"

"Apparently not." She laughed, reached across the table, and took his hand for the first time. But when he didn't loosen to her touch, she let him go.

The next week, she dropped into his furniture store just before closing. Charles seemed to have a great deal more courage as he walked briskly through the endless rows of desks, filing cabinets, and computer tables to meet her. "Welcome," he said, smiling, at ease in his suit and tie. He led her around and made her sit in multiple styles of waiting-room chairs and ergonomically designed stools for typists and receptionists. The repetition and sameness of objects—chair after chair after chair—spooked her a little. "You think it's terrible," he said. "What I do."

She denied it at first. Then said, "It does seem a little . . . lonely. All these human objects without the humans."

"You want to see lonely?" he said. He walked her into the back: a gray, dimly lit storage facility, in the middle of which stood a forklift surrounded by towers of boxes. The place was remarkably vacant of warmth and life, and a soft roar of wind and emptiness seemed to hum at its center.

She admired his comfort here, his sense of dominion. "I don't mind it. It's quiet. It's like going to the park. It's an escape."

Later that week they strolled through the arboretum, where the trees had begun to turn and where they lingered beside a glassy, shallow stretch of the Huron River, the pink, unmarked evening sky laid out over its mirror. Two hippie kids in loose clothing sat on a log, holding each other, kissing, giggling. A muddy-colored dog with a red handkerchief knotted around its neck leapt into the river and began drinking. When Kate took Charles's hand and pulled herself close to him, he was trembling. And somehow, just after Kate kissed his cheek lightly, she caught it, too; a rush of fear shook her. She was breathing shallowly when Charles bent down and kissed her on the lips. "I hope that was all right," he said.

When she nodded, he seemed immensely relieved, his step lighter now as they walked hand in hand, swinging their linked arms, up a dirt path until they came to a clearing in the trees. Startled, a deer sprinted through the high grass, dove into the trees, and was gone. In the orange evening light, Charles looked larger, less meek, and Kate couldn't help wondering what this gentle man would be like with a gun. "What's it like to kill something?" she asked.

"You might not like me as much if I told you the truth."

Kate laughed and squeezed his hand. "I promise I'll still like you."

"OK," Charles said. "It's thrilling. It's why you go out there. It's the fun part."

"It's fun to kill?" If she didn't like him less, it still wasn't the most pleasant answer, nor one she understood.

"Perhaps 'fun' isn't exactly the right word."

On their walk back, the temperature dropped sharply, and Kate was shivering so violently that she had to wonder if her vulnerability to the cold had to do with her illness. Was she weaker than she'd suspected? When they parked in front of Kate's house, she kissed him once, but pulled away when he wanted to continue. "I should tell you something," she said, still shivering. The dark inside the car, the fact that she could see only the outline of his face, made it easier to lie to him. "I'm recovering from cancer. Breast," she said, stopping so that odd word stood alone. "Recovered, I mean. I wouldn't mention it, but I need to tell you that I have a scar."

"A scar?" he said.

"I had a mastectomy. My left breast." She hated the feeling of shame that accompanied what she had just said. It was merely a fact, and she should have had the presence of mind to treat it as such.

There was a pause before he said, "I'm sorry."

Kate couldn't see the expression on his face, but she sensed that something was different between them. An ease, an excitement was gone. "Does that change things?" she asked.

Again, he took time in answering. "I don't think so."

"You don't think so?" The anger in her voice half surprised her. She didn't know him well enough to be angry with him.

"It's just that . . ." He stopped himself and reformulated his thought. "This was supposed to be a light thing. No commitment. Nothing serious."

"What does this have to do with commitment?"

"I don't know," he said. Then he bumbled out, "It seems serious. It seems . . ."

"All right," she said. She got out of his car, and before she'd closed the front door behind her, she heard him say, "I'll call you."

Inside, she found Melissa and Mark on the couch watching a movie in the dark. It was a school night, and they were openly defying the rule she'd set down. She turned the lights on, and they looked at her, squinting in the brightness. "Mark has to leave now." Her anger was too pronounced, too obviously out of proportion. Their response to it was to remain frozen in each other's arms. Kate wanted to throw something at them—a shoe, a book, even her purse would have worked. "I said now," Kate said. Mark finally sat up and rushed to put his shoes on.

"Did something happen on your date?" Melissa asked.

"I didn't have a date."

She expected a fight from Melissa. But instead her daughter sat up slowly and kept her eyes cautiously on Kate.

Charles called all week and left pleas on the answering machine that Kate tried her best to ignore. He was blunt. He stuttered and repeated himself. He admitted that he'd been thinking of her. He regretted the words he'd spoken that night. "I'm calling from the back of the store," he said in one message. "From the warehouse phone. You were right. It is lonely back here." In another, he became almost desperate. "I guess I just miss you. I hope I'm not saying too much. I realize this is just an answering machine. I realize that I'm begging." He sounded as hurt and alone as she had felt in the car that night. Nonetheless, she was done with him, until he made what was obviously his final call, the sad bass-tone of resignation in his voice. "I'm sorry things didn't work out," he said. When she picked up the phone, he began once again to express his regrets, and because she couldn't listen to one more simultaneously rambling and halting apology, she said, "OK, Charles. Apology accepted."

He wanted to see her as soon as possible. That afternoon he and his son, Ryan, had planned to shoot skeet at the gun club. And so Kate ended up on the edge of town, shouldering a shotgun for the first time in her life and wearing wax earplugs as she blasted away at a "clay pigeon," a little black disk, and tried to follow the instructions Charles shouted out at her to lead the pigeon by at least a foot. The gun club was in the center of an abandoned field, which looked dead, yellow, and already ravaged by winter. It was a gray day, the air like white smoke, and Kate was surprised by the pleasing and substantial weight of the weapon in her hands, the delicious, earthy odors of cordite and gunpowder after each blast, the sense—there was no mistaking it—of power and control the weapon gave her when she finally obliterated her target. She did so twice, then three times, awed as the disk disintegrated in the air. Behind her, a small boy of about ten, who wore a camouflage baseball cap and chewed a huge wad of pink bubble gum, pressed a button that released the pigeon every time she shouted the word "Pull!" She handed the shotgun, its barrel hot as a stovetop, to Charles and stood behind him—"Always stand behind the shooter," he'd told her earlier in a grave voice—and watched now as he meticulously hit pigeon after pigeon. She hadn't anticipated her excitement at seeing Charles's skill, the quickness with which he trained the barrel on the target and destroyed it. His arms seemed thicker, more powerful, his shoulders broader. There was no sign of weakness, of hesitancy or doubt, and she was awed to see this unexpected competence in a man who, as she was seeing that afternoon, could barely keep his son in check.

Ryan was a tall kid with deep-set eyes that seemed on the edge of rage every time he looked at Kate. His mohawk, high and stiff and died salmon pink, and his multiply-pierced ears, lined with studs and hoops, made him seem menacing, especially when he took the shotgun in hand. On the way out to the club, when Charles had stopped for gas and left Kate and Ryan in the car alone, the boy resisted her every attempt at conversation, and then, after she had given up, he smiled at her and said, "Are you fucking my dad yet?"

"I'm not going to answer that question."

"None of my business, right?" he said. "You've probably already seen that he's a wimp. He lets people do whatever they want to him. He just takes it."

"I'm not that kind of person," Kate said.

Ryan nodded. "Sure you're not."

Whenever Ryan missed his target that afternoon, he cringed and swore, sometimes under his breath, though more often out loud. "Fuck me," he half shouted once, to which Charles merely responded with a warning glance. Kate would have sent him to the car at the very least. Ryan had certainly been right about his father: He did seem willing to take just about anything.

Kate was relieved when they dropped Ryan at home later and went out to a pleasant dinner with wine. When late in the meal Charles sighed and said, "I'm too easy on Ryan. I let him get away with everything," Kate lied.

"I'm not so sure that's wrong," she said. "Every kid needs a different approach."

He shook his head. "My motives aren't that noble. I just want him to like me again."

They joined hands across the table now. Kate felt terrible for this worried father, this man who just wanted to be liked, and her pity quickly transformed into attraction. She knew already that she wanted to sleep with him that night. She was blushing when she stammered out an invitation. "You can say no," she added.

But he didn't say no. Kate hardly knew how she'd imagined herself behaving then, though she hoped that passion and desire would take over, that she'd know what to do. Instead, she and Charles waited for the bill in utter silence, which persisted as they drove toward Kate's place, the black trees and the proper Victorian homes rising on either side of them in the dark. "Let's talk," Kate said.

"OK," Charles said. But they didn't say another word until they stood facing each other across Kate's bed. For a change, Kate was relieved that Melissa had once again defied her and was out that night. "We don't have to do this," she said.

"I want to," he said, though he didn't sound as if he did.

When she came out of the bathroom wearing a man's white T-shirt that fell to her thighs, she didn't feel at all attractive. Charles sat on the edge of the bed in his tank top and boxer shorts, his legs skinnier, paler, more covered in thick, dark hair than she'd imagined. His arms were crossed, as if protecting himself from her. "I don't care about your scar," he said.

Kate knew he'd meant to say something that would sound nicer, more romantic. "I want to keep this on," she said, pointing to her shirt.

In the dark, everything became a little easier. He began to kiss her—her face, her neck, her arms—all the while carefully avoiding the place of her absent breast. His mustache tickled. She found his erection without meaning to. It was just suddenly there in her hand, and she couldn't help but think of the shotgun she'd been handling earlier that day. Guns and penises. She let out a silly, adolescent laugh. "Is something wrong?" he asked.

"I haven't done this in so long." Now that she held him, she didn't quite know what to do with him. She tried the very act she'd seen her daughter perform only weeks before, but she was indelicate and Charles let out a whelp of pain and then began to laugh.

"Is this all right?" he asked when he finally mounted her.

Her left thigh began cramping, but she nodded as the pain gathered into a dense ball. "It's all right," she said. His caution, his concern moved her. If not passionate, it was deeply tender, just as he had promised, and she lifted herself a little to kiss his shoulders, his neck and cheeks. It took him a while—Kate could have hoped for a briefer first time—but as soon as he was finished, he rolled over and said, "You didn't, did you?"

"I will next time."

"I'm sorry."

"Don't be. It was . . ." She paused, looking for a word, and when she finally said it, the fullness and enthusiasm in her voice embarrassed her, "Lovely." She felt a deep and heavy laziness of body. Their legs were tangled. Off in the darkness beside her, the fingers of her hand caressed Charles's neck. She had forgotten for a moment what was happening to her. She was dying, she remembered now. Again. For the second time. And for some reason, it was easy to know. She wasn't afraid, even as she was certain that the fear would return soon. For now she lay next to a man who must have been as spent and physically oblivious as she since he let out an enormous, accidental belch. "I'm sorry," he said.

Half-asleep, Kate giggled lazily. "I'm happy," she said.

The next morning, she was dizzy and experiencing double vision. In her bathroom mirror, she saw that her left eye had fallen toward the lower outside corner of its socket. She looked monstrous, and she wanted Charles, who lay slumbering in her bed, out of the house. When she prodded him awake, he rolled over and smiled at her, seeming to expect the kisses and friendliness of a lover. His breath was less than pleasant and his hair was lopsided. She kept a hand over her eye, and when he asked about it, she said something about an infection and eye drops that he didn't question. "I've got to get to work," she said, after which she stood by him while he dressed.

"Is something wrong?" he asked, standing on the porch in a warmish rainy morning. One of his shoes was still untied, and his shirt was partially untucked. He waited in the drizzle until Kate gave him a peck on the cheek. "Something's wrong," he said. "Tell me what's wrong."

"I'll call you," she said, and then closed the door.

Kate stayed home from work for the next few days. With the house empty, she thought of Charles more than she wanted to: his ease with a shotgun, his pale, gangly nakedness, his postcoital belch, his laughter and patience in her bed. He left four messages on the machine, but she didn't call him until two days later. It was three in the morning, and she'd woken with a dull, throbbing pressure in her head that verged on pain. She was hot, drenched in sweat—a side effect, her doctor had explained, of rapidly growing tumors—and opened her windows, but the breeze moving in the curtain sent shadows rushing through the dark of her room—walls of blackness falling on top of her. "Kate," he said sleepily.

"Would you consider coming over here . . . now?"

He was in her bed in fewer than twenty minutes. She could only cuddle that night, and he seemed more than happy to oblige her. "This isn't going to be serious, right?" she asked.

He kissed her ear. "OK."

"It will be pleasant. It will go until one of us says enough," she said.

He moved in closer, sealing their bodies together. "Sure. I mean, unless we decide otherwise."

"I'm pretty sure that I won't decide otherwise."

"That's fine," Charles said.

On subsequent nights, they returned to their lovemaking, vigorous, athletic, more skilled and certain. They did everything they could think of with the eagerness of discovery and the fumbling skill of those who'd done it before. Charles took her from behind with an enthusiastic brutishness—his arm hooked around her neck and his pelvis pounding into her—that left her feeling pleasantly ravished. Kate remembered how to come, straddling Charles and using her thigh muscles to focus on the pleasure. Charles became, at times, almost too fearless, letting out loud howls so that Kate put a hand over his mouth and whispered, "My daughter will hear." In moments of physical exuberance, Charles tried to lift her shirt, but she grabbed his arm forcefully and pushed it back down.

After a week or so of adventurous nights together, Kate was exhausted. Her body felt leaden, fatigued, not exactly sick, but not well either. She wanted closeness, not pleasure, which Charles sensed easily. He spooned her, the weight of his arm folded over her—a good, blanketing weight—and fell asleep more often than not hours before Kate, who lay awake watching the lunar sweep of headlights pass through the room. Charles spoke out of his dreams, which were sometimes comforting, as when he asked repeatedly for more gravy, please. "Delicious," he would say. And sometimes terrifying. "Stay away!" he shouted one night. "Away! Away!" When she woke him, he looked at her, and she saw the terror pass from his face as soon as he recognized her. "Love," he said sleepily, and then held on to her for a desperate and needy moment before he fell back asleep.

Toward the end of October, Kate arrived home from work one afternoon to find her daughter in tears at the kitchen table. Sitting across from her, Mark looked pale and unwell, and Kate assumed that he had finally broken her daughter's heart. Kate had had a good day and was hardly prepared to deal with this sadness. She'd felt strong, invigorated right through this sunny, slightly chilly afternoon. At lunch she had seen a group of schoolchildren dressed as witches and vampires grasping a rope as their teachers herded them safely across Huron Street. Walking home, she took note of the fat pumpkins, gapped-toothed and grinning on porch steps, and thought of this holiday that contemplated darkness and fear and death. She'd felt both aware of and pleasantly removed from what was about to happen to her. And now, facing her weeping daughter, she was about to rush upstairs and leave the kids to themselves when Melissa lifted an open letter from the table. "You didn't tell me. You didn't say anything."

"Is that my mail?" Kate asked, setting her briefcase down. From the torn envelope on the table, Kate knew it must be a letter from the hospice where she had decided she would die, in part to give Melissa her own safe space at home.

"You lied."

"I think Mark should go home," Kate said calmly. "I think you and I need to talk."

"He's not going." Kate's daughter reached over and grasped Mark's hand.

Mark looked shaken, uncertain. He wore a Mountain Dew T-shirt, a new pair of bright blue Nike running shoes, and the same sort of blue sweatpants that Melissa was wearing. They had just returned from swim-team practice and had that sallow, washed-out look of kids who've been in water for hours. A box of Raisin Bran was out on the table, and they'd no doubt eaten two or three bowls each before Melissa had opened the letter. This time of the afternoon, with the kids gorging on toast and cereal, then sitting in front of the TV or working on homework, could be Kate's favorite part of the day. She enjoyed the house most when they were there, when she felt their presence, which was another reason she never should have put her foot down weeks before. "Should I go, Mrs. Harrison?" Mark asked.

"He's staying," Melissa said again.

"He might want to go," Kate said.

Mark looked timidly over at Melissa. "Maybe I should go." Melissa shook her head and pulled him so forcefully toward her that Mark had to scoot his chair over. "I think I should go."

"Please just . . . ," Melissa growled, unable to finish her sentence.

Kate sat down at the table. "I didn't tell you because I needed some privacy for a while. I needed to get used to it again."

"How long?" Melissa asked.

"Maybe three months. Maybe six. The doctors can't be certain."

"You don't look sick," Melissa said suspiciously.

"I don't feel very sick. Yet."

"Maybe it won't happen. It didn't happen last time."

"Maybe."

Sitting beside Melissa, Mark seemed to squirm in his chair. He had no freedom to move with Melissa clinging to him, and Kate saw how intensely he wanted to escape. She sensed that this second occasion of her dying might be too much for him. She hardly knew if it was a selfish and calculating impulse or true desperation, the better motive by far, that made her say, "You can spend as much time with Mark as you like, Melissa. He can even sleep over now and then. I just ask that you not disappear this time."

Melissa's gaze was cruel. "You lied to me."

And because Kate couldn't fight, especially over this, she got up and left the room.

Kate was not surprised when her daughter disappeared after that. She came home from school late and left first thing in the morning, hopping into Mark's car. She stopped talking to Kate, or only talked to her to say the most prosaic things. "Got to go. Be home later." Kate could do nothing but watch as her daughter grew distant, watch and hope that Melissa's fury would subside.

It was around this time that Kate began testing Charles, though she was only vaguely aware of doing so. One morning when they woke up together, Kate kissed him and then asked him to shave his mustache. "I'd like to see you without it. It tickles a little."

He touched it contemplatively before retreating to her bathroom. After a moment, she heard his electric razor, which he'd brought over hesitantly the week before and only after asking her permission. "It's an extra," he had said. "I have another at home." As if that somehow made a difference. Kate had smiled and said teasingly, "As long as you don't think it's too dangerous." When he came back out of the bathroom now, his face was leaner than she'd expected, though she knew she'd get used to it. What surprised her even more was how willingly, how quickly he'd done as she asked.

She made other requests, too. She asked him to part his hair on the left side rather than in the middle, and he did it. She asked him to wear red, the color that suited him best, and discouraged him from ever wearing gray, which washed him out. She woke him at two, three, four in the morning and made him leave without explaining herself. She called him at the same hours and pressured him to come over and get into bed with her. He came and he left when she asked. And though she wasn't always sure why she made her requests, she was sure that Ryan had been right about her. She was taking advantage. She was pushing him around.

The first weekend in November, Charles took Kate hunting. He'd proposed that she hike with him through the woods while he hunted, and had been surprised when she insisted on participating. She left a note for Melissa, to whom she hadn't talked in days. "Gone hunting. Will return on Sunday." Kate felt startled by the note even as she wrote it: how odd, how unlike herself it sounded. Would Melissa laugh when she read it? Would she worry?

Charles picked her up at five on Saturday morning in what he called his "rig": a huge pickup with a camper on the back. It was dark out, freezing, and Kate felt frail and groggy as she locked the front door and pushed herself through the cold air. The truck was warm and smelled of boot leather, wet wool, and another odor that Kate could identify now as guns—oil and cordite. A mist clung to the roads and made the dark houses on Washington Street appear caught in spools of web. Kate struggled to stay awake and talk to Charles, but she felt unwell, and the pull of sleep and the pleasure of succumbing to it were too much.

She woke in a little town called Mio, where Charles bought her a hunting license from a large man who wore an orange hat with earflaps and smiled at Kate. "Wish I could get my wife to hunt. But she won't have it."

"I thought I'd try it this once," Kate said. She felt a little strange and improper, going out into the woods to kill things.

Outside Mio, they entered a tract of forest that Charles knew well enough to navigate without a map. By ten that morning, Kate had donned a hunting vest, its pockets weighted down by twenty-gauge shells, and was cradling a shotgun and trampling over a forest floor carpeted with bark and dead leaves. Charles was twenty yards to her right. Their quarry was grouse, and Kate was tense, conscious of wanting to shoot something, though she didn't necessarily want to kill it. The day was sunless and cold enough that Kate could see her breath. When the first bird rose in front of her, the muscular beating of its wings startled her. She shot and missed, after which

Charles took the bird down in a cloud of feathers. The grouse, dark gray and nearly the size of a chicken, was still alive, driving itself into the ground as it flapped one wing. Charles ran to it, took its head in hand, and snapped its neck with a flick of his wrist, then stuffed it in his game pouch. "You want to do that right away," he said. "There's no reason to let it suffer." How simple, how quick it was. It sickened Kate even as it excited her, even as it made her want to shoot more surely the next time.

The second bird that got up, she missed, as did Charles, who shot after her, and she was relieved to see the bird soar above the tree line and escape. But early that afternoon a grouse burst out of a tree no more than five feet in front of her. She was quick to train the barrel on it. The bird went down and immediately began its broken dance, hopping on a leg, leaping into the air and falling again. She ran to it, then stood back when she saw the ripped-open wing, the bleeding flesh to which bits of feather stuck. Charles reached her and offered to finish the panicky creature off. "I can do it," Kate said. She grabbed it by the neck, struck by its weight, its absolute terror as its one good wing insisted on struggle. She tried to flick her wrist, as she had seen Charles do, but the bird was stubbornly heavy, one grayish, unreadable eye trained on her as she flopped its too-solid body about. Feathers fell to her feet. Blood flecked her forearm and left dark spots on her jeans. The bird's stupid determination enraged her, and she tightened her grasp around its neck and flung it down like a heavy bag of laundry. She felt its neck snap, as distinct as a pencil breaking. Finally, it was dead, and Kate felt guilty for the sense of accomplishment killing it had given her. She had overcome the bird. She was the stronger. And this feeling was overshadowed only by her desire to clean herself up, to get rid of the mess, the blood and feathers, of her stupid bird.

That night, Charles opened a nice bottle of Cabernet and prepared a modest feast of wild rice, zucchini squash, and grouse breasts, which were thankfully small. Kate's appetite was poor. Though the bright interior of the camper was warm and cozy, she battled a nearly irresistible fatigue that seemed to arrive earlier every evening now.

Charles offered a toast to her hunting skills. "To your successful first day out," he said. "We'll do this again."

He was glowing, overjoyed by the success of the day, by the belief that there would be other such days, and Kate felt the urgent need to dim his happiness. But it was too late to tell him with any justice what he should have already known. "I'm not sure," she said. "Hunting is a little dirty for me."

It stormed that night, wind and rain pounding the thin camper walls. In bed, the darkness was all-encompassing, pitch-black as it could only be away from city lights. Kate could see nothing in it. No sign of Charles beside her. No sign of her own hand in front of her. And as the wind continued to rage, Kate thought of the grouse out there clenched like fists in the shelter of trees and covered over in the same darkness that seemed to be smothering her. She felt his touch then, his soft fingers settling over the place where her breast was gone. It was not a sexual touch. It was tender. It wanted only closeness. And when Kate tried to remove his hand, he held her more firmly, and soon she let her hand rest over his, let herself be held in a darkness that felt safer now.

In November, Kate found it almost impossible to work through a full day at the bank. She was having pressure headaches that made even light physical activity unthinkable. Her double vision and dizziness worsened. At times, her left hand stopped functioning. She couldn't make the fingers close, and so for hours at a time she would keep this hand in her lap and hope no one noticed. To a degree, these signs of her illness relieved Kate. Certainty was good. It precluded hope. It precluded delusion and disappointment. And then, for a day, even two or three, the pain and fatigue would lift and she'd feel remarkably well again. She'd eat large dinners with Charles and make love to him. She'd take long walks with him and stay up late watching rented movies. She'd laugh loudly at his jokes, which were admittedly not so funny. But the pain would always come back, and she had to prepare herself for its return. She had to remind herself that she would die, which she did by handling numerous practicalities with the same dispatch and efficiency she brought to everything else in her life. She prepared her taxes in advance, contacted a lawyer, revised her will, set up a checking account for Melissa, who would turn seventeen in six months and would live alone in the year before college. Kate arranged a very brief and affordable funeral, at which, she had decided, no physical remains of her—in a jar or coffin—would be present. Kate found comfort in these tasks. They made death accomplishable, something she could do rather than something that would be done to her.

One morning, after four days of what felt like perfect health, Kate got up from bed and collapsed before she'd gotten halfway to the bathroom. Charles was helping her up when she realized what had happened. She was unhurt, and as soon as she could stand on her own, she pushed Charles away. "Please don't cling to me," she said.

"You just fell."

"I stumbled. I'm fine now." She went into the bathroom, and when she came back out, Charles was sitting on the edge of the bed looking up at her with too much concern in his eyes.

"Is something wrong?" He paused, seeming to realize the danger in his question. "Are you unwell?"

She slammed her underwear drawer, panties and a bra clenched in her fist, and began rifling through dresses in her closet with a physical vigor that was meant to be definite proof of her wellness. Charles flinched when she threw a dress down on the bed. "I am not unwell."

"You just collapsed."

"I tripped."

"Your knees gave out from under you. I saw it. You've been tired lately. I've seen that, too."

She turned her back to him and kicked a stray house slipper into the wall. "I'm dying." She was furious at him for making her say it. But in the long silence after her admission, her anger faded. "I lied to you earlier. I'm not recovered. I'm sick."

"Dying," he said flatly. "Dying when?"

"I'm dying now."

"When?" he asked again. "How long?"

"Not long." She turned around. Charles was naked save for his boxer shorts. His pale shoulders were drooped in a sad way that made her want to go to him, and through the slightly open slit of his shorts, she glimpsed a small part of his limp penis, the sight of which left her feeling tender and proprietary toward him. He was hers—her lover, her friend, her companion.

"From what?" he asked.

"Cancer."

He nodded.

"It's gone to the brain," she said. "That's why I get dizzy."

"Jesus," he said.

"It'll get worse," she continued, unable to stop herself. "Before it's over, I might not be able to make facial expressions. I might not be able to pronounce words correctly." She shrugged. "I'm sorry," she said.

"You didn't tell me any of this."

"We were having a fling," she said. "That was our agreement."

She sat down next to him, but he moved away and then stood up and began hurriedly dressing. "No," she said. She hadn't meant to say that.

He struggled to tie his necktie, finally just letting its ends fall. "I've got to go for a while," he said. He picked his shoes up from the floor, walked into the hallway in his socks, and closed the door behind him.

She hadn't expected the heartbreak, the thoughts of him, the simple, unrelenting desire for an absent person. She called twice and left messages. In the first, she asked him to please call. In the second, she was blunt. "Call me, Charles. Call me today." She was shocked by her aggression, her outright command. But she was even more surprised by the fact that he didn't call, not on that day and not on the next. The third time she called, Ryan answered with a flat, face-slapping, "Yeah, who is it?"

"Kate," she said softly. "I'd like to speak to your father."

"What did you do to him?" She'd expected the rudeness, but not the defensiveness, the obvious anger in his voice.

"I'd like to speak to him."

"He's not here." He paused. "What did you do to him?"

"I don't think that's really your concern."

"He was crying the other day. He was just sitting at the table crying. I guess you found out just how much you could push him around. I'd say you're an expert at that."

The rage in Ryan's voice left her both overwhelmed by guilt and glad that there was love for Charles mixed in with his son's bitterness. "Please tell him I called."

"Maybe I will," he said, and then hung up.

By mid-November, the beautiful portion of fall had ended. The winds came and blasted the leaves from the trees, and the rains turned them to brown gutter slush. The dark fell early, and more often than not Kate woke to gray mornings and the wet sounds of cars driving through water-drenched streets. Melissa continued to stay away, arriving home late in the evenings and slipping out of the house with her book bag early in the mornings. Kate worked half days now at the bank. She'd told her bad news to her district manager, who was happy to let her work until she no longer could. She spent her solitary afternoons at home rereading old mysteries and watching stacks of rented movies. She slept. She hoped that Charles would call. And she prepared herself for what would be a quieter, lonelier death than she'd expected.

Just when it seemed things would go on in this way, Kate came home from work one afternoon to find Melissa on the couch hugging her knees. She was in her favorite pajamas—thin yellow cotton with blue polka dots—and her eyes were raw from crying. In the crook of one arm, she held her worn-out teddy bear. Kate sat down on the opposite end of the couch. "Where's Mark?" she asked.

"He's gone."

"Home?" Kate asked.

"Gone," Melissa said. "He dropped me."

Kate felt a rush of guilt. She wanted to go to her daughter, but Melissa made no gesture or sign of wanting her. "I'm sorry, sweetheart."

"I scared him off," Melissa said. "I was too intense for him, or something."

"I don't think it was you," Kate said. "I think it was the circumstances. Sixteen-year-old boys don't particularly want to be around a house where the mother keeps taking to her sickbed."

Melissa shook her head. "I don't want to talk about that."

"OK," Kate said. "There are other boys."

"It doesn't matter," Melissa said, beginning to cry again. "I was just using him. That's what he said, and maybe he was right. He was my protector." She looked up at Kate. "From you." She stopped crying then and sat up straight and made an effort, Kate could tell, to be brave. "I'm going to try to be around more."

This news caught Kate off guard. She didn't know what to say, and was just as surprised when she felt the tears come. "I'm sorry," she said.

"I can't be here all the time," Melissa said cautiously. "But I'll be here after school, and I'll be here for dinners."

"I know what to expect this time," Kate said. "I'm going to be better. I'm not going to . . ."

"You went hunting the other weekend," Melissa interrupted.

Kate nodded. "I actually shot a bird."

Melissa laughed. "I can't picture it."

"I did. I shot it and Charles roasted it and I ate it." Kate and Melissa both laughed at the thought of it.

It took Charles three weeks to call. He left a message on the machine asking Kate to coffee at the café where they'd first met. That afternoon, the temperature fell below freezing, though the sun was out, and people hurried over the sidewalks, bundled in heavy coats. Wanting to look her best, Kate went without a hat and suffered for it, her ears numb by the time she entered the warm, mostly empty café. She found him seated in the same sunny corner where they had met, though he looked different now. After three weeks of not seeing him, he looked paler, thinner, slighter than she'd remembered him. He sat clinging to his coffee cup as if for warmth. His mustache was back, for which she was glad. In truth, she preferred him with his mustache. "Thank you for coming," he said after she'd sat down.

She could hear the fear in his voice and was at first reassured by it. "I've missed you," Kate said. It was a great relief to have said this, to have let it out.

He smiled, but his smile didn't last. "I'm not good at this."

"Good at what?"

"I don't know," he said. "I don't know what I want to say."

Kate already knew from his tone what he wanted to say. "Sure you do. I don't know why you had to make me come out in the cold to hear it."

He shook his head as if he were trying to rid himself of a thought. "I'm very sorry about your . . . about your being sick. I wanted you to know that."

"Thank you," Kate said. "I'm sorry, too. About not telling you." But she couldn't make herself sound sorry. And once again, she was surprised by her anger. She wanted to strike out at him now. Instead, she sat back in her chair and waited for him to speak.

"It's nice to see you. I've missed you. That's true for me, too. But I don't think I know you well enough to . . ."

He was going to make her finish his thought. He didn't know her well enough to watch her die. "I suppose not," she said. And then she added, with more anger in her voice than she'd wanted, "Your electric razor is still in my bathroom."

"Oh," he said.

For a moment, she remained silent and fought off an urge to weep. It stung to see this man who had giggled and tumbled in her bed now hold himself at a distance. And when she was sure she would not cry, she laughed. "It was just a fling, right?" Her voice sounded fake, and though she knew this pretense made her ridiculous, she couldn't help herself.

"Sure," Charles said. "I just wanted to see you again." He put his head down, and for a moment Kate thought he might cry. But when he looked up again, he managed to smile briefly. "It was nice," he said.

He wanted her to agree. He wanted her to say something equally fake and cheerful, but she didn't.

Melissa came back to her, as she'd said she would. In the late afternoons, she opened her books on the kitchen table and worked while Kate prepared dinner. One afternoon, Melissa brought dozens of college brochures home from school, and Kate and Melissa paged through them, talking about whether a large or a small college experience would suit Melissa best. Did she want a school with a Greek system? “That’s not for me,” Melissa said. And Kate, who didn’t want to be too influential, was inwardly glad that her daughter would not be a sorority girl. It was far too early to be so absorbed by these questions, but Kate was grateful for any opportunity to talk about her daughter’s future, and Melissa seemed to know this and indulged her.

In December, Kate’s double vision worsened and she finally left the bank for good. Her doctor recommended that she tape her left eye shut and wear a patch. And so this small part of Kate was already dead. Once or twice a week, she would suffer headaches that were bad enough for morphine. But for the most part, dying was surprisingly painless. More than anything else, it was exhausting, so exhausting that merely standing up was a struggle. At times, death seemed more mundane than frightening. The drawn-out brightness of the mornings, the length of midday and of the late afternoons when she lay on the couch alone waiting for Melissa to come home from school left her fatigued and drowsy.

Kate still had her bursts of energy, though they’d last now for hours rather than days. When a blizzard descended on Ann Arbor, Kate and Melissa put on their fattest winter coats, gloves, and hats, and walked for more than an hour in the new snow.

Melissa and Kate almost never spoke of what was happening—and what would soon happen—until one afternoon when Kate was especially sick. She lay over the couch, groggy from painkillers and covered in blankets. Kate had been discussing as lucidly as she could the virtues of Carleton College, while trying to hide the fact that this was the school she would choose for her daughter, when Melissa stopped her with a blunt question. “Does it hurt?”

Kate looked at Melissa for a moment. “You’re sure you want to know?”

Melissa nodded.

“Sometimes,” she said. “But not as much as I thought it would.”

“But it hurts.”

"Yes."

"Will it hurt when it happens?" Melissa wasn't looking at her. She was paging through a glossy college brochure.

"No," Kate said. "I won't be awake."

Melissa shook her head. "I don't think I want to be there then. If that's OK."

For an instant, Kate wanted to beg her daughter to be there, to stay with her, above all, at that moment. Instead, she nodded. "I'll be asleep. I won't know who's there."

"Is it OK?" Melissa asked.

"It's OK," Kate said.

It was raining out when someone knocked. The day nurse had just gone home, and Kate had to summon all her energy to rise from the couch and answer the door. A cold in-suck of air filled the entryway, and despite the grayness outside, the light had a raw brightness that Kate had to turn away from. Charles was wet, and the stringy flatness of his hair made him appear desperate. He held a small bunch of drenched tulips out to her, and she managed to carry them back to the couch. Looking at the flowers—their dramatic mess of color—exhausted her. "I got caught in this," he said. Water dripped off his coat and onto her wood floor. "I'm sorry," he said. Then he explained himself: "I just wanted to visit. As a friend."

"I'm tired, Charles," she said. "I won't be able to say much." As usual he was nervous, and for the first time Kate was irritated by his fear rather than touched by it. She knew that he was merely afraid to be in the presence of a dying person. He seemed so reduced: every inch the furniture salesman. She should have offered him tea or coffee, but she could not imagine how she would get up from the couch again. She was in her robe, for God's sake. "Your eye," he said. "Is it OK?" She'd forgotten about her patch until then, and now felt humiliated. She didn't want him there. She didn't want him to see her dying. He had been right: They didn't know each other well enough.

"No," she said. "It's not OK."

"You look good."

She almost laughed, but stopped herself when she realized how horrific laughter would sound coming from her. For a time they were silent until Kate finally said, "I'm tired."

He nodded. "I hope . . . I hope I wasn't unkind. I hope I didn't mistreat you. I hope . . ."

Kate understood now why he had come. She shook her head, and because he looked so achingly vulnerable, so convinced of his guilt, and because he was so extremely kind that he believed he was in the wrong when he wasn't, she said, "Of course not." And though she was too exhausted to summon the requisite tone of penitence and regret, though she wasn't sure it was entirely true, she remembered her daughter's recent courage and summoned her own. "I suppose I used you . . . a little. I didn't want to end up alone. I didn't want to end up"—she paused and let her head sink into her pillow—"like this." She smiled. "It's not as bad as it looks. It's not as bad as I thought it would be. I have my daughter." And now that she had said it, she thought it was true.

His shoulders lifted as if a chain had just come off him. How easily people might push him around. How easily she might have delivered a blow to him right now, had she wanted to. "It was just using me?" he asked.

"Not just. It was more than that, too." The truth of these words was in the sudden enthusiasm and fullness of her voice, and his smile and the lift in his face told her that he had heard it. For a moment, she wondered if he deserved to be this happy given what would soon happen to her. But the moment passed.

"I'd rather you not come back," she said. "I'm going to get worse, and I'd rather you remember me as the woman you took to bed and not the woman with an eye patch."

"Sure," he said. She wished he'd struggled more before saying that.

"I'm tired," she said again. But she wasn't prepared for how quickly he kissed her forehead and then turned around and left.

Her heartbreak continued. When she was especially lonely, in the long hours of daylight, she thought again of his lanky nakedness, his surprising competence at killing, his melancholic voice on her answering machine asking to speak to her. How odd to be heartbroken at this time in her life. How odd to be left with desire. It was a relief and a luxury to know that she did not want the actual man. Not now. She liked him best in her thoughts. He was more vivid, more alive that way. She could spend hours thinking of the soft, contemplative way he'd touched his mustache from time to time, and the way he'd told her, "Always stand behind the shooter," making it clear with his paternal tone of voice that her safety was his foremost concern. She would see them making love and be surprised again by his athleticism, his volume, his surprising confidence in bed. She would see years into an imaginary future with him; how annoying his passivity and meekness would become, annoying and also endearing. She would exhaust herself protecting him from those who'd take advantage of him: his son, his business partners, even herself. She would think of him as a hunter, too, a gentle hunter with great respect for his prey. How quickly he got to his wounded bird and snapped its neck. She would think of how he had lifted his wine above their small feast of grouse and toasted to her success, to their many hunts to come; and how he had lain beside her that night, his hand—the same one he had killed with—touching her scar in a darkness that was, for the time, easier to bear.

REAL GRIEF

Holly Morris was thirteen and not behaving herself at her grandmother's funeral. She made the few children in attendance—only there because the counselor from the school district had advised it—play patty-cake with her on the couch while the adults lined up in front of the large, glossy black coffin. Everybody knew that coffin had cost a lot more than the Morris family could afford. And because a funeral home was too expensive and Bethel Mount Chapel, the church where the Morrises and my family and every other family at the funeral went, was no more than a room with gray metal chairs, the Morrises had moved their TV out of the way and put the casket, with its upper lid open to the dead woman, in their living room. Everybody on the front porch and back patio was whispering about the cost of the coffin, not to mention the reconstructive work done on the old woman. The coffin was polished metal and wood with what Larry Truman, a carpenter in Wilford, knew was cherry trim. "Precious," one woman said about the interior fabric and cushions. People seemed to agree that the expense must have nearly destroyed the Morrises and would not have been necessary had Holly's grandmother died in a more peaceful way. But they also had to agree that they might have done just the same had it been their tragedy.

Jack Rogers and I tried to understand the cost in our terms—the number of trick boards and soft-wheels with Speedo bearings and Tracker trucks that kind of money might buy. We both had Kmart specials, plastic held together with rusty bolts. You could have bought twelve or thirteen flexwood-fiber fat boards for what the Morrises had spent on that funeral. "At least that many," Jack whispered, and I didn't argue. From the back of the living room, we had both glimpsed, through the throng of adults, the long, narrow box. The three Morris men were kneeling over their mother, weeping, and doing something desperate and inward—praying, talking to the dead woman—while Holly and Belinda Green, who even at eight must have known better, clapped hands and sang out from the back of the room, "Say, say, oh playmate! Come out and play with me!" Finally, Mrs. Morris seized Holly's wrist and led her away. But as soon as Mrs. Morris returned to her sobbing husband, her daughter was back, recruiting every kid she saw for a game of carpet tag, in which you take your shoes off and drag your socked feet over the shag carpet and shock the hell out of another kid. Holly also rounded up Jack, the Watkins brothers, and me, though in our early teens we were all too old for nonsense. So we stood back while the little kids tore their shoes off and began motoring around that part of the living room to fill themselves with electricity. By that time the adults were no doubt questioning the wisdom of bringing the few children who had come—the ones who'd witnessed what happened to old Mrs. Morris. Never mind that the woman counselor from the school district had advised it, had asked our parents to talk to us, listen to us, let us decide whether we'd like to come to the ceremony. "It might help give you closure," Jack's father had told him earlier that day, though "closure" was not a word we'd heard our parents use before. And now the Hedge and Bibs and Scott parents grabbed their kids and hauled them down the street and into their homes.

Standing alone at the back of her living room, Holly Morris swung her arms in circles, as if about to start jumping an invisible rope. "That is entirely enough now," Mrs. Wills, a close friend of Holly's mother, said fiercely. But Holly just smiled and wore this I-can't-hear-you face. Feeling stiff in our hand-me-down suits and ties, Jack Rogers, the Watkins brothers, and I stood there, waiting, knowing something had to happen. "That child needs to be hit," we heard Mrs. Wills whisper. Under normal circumstances, with all the families present going to the same church, living in the same neighborhood, working similar jobs, someone might have done it and let Mrs. Morris grieve. But there was something manic and unapproachable about Holly Morris—her openmouthed smile, her loud, hard giggling, her shouts, moments ago, of "You're it! You're it!"—that made her glee unstoppable and challenged any authority so completely that the adults seemed to back away from her and doubt themselves.

Finally, Mrs. Morris came away from the coffin again. She grabbed her daughter's wrist, twisting until Holly bent with pain, though the girl didn't stop smiling the whole time her mother dragged her down the hall. Mrs. Morris was a large woman with thick ankles and a fleshy round face, not at all like her thin, blond daughter, all sleek tan arms and legs. Even at thirteen, she had real tits that stood out from the rest of her, a fact that had not at all been lost on Jack Rogers, me, and the Watkins brothers, since she was one of the few girls at Wilford Junior High with a woman's body. The mother tossed her in a room and locked it with one of those old-fashioned keys that she put in her pocket. On the way back down the hall, Mrs. Morris was crying hard. "God bless you," Mrs. Tucker said. Like many of us, Mrs. Tucker had been there the day of the death, had seen everything, and had some idea of the uncertain rage Mrs. Morris might feel toward Holly. Those who had not seen the event had heard about it, and even as Pastor Lamb took his place at the head of the old woman, straightened the flower in his lapel, and began to speak, I couldn't help imagining how the part that I hadn't seen had happened: how Holly and her grandmother had just gotten into the Buick and were off to Holly's soccer practice when the old woman remembered she'd left her purse inside. I saw it all take place then as Pastor Lamb said a eulogy for the joyful elderly lady who'd so willingly driven neighborhood children from event to event, who'd kept the Morris garden up, who'd fed the stray cats of Wilford, who'd had an inspiring passion for the lost and needy. I imagined how surprised the old woman must have been when, right after stepping out of that car, she'd turned and seen the Buick rolling slowly down the slight grade of the driveway—so slowly that the eighty-three-year-old grandmother thought she could catch it, get inside, and stop it. She'd taken hold of the handle and been about to open the door when she somehow fell and ended up under the car, which kept rolling even as Holly sat in the passenger seat watching it happen. She no doubt saw the panic in her grandmother's face as she went down, perhaps heard something like a scream and felt the give-and-take of the car as it rolled on for a moment before settling, unimaginably, in place. How quiet the inside of that car must have been for Holly Morris. Mrs. Scott had seen the event from her kitchen window as she scrubbed a plate. Her husband had called 911 and rushed outside, but he couldn't get Holly to unlock her door. She stared right through him, then looked the other way when he knocked on the glass. As soon as he headed around the car—which he'd wanted to avoid doing because he'd already seen the old woman over there once and didn't want to have to see her twice—the girl reached over and locked that door, too. They, Mr. and Mrs. Scott together now, shouted at her. When their efforts failed, they even enlisted a policewoman, who had just arrived and was a mother herself, to say in a really nice voice through the window that Holly needed to unlock the door, sweetie, and come out now.

But the girl didn't hear a word of it. She turned the radio on to a high volume, so high that the Browns and Meyers and Jensens, who had come out to help, could hear the evening news, the weatherman predicting in his too-perfect radio voice that the Indian summer—the blue skies and mild temperatures that seemed so wrong for a day like that—would continue into the first week of October. When the fire truck arrived and a team of rescuers—all local men, amateurs from Wilfred, who quickly saw that there was no one to rescue—began lifting that Buick off the old woman with a hydraulic jack, Holly turned her grandmother's AM radio up still higher to a top-ten pop song countdown to which, her eyes closed, she swayed slowly as she mouthed the familiar words of a song she had danced to many times at one of the Wilford Junior High stomps. When finally, after more than twenty minutes of trying, a rescue worker managed to jimmy the lock on the driver's side, Holly simply reached over and slapped the lock down again before he could open the door.

By that time half the neighborhood was out there, including me and Jack Rogers and the Watkins brothers, all on our boards and trying to get a glimpse of Holly locked in that deadly car and moving to Cyndi Lauper's "Girls Just Want to Have Fun." We walked around to the opposite side of the car and, along with other neighborhood kids, all younger than us, saw what was left of the old woman, her legs extending from beneath the Buick with a pair of clean, brand-new, bright red tennis shoes—she'd always worn loud, youthful shoes—on her dead feet. The little Brian girl with strawberry-red hair and her friends, Carrie and Shana and Belinda, who'd been jumping rope in the Johnson driveway, as well as Ricky Hedge and Martin Bibs and a bunch of kids on their tricycles and Big Wheels with rainbow-colored tassels streaming from their handlebars, were there and witnessed that sight too. Most backed off and wandered down the street in a daze. Others lingered, staring, transfixed until an emergency worker said, "They shouldn't be here. Somebody get rid of the kids!" A few parents came, covering their children's eyes with a hand, and a cop shooed the unaccompanied ones away. The cats remained, though. She'd fed them for years, and no doubt they recognized her, even became hungry at the sight of her, which might have explained why the rescue workers, kicking and yelling at the twenty or thirty scraggly strays, could not scatter them or quiet their repetitive mewing. The animals dashed at the old woman's legs and darted under the car, where they crouched, just out of reach and close to their provider.

We were smart enough to stay back, just within eyeshot across the street, where Gary Watkins threw up in a bush while the rest of us watched Holly swaying to that music. We had all told lies about this girl with tits and a tight ass and a soft child's face. She and I had locked ourselves in the janitor's closet in the school basement, where I'd held onto a mop handle while she gave me a very slow, torturous hand job, licking her palm just to make it better for me, I'd told Jack Rogers, who'd told the Watkins brothers, who themselves had received what they called "twin blow jobs," pushed up against her picket fence one midnight. We'd taken her through every motion we could imagine in our lies. We'd made her body the target of a point-system game we played. A piece of Holly Morris's ass—a caress or pinch or feel—was worth ten points, the highest by far at Wilford Junior High, where copping a feel from any other girl would get you only five at most. (And because points could only be earned when all of us, Mark, the Watkins brothers, and I, were present to witness the act, our lies didn't count.) I'd scored 200-plus on Holly, and Jack Rogers was just behind me with 180; the Watkins brothers were slower, more shy and scared, though that obviously didn't stop them from lying about blow jobs. The last time I'd touched her, slipping my hand on her butt as I stood behind her in the school-bus line, she'd turned with rage in her face and jabbed a mechanical pencil at me. "Get your little pussy fingers off me, Billy Munroe," she said. I'd never guessed at the fury she'd had in her, and when I got home that day I couldn't help but look at my hands and feel a little disgusted at what she'd called my "pussy fingers," even though I knew that I was out in front in our game, that point-wise Holly Morris was mine.

But she didn't seem to belong to anyone that day as we watched the unpracticed Wilford rescue squad, who just weren't used to dealing with disasters, fumble their efforts to retrieve what was left of Holly's grandmother. The car, a huge sky-blue American cruiser, slipped off the jack twice before they recovered the old woman and began the messy task of putting her away. "Someone get the girl out of the car," a worried neighbor—it looked like Mr. Brown—shouted at the men. But the workers didn't budge; they'd already tried and failed. She wasn't bothering anyone. At least she hadn't been until her father returned from work, parking his old Ford truck across the street, to witness the aftermath of the accident.

Mr. Morris was a large man, tall and thick and bearded, not in the least known for his gentleness. He stood with his clipboard in one hand, a ballpoint pen resting behind his ear, his BF Goodrich namebadge rising and falling with each breath. When he crossed the street, Mr. Brown and Mr. Scott both backed away, seeming to give him space to comprehend the tragedy that had killed his mother. The rescue squad had mostly zipped old Mrs. Morris up in a brown plastic bag, but Mr. Morris could still see the worst of her. A great weight seemed to force him to his knees. The whisper of a policeman in his ear made him weep. The sprinkler in the middle of the lawn came on then so that a hard rope of water slapped Mr. Morris in the side, his shirtsleeve and pant leg suddenly dripping. An adult seized five-year-old Marty Green and turned off the faucet the child had been fiddling with. "Get away!" Mr. Morris yelled, and his friends and neighbors retreated. "Get the hell fuck away!" People returned to their houses then while we withdrew behind the bush that Gary Watkins had hurled on earlier. From there, we watched the kneeling Mr. Morris, his whole body dripping, his whole body seeming to grieve, as he noticed his daughter locked away in her odd, unchanged world.

His real anger began then. He pushed his way through two police officers, beat the hood of the car with his fist, and became more enraged when his daughter didn't so much as flinch. He cursed her, demanded that she turn that music off and step out of that car or he'd kick her ass to he didn't know goddamn where, though all he did was smash a dent into her locked door with his foot, turn around, hold his face in his hands, then kick the car again while Holly's seated dance became more animated, her forearms raised and swinging double time and opposite the back-and-forth sway of her head, graceful, skillful in a way that my friends and I had never come close to on the dance floor. She moved in perfect sync to what Mr. Morris and all our parents felt was the frivolous, sexual beat of godless music, the sort of music his daughter locked herself into her room for hours to listen to. It wasn't Christian, Mr. Morris knew. It wasn't good, and so perhaps it was easier to hate his daughter for loving filth like that than to feel whatever he'd been feeling for his dead mother. He hadn't gotten along with Holly, as the whole neighborhood knew, for the better part of a year, and his growing fatherly rage came out now as he continued to beat the hood and to curse Holly, no longer his little girl, not after she'd repeatedly sneaked out of his house at night, not after he'd caught her and an older boy he'd never met sharing a cherry Slurpee spiked with vodka at the Wilford Mall. He suspected she'd done other things, too, and so he hated her that afternoon, the dirty, rebellious girl whom his mother had always been so willing to drive around town—to the mall, where he'd caught her with that boy, to the movies, where she'd done God knew what, to soccer practice, to anywhere she'd wanted to go—which might have been the thought that made him shout, "You killed her!" And maybe it was those words that made him stop and put his head down on the hood of the car. His wife, who had been approaching the scene hurriedly from a block away—she'd been having coffee with Mrs. Eliot, the neighborhood piano teacher, and had arrived just in time to hear her husband call their daughter a killer—slowed down to learn from a nearby policeman what had happened. She cupped a hand over her mouth. She shook her head. She went to her husband and held him then. "I'm sorry," he said.

"Your father says he's sorry," Mrs. Morris shouted at the car window so that Holly could hear her through the music.

"She won't come out of there," Mr. Morris told his wife.

"Please come out now, Holly!" Mrs. Morris shouted.

"Come out now, Holly," her father said.

"Sweetheart," Mrs. Morris said. But Holly was gone, far away from them, and finally they had to leave her there and hold each other while the same policewoman who'd failed to lure his daughter out of her trance—or whatever she was in—asked Mr. Morris questions and had him sign papers that made him cry still more loudly. We'd come out from behind the vomity bush since nobody seemed to notice us anymore. All the same, we shouldn't have been watching. This was private and shameful, we knew. But we couldn't not watch. Others had gone in and Mrs. Allison came out on her porch to tell us that this "happening" wasn't for us boys to see. We told her that we were just skating, which was sort of true. Mark Watkins was riding the nose of his board with skill and easy cockiness until his brother knocked him off and said, "Not here, dumb ass. Not now."

"She's fucking crazy," Jack Rogers said.

"Shut up," I said, thinking about the 200-plus points I'd scored on Holly's ass and feeling both famous and ashamed about it. I would have fought for her then. I would have smashed Jack Rogers's face into the ground and stood on his head to keep him from saying anything more about her. I wasn't at all sure what I was protecting her from, and later, after what would happen between Holly and me at her grandmother's funeral, I'd see that I really didn't want anything to do with her. But Jack Rogers backed off, and nothing happened.

The fire truck had gone, as had the ambulance with the Morris grandmother. The counselor, a woman wearing a dress suit, had arrived to convince Holly to leave the car, though finally she retreated inside with the Morris parents. One of the more beautiful sunsets we ever remembered seeing—then or years later—was beginning to light the sky a deep purple that made our shadows into twenty-foot lanky giants, their shapes falling across yards and out into the street. Just as we were about to leave and go home to our separate dinner tables, we saw an amazing thing. The music inside the Buick turned off, and Holly Morris stepped out—the long, spooky, dark lines of her shadow unfolding and preceding her across the grass—and went into her house. The amazing thing was how she walked on air all the way to the front door, taking these light, easy steps so that you could hear the crisp, brief click of her soccer cleats, heel to toe, against the concrete. Jack Rogers, who still talks about that day more than a decade later, never mind that Holly Morris long since left town and never came back, claims now that he saw her take a gleeful skip between steps. A quick, happy little kick. But he overdoes it every time he tells that story. She was just walking as if something nice and sweet as hell had happened to her and now she felt better and more beautiful than she usually did.

It didn't take long for Holly Morris to get out of the room where her mother had locked her away. She must have climbed out the window and had a rough landing since she walked back into her grandmother's funeral through the front door with a nylon ripped all the way down one leg, a smudge of garden dirt on her cheek, and an excited, invigorated look on her face, the sort of look you get when you're free again. I tried not to notice her. I was in line then to view the old woman. This would be the closest I'd ever come to a dead person, and I was watching the adults ahead of me—the way Mr. Almer bowed his head and said a few silent words—so that I'd know what to do when I got to her. I'd watched the Morris men—who'd viewed her first and for a long time—touch her, lift her hands, lace their fingers—or try to—in her too-stiff ones, lean into the casket and kiss her, nudge their cheeks against hers in a display of physical affection for the dead that scared me and made me nervous about my own turn with her. But when Mr. Almer backed away, I found that I knew exactly what to do, how slowly, quietly to approach, bow my head, look and feel solemn, say a few silent words to myself. This was how to grieve and help my neighbors grieve their loss. I felt the pressure of a hand on my shoulder and looked over at Mr. Green, a good friend of my father, who said, "Hi, son" in a dusky half-whisper before he looked down, shook his head, and said, "Oh, Christine," which had been the old woman's name, then left me there alone with her. I knew next to nothing about Holly's Grandma Morris save what Pastor Lamb had already said about her feeding cats and driving neighborhood kids around, about her love of gardening. And because Pastor Lamb had asked everyone present that day to contemplate one thing they knew that made Christine Morris unique and human, I treasured what seemed to me the saddest thing about her by saying to myself, "She had a passion for stray things." A real reverberation of sadness moved through me, and I stood there for a moment until I heard the slight thud of something against the foot of the coffin and turned to see Holly, the streak of garden dirt still on her cheek, smiling at me and holding a bowl of green olives she'd brought from the kitchen, where dozens of casseroles and other food neighbors had delivered crowded the counters. She selected an olive, aimed, then launched it. It hit my chest and rolled over the shaggy carpet. She smiled at me very nicely again, her eyes saying something like, "Hi, you." Then she turned and flashed the same look at Jack Rogers and the Watkins brothers before throwing a cluster of olives at them, forcing them to retreat down the hall and out of range. Holly saw that, with the dead woman behind me, I had nowhere to go. Standing in a sassy, smart-ass way, all her weight on one hip, she tossed another olive at me, this one flying over my shoulder. Mrs. Morris blasted down on Holly then, using too much force right there in the middle of the room and in the presence of that beautiful and expensive coffin. As if wielding a hammer, she swung the flat of her hand down on Holly, who willingly bent low and gave Mrs. Morris an easy target, even hiking her lemon skirt over her hips so that we could see—Jack Rogers and the Watkins brothers staring from their safe place down the hall—through the white haze of her nylons the tight turquoise panties covering what to us had been her ten-point ass. Mrs. Morris was winded and had to stop, and only then realized what her daughter had done, what had happened to that room: Many mourners had looked away from the old woman, surrounded by banks and reefs of flowers, and fixed their eyes instead on what her daughter was displaying. It was full and perfectly shaped with a red blotch of torn skin just above her thigh where her nylon had ripped. Mr. Brown, Mr. Almer, Mr. Green (who had just touched my arm), Mr. Watkins, my father, Mr. Lemon, and other men—and some women, too—were looking and kept on looking until they realized what they were doing and realized that Mrs. Morris, still breathing hard from the exertion, saw them doing it, which was when the entire room looked away. I averted my eyes, too, for a long time, putting my head down and feeling the rush of blood and shame to my face. When I looked up again, my neighbors were shaking their heads and whispering. Some wept quietly. Others stood in line to view the old woman a second time. Mrs. Morris was now the only person looking at Holly, who had stood up and was smoothing the front of her skirt. Her mother stared at her with quiet disgust until her husband, his usual bad temper subdued by exhaustion and grief, took his wife's hand and led her into the kitchen, where they would no longer have to watch their daughter misbehave.

Now that Holly was free to do as she liked, she tossed a final handful of olives at a circle of women standing in an opposite corner, many of whom moved uncomfortably, shifting, trying not to look at the girl. Mrs. Mathers wiped her left cheek with a napkin where one had hit. But no one turned. No one acknowledged the girl. All at once, Holly gave up, put the bowl down, and looked around for someone or something. She looked from one corner to another until her eyes found me. She smiled and blew a kiss off her fingers in my direction. I wanted to turn and join the line in front of the coffin again. I wanted to join Jack Rogers and the Watkins brothers. But they had left the room, gone down the hall or out the door, and Holly was already in front of me, had already taken my hand. She pulled me out the front door and around the side of the house, hungry, dirty cats following us the whole way. "We'll use Grandma's gardening shed," she said.

"I should go inside," I said. But when I planted my feet, she yanked me forward with both hands. A group of men on the back porch smoking didn't seem to notice us. Starving stray cats mewed loudly, aggressively, at our feet. Holly kissed the side of my neck lightly and squeezed my hand so tightly that the bones hurt. Cats brushed against my legs. "They get bitchy when Grandma doesn't feed them." She kicked one out of our way, opened the door, and pushed us into a darkness so thick I flinched, moved my other arm out in front for protection, and found only cold air.

"I need to go back," I said. Her hand on my face pushed me against a wall. The shed smelled of earth and dampness and old metal tools. With a kick of her leg, the shed door slammed shut and the small triangle of light became a chink. "Please," I said.

"Coward," she said. I couldn't see her, though her hand darted from my neck to my crotch, where she pulled up sharply until it hurt. "You little ass-kissing . . ." She let go of me, then dug her hand into my butt and pushed me against her. "Ten points, Billy," she said. She wedged her knee forcefully between my legs. "Kiss me now." And even as her tongue entered my mouth and our teeth clattered and her hands tightened on my face, clawing at the bones, I wanted to be inside standing above the dead woman, anticipating the proper thoughts and feelings, and then, looking down at her white, reconstructed face, thinking and feeling them.

THE ANIMAL GIRL

1

The summer job Leah was interviewing for at the university biomedical laboratory did not exactly require her to kill anything, but it did involve the deaths of animals, several of them every week. Franklin, Leah's father, who had been a research doctor and was now an administrator at the University of Michigan Medical School, had gotten her the interview. It was part of his recent campaign to jolt her out of her slump, to revive, educate, and edify Leah, who at seventeen was friendless, had no direction, no interests, was homebound out of choice and very much in the way of her father and his new girlfriend, Noelle.

Leah was unpleasant to be around, and she knew it. Franklin was too much in love. Only three years ago, her mother, Margaret, or Maggie, as everyone had called her, had died and left Leah and Franklin devastated. Leah wasn't ready for her father to be happy again. How weird and stomach-turning it was to see him emerge in the mornings from his room, still in his pajamas, with a full smile above his thick beard—all that bushy facial hair he'd grown in the last years because he'd been too grief-stricken to trim it. And now he was smiling, too often and too obviously. He'd been nagging at her to make more of a social effort, to go out. "Boys aren't against the rules, you know," he said. "You're allowed to be interested in them."

She'd shrug. "Whatever," she said. Once, she had let him have it. "I don't need to fall in love, okay? Maybe you do. But I don't." He'd backed off and left her alone.

So when he asked her to consider the job, she said no. "Please, Leah. You already have an interview. It's a chance for you to learn about science, to see what's going on, to get some exposure."

"I'm not interested in science."

Franklin slumped over in his chair. He was a large man, six foot three, with big bones and a soft midsection, and seeing his thick, ungainly body fall in disappointment, seeing his hands, large as bowls, beseechingly laid out on the table, had its effect on Leah. "Okay," she said. "I'll go. Then I'll say no."

"Thank you," Franklin said.

Leah showed up at the interview looking as she usually did: dumpy in her overlarge Levi's and white T-shirt. The laboratories were subterranean, windowless, a labyrinth of narrow hallways with exposed water pipes running the length of the low ceilings and long fluorescent-tube lighting that coated everything in a naked whiteness. The close, unnatural odors of chemicals hung in the air, despite the respiratory whirl of the ventilation system. Max, an old colleague of her father, was the researcher she'd be working with. He kept his office dark: Two desk lamps and the bluish glow of his computer screen gave the space a cavelike dimness. The air was a complex mix of smells: tennis shoes, coffee, and microwave popcorn. "The last time I saw you, you were this high." He put his hand out at waist level and laughed. Leah remembered him, too: the picnics years ago at his yellow house and his then-young wife.

He started by explaining that his work involved animal experimentation. "I want to be frank with you," Max began. "We've had a lot of people quit this job after a few days. It's not for everyone."

"Oh," Leah said. She hadn't expected to be discouraged, to be warned away.

"I wish I could tell you that you'd be doing a lot of science. But I'm afraid you won't be. Of course, I'll be happy to tell you all about what we're up to here. But your job would be taking care of and feeding the animals."

He had big, fleshy lips and heavy eyelids that made him look both morose and jolly. Leah liked his thick sideburns and unruly hair. She had immediately sensed something in Max, something both depressive and good-natured, that she wanted to be around, and that suddenly made this job more appealing. "That's all right," she said. "I enjoy animals. Working with animals will be great."

Max smiled sadly. "The animals will die," he said. "So if you enjoy them . . ."

"They're dying for science, right? I won't give them names or anything." Leah had just noticed two anatomical diagrams, one of a human and the other of what seemed to be a small cow, hanging on Max's wall; and looking over them, she was struck by the crammed complexity of innards—vessels, organs, layers of muscle, fat, and skin—and felt a visceral unease at knowing that she too was made of this mess. On the wall opposite his desk, Leah saw something she hadn't expected in a scientist's office: a poster of Clifford Brown, eyes closed, blasting his trumpet as curls of cigarette smoke rose between the valve casings. "I'm into jazz, too," she said. "It wasn't fair he had to die so young. If he'd lived, we wouldn't have to settle for that terrible amplified funk Miles started playing at the end of his life. He would have been too embarrassed to play music like that with Clifford around to hear it. Clifford would have kept him honest."

Max grinned and put a hand thoughtfully to his fleshy cheek. Leah was trying to figure out what she liked about this bearish man who couldn't have been much younger than her father and who wore an old yellow T-shirt, untucked, beneath his lab coat and a pair of frayed Adidas with brand-new, superwhite laces that clashed with the dirty off-white of the old leather. "Maybe so," he said.

"Is that a baby cow?" Leah asked, pointing to the anatomical poster.

He shook his head. "That's a sheep. We work with sheep and dogs. The sheep seem to bother people less than the dogs, for obvious reasons. Our animals don't stay with us longer than a week. You won't be involved with the elimination and disposal. We have somebody else to do that. You'll be responsible for feeding them, cleaning out their cages, and doing pre-op." Leah didn't know what pre-op was, and she wasn't going to ask. "You won't have to be in the lab during any procedures, if you'd rather not see them." He paused then, seeming to give Leah time to think. "You're sure the job won't bother you?"

"Will the animals just die sometimes?" she asked, trying to sound as clinical as he and failing. "When the bigger experiments are performed, I mean."

"I'm afraid they always die. That happens to be the nature of our work."

Leah took in a deep breath before she said, "It won't bother me."

The morning Leah was to start her new job, Noelle and her father ambushed her with her favorite meal—strawberry crepes and fresh whipped cream—and Leah knew they had difficult news for her. They had already showered and dressed. Noelle, who was in real estate, wore Franklin's apron, which said "King of the Kitchen" on it, over her gray suit. She poured the batter while Leah's father stood in sunlight slicing strawberries and humming. The table was set, the orange juice in glasses. The aroma of brewing coffee mixed with the warm pancake air of the kitchen. "What's happening?" Leah asked. "Something's up. You're going to tell me something."

"Why don't you sit down, Leah?" Franklin said. He'd just had his hair and beard trimmed, and his neatness and good grooming made him look more and more like he belonged to this woman.

Leah didn't sit down. "I've got my first day of work. I can't eat."

"Your father told me. Congratulations," Noelle said. She really was a sweet woman, and Leah was at times disgusted with herself for disliking her. "What exactly will you be doing?"

"I'm an executioner. I'll be killing animals." This answer silenced Noelle so completely that Leah felt compelled to take it back. "I'm working at a lab where they do experiments. I'll be feeding and cleaning up after the animals they use. Sheep and dogs."

Noelle placed a plate of stacked crepes on the table, and Franklin followed her with bowls of strawberries and whipped cream. "So," Leah said, "I suppose you two are getting married. That's the news, I bet."

Standing behind his chair, Franklin's face turned a deep red. Leah couldn't remember ever seeing her father blush, though she had seen him weep, his eyes raw and beaten, until he could cry no more. "Not quite," he said.

"So what's the good news? Why are you bribing me with strawberry crepes?"

Franklin all at once was nervous and started playing with his fork.

"Noelle and I have been talking about the possibility of her moving in with us."

"The possibility," Leah said. "Are you asking me?"

"How about sitting down and eating a crepe, Leah?" Franklin said.

When she didn't sit, he turned to Noelle, who'd taken her apron off and looked powerful and businesslike in her gray suit. "No," she said. "We just thought we should let you know."

"Great. That's great. Congratulations." Leah felt her throat catch and the tears rise to her eyes, despite her best effort to hold them off. "I'm being a baby. I'm sorry for being a baby," she said. Then she rushed out the front door.

On Leah's first day, they gave a sheep a heart attack, though Max and Diana, Max's graduate student, called it a minor infarction, which Leah gathered was not quite the same as a heart attack. Leah was afraid she might relate to the animal, care for it; and so, midway through her workday, when she stood next to the sedated sheep and watched it jolt and begin to die on the operating table, she was proud of herself for feeling so little. It was a large animal, after all, so obviously alive, stinking with aliveness, with barnyard odors that permeated the laboratory. "Why are we doing this?" she asked, a question that Max, absorbed in the careful killing of the animal, had seemed not to hear. She didn't ask again, though she did want there to be a good reason for destroying this creature, which she and Max had had to force down every inch of the hall between its pen and the operating room. From the moment Leah had sheared the wool from its left foreleg, where Max would insert the lethal device, an inflatable catheter, the sheep had seemed to guess its fate. The sound it made as they pushed it down the corridor was not unlike a child crying, though there was something purely animal and stupid in it. This beast wasn't smart enough to care about, she told herself. Halfway to the operating room, it stopped, eyes athwart and glaring fixedly at nothing. Leah felt the warmth on her leg before she looked down and saw that it had shit on her. Then it pissed, the linoleum floor suddenly slick as ice with the warm flow of urine. "That wasn't supposed to happen," Max said. "They weren't supposed to feed or water it last night." Evidently, the person for whom Leah was taking over had been incompetent.

When they finally got into the operating room, Diana, a beautiful if slightly heavy woman, whose neat, made-up face contrasted oddly with this place and the jumbo syringe in her hand, administered the anesthetic. It took the three of them to lift the animal, now docile and drowsy, onto the table. Once the sheep was completely out, they began to kill it in a very slow and complicated way. Max inserted the catheter along with a microscopic camera, which relayed a black-and-white image of the sheep's artery and the pathway of the catheter onto a computer screen fixed to the wall. Max studied the screen as he worked the catheter meticulously through the artery and into the animal's heart. "Bingo," he said. "We're in." Leah knew what would come next. They would inflate the catheter and induce a heart attack. But before they did, Max, who evidently thought Leah was a wimp, said, "You don't have to stay. This isn't part of your job."

"I'd like to watch, if that's all right." Max nodded, and Leah stayed, though in truth she wanted to leave and would have if some part of her didn't wonder what it would be like to watch something die. Besides, she liked being near Max, especially when he worked. Max's lumbering body became focused and alert as he directed the catheter. He kept his eyes on the echocardiogram and the computer screen at the same time, seeing a great deal where Leah saw only a whirl of gray images. Max put his hand on the animal's heaving side for a moment, as if to prepare it, then took his hand away and pressed the button that would kill it. Leah was impressed by her indifference when the animal suffered a heart attack on the table, its body jolting, its legs kicking so suddenly that Leah stepped back and watched its sleeping struggle wane, now only its rear legs paddling a little, then becoming still again. "It can't feel anything, by the way," Max said.

"It doesn't bother me," Leah said, unable to suppress a tone of excitement. "Is it dead yet?"

Max was leaning forward, his eyes still on the screen, when Leah was tempted to touch him. Under the circumstances, this impulse seemed all the more wrong. Nonetheless, she felt it. Her back to them, Diana was watching a printout of the EKG. And so Leah placed her hand on his shoulder, as if momentarily balancing against him. The simple presence of him, his solidity, his body heat, was astonishing to her, and she left her hand on his shoulder for a long moment before lifting it again. He made no sign of noticing, and Leah was thrilled and suddenly nervous. "Nope," he said. "We don't want to kill it. Not right away. That's not the point. We're giving it a minor heart attack, causing an infarction, in order to kill some cardiac tissue. We use the balloon to simulate a thrombosis—a blockage of the vessel—long enough to bring about necrosis. To kill or damage the tissue. Then we deflate the balloon and measure the capacity of the damaged heart. How long can he live on this heart, and how much of the tissue in the affected area is necrotic? How much is still healthy? How much is damaged but capable of healing? He might live for hours or even days. He might even experience a full recovery. He might not die at all, in which case we'll have to do that part for him."

"Why?" Leah asked.

"We need his heart," Max said. "After all this is done, we remove it and study the extent of tissue damage."

Later in Max's office, after they'd left the sheep on the table with an IV dripping lactose slowly into its body and a partially dead heart keeping it alive for now, Max and Leah ate their sack lunches together. Max had put on a Charlie Parker CD, and they listened to the high-velocity riffs of Bird's solo to "Now's the Time" while Max ate his tuna-fish sandwich and told her more about the experiment: how the sheep heart is similar enough to the human heart to be helpful as a model, how minor heart attacks in humans are much more common than major ones, and therefore very important to understand, how they'd be inducing thousands of heart attacks of varying severity, involving different parts of the cardiac muscle in an attempt to be "comprehensive." Finally, in a later stage of the study, they'd be testing different strategies of emergency treatment, designed to minimize the area of necrosis. Max became animated, spoke with his hands, and forgot about his lunch as he spoke. "A patient with a history of heart disease comes to the ER complaining of chest pain. He's most likely suffering a minor heart attack. So what should the physician do first, and how quickly does he have to do it in order to reduce permanent damage? What's the window of time the physician has to make his decision? And what are his"—

"Or her," Leah interrupted.

Max nodded and smiled. "Or her," he said. "What are *her* best options for treatment? Hopefully, our work will suggest some answers."

Before they finished their discussion, Max took out a plastic model of a sheep heart from a deep drawer in his desk and started to disassemble it and lay its parts—the auricles and ventricles—on the desk next to his half-eaten sandwich in order to show Leah where thromboses typically occur and the different areas that would be affected by infarction and what they might learn about the resulting tissue damage. While he talked, Leah took him in: his chubby, unshaven cheeks, his thick, ruffled hair, the circles of sweat that had begun to form in the pits of his lab coat while he'd been inducing the heart attack just at the right time and in the right way; and again something about him—big, sloppy, soft-bodied Max, who had whole-wheat crumbs in his mustache and who cared passionately about things that were a mystery and just a little boring to Leah—kept pulling at her. "Necrosis," she said, repeating the word he had just been using. "That means death in Latin, doesn't it? I'm taking Latin right now."

"Actually, it's Greek," he said.

And then, maybe to arrest his obsessive focus on science, maybe to prevent what might become a lengthy and unwanted lecture on a Greek word, maybe just to change the subject, maybe to shock him, to show him she wasn't just his high-school helper, his inquisitive animal-keeper, maybe to get his attention, maybe for no reason at all, she said, "My mother died of leukemia. Aggressive leukemia. Three years ago. Really quickly. The doctors just thought it was anemia at first. They gave her iron, and she seemed to get better. Then she got sick again." Leah almost snapped her fingers to show him how quickly it had happened. "It only took her three months to die."

Max put down the plastic pieces of the heart and folded his hands. "I'm sorry," he said. "I heard something about that. I heard it was awfully tough on your father, too." He smiled as he had when he'd warned her in the interview that the job might not be for her. A heavy, soft, sympathetic smile, so sympathetic that Leah wondered what her father might have told Max about her: his brokenhearted, sullen daughter who needed to get out of the house more often, who needed all the pity and charity she could get. "As I remember, your mother was a very nice woman."

"I don't know why I told you that. I shouldn't have." Leah shrugged. "Anyway, this work doesn't bother me. Seeing that animal dying was just fine."

Max nodded and seemed, for a moment, slightly awkward before he said, "That's good."

"What about you?"

"What about me what?"

Leah felt that she'd just earned the right to ask the question now. "Why don't you have pictures of your wife out? Your family? I remember you had a wife." In fact, Leah was prying. She remembered her parents talking about Max's divorce several years ago.

"Oh," he said. He took a big bite of his sandwich and chewed for a while. "Sharon, you mean." He shook his head and looked a little annoyed. "That's a bit personal." But then he answered her: "That didn't work so well. Sharon went her own way a few years back. She's remarried. I'm good at science, but not . . ."

"You'd be a good dad," Leah said, hoping to cheer him up. But that statement was evidently too personal as well, and he let her know by looking at his watch and announcing the end of their lunch hour.

On the way back to what she thought of as her animal basement, she passed through the operating room, where the sheep lay fatly on its side, heaving with life, and again she stood over it a moment, asking herself what she felt, which was, to be truthful, a little more than nothing—an *oh-well*, a *what-can-be-done?* kind of feeling.

She spent the rest of her day with the animals in her windowless room down the hall. It had a blankness that she found quieting—off-white walls, a rectangular block of fluorescent lights on the ceiling, a concrete floor with a drain at its center, and a large tublike industrial sink in the far corner, next to which bags of feed—dog food and grain—were stacked. The one anomaly, and the thing she liked most, was a large clerk's desk, which she tried to budge. It was as heavy and unmovable as a boulder, and made her animal basement feel oddly like an actual office, a place where things were to be written and thought about. The animals stayed at the back of her narrow room in cages, their floors covered with blond wood chips that gave off a musty, earthy odor tinted with urine and animal heat. There were a dozen cages, though on that first day she had only three animals (now only two, since one of these was dying slowly in the room down the hall). She had one sheep and one dog—a boy dog, she could see when she bent to look at its underside. Each animal had its own folder, filed in the left desk drawer under two categories, Canines and Sheep. The folders contained the age of the animal in months, its gender, its color, weight, and height, and an identity number; the canines had three digits, and the sheep had four. The dog she had that day was 013, an unlucky number. It wagged its tail and looked up at Leah with an oddly human and expressive gaze that said something like, "Hi, there."

"You're going to die," she said to it. But 013 just kept wagging its tail. Leah stuck her fingers through the grate of the cage, and the silly animal licked them.

The beginning of that summer had been wet and cold. A colorless arctic gray began and ended each day until the first week of July, when the heat came all at once, only a few days after Noelle's arrival, in a burst of sun and humidity that was almost tropical. This shift in seasons somehow gave Noelle more power and presence, as if she'd been there a very long time, through the short days of winter, the gradually lengthening days of spring, and then into summer. She came with her dishes and her shiny pots and pans, so much more numerous and better than the odd assemblage of dull stuff Leah's mother, never much of a cook, had used for years, all of which Franklin put into boxes now and stored in the basement. She came with her fancy olive oils, fancy French and Italian cheeses, and a spice rack for which Franklin, who had never been handy, nonetheless got out his tools—a level, a power drill, and plaster screws. Finally, after drilling three sets of unnecessary holes, he attached it to the wall, and Noelle applauded. Noelle loved to cook, and judging from

Franklin's praise, Leah guessed she did so expertly, which was all the more reason to avoid the dinner table, Noelle's dinner table, made of cherry wood and caressed with lemon oil at least once a week, and, yet again, so much better than the rustic, square table Leah's family had once used, which also ended up in the basement. She kept her distance from Noelle and Franklin at the dinner hour—at all hours, really. She was busy, she told them. She had to work. Or she felt a little sick. She remained in her room listening to Thelonious Monk, Duke Ellington, early Miles. Or she practiced her clarinet, working through major and minor scales, through exercises, even flat-footedly improvising to a Jamey Aebersold CD turned up loud on her stereo. Though she listened to jazz, she couldn't play it. She couldn't swing. She was stiff, right on the beat, her every note brittle and staid against the laid-back drums and piano on the practice recording.

Only once did Noelle and Franklin insist and force her to join them for a dinner of broiled salmon, dill potatoes, asparagus, and a sauce in a very hot dish, which Leah put down in the middle of the table, where it marred the wood. It had been an accident, she falsely argued. She hadn't meant to. Noelle nearly screamed, "Did you do that on purpose? Did she do that on purpose, Franklin?" Leah worked herself into tears, denying this, and Franklin looked powerless, seated at the table and trapped between two angry women. Unbelievably, Noelle visited Leah's room later to apologize, and for the shortest moment Leah felt guilty for her lie, though not guilty enough to do more than remove the headphones of her Walkman, hear Noelle out, and then, without conviction, say that she too was sorry for having gotten upset, when in fact she was wondering why Noelle had to be so damn conciliatory, so damn sweet and determined to get along. It made Leah feel all the more petty, childish, and, something she hadn't anticipated, helpless.

Noelle was athletic, too. And so she came with her bright, souped-up mountain bike, her tennis rackets (the second one she'd bought for Franklin as a present), even her otherworldly scuba gear—a tank, face mask, and flippers. She was a healthy, attractive woman with a small waist and noticeable boobs, more noticeable than Leah's mother's, though her mother's face, soft and expressive, was far more beautiful than Noelle's, which was pretty but too lean, too harshly featured. Noelle had even inspired Franklin to buy his own mountain bike and spend every other weekend cycling with her through different areas of northern Michigan. They invited Leah along on every trip and Leah always gave the same answer: maybe next time.

What bothered Leah much more than Noelle was what was happening to Franklin. He was changing. He was becoming another person, someone she didn't know and maybe couldn't know. It wasn't just that he was no longer sad, that he had trimmed his beard and scheduled regular haircuts, that he dressed nicely, even on weekends, that he played tennis, hiked, cycled, took beginning scuba lessons at the Y, none of which the old sedentary Franklin, the man who'd been seemingly happy and in love with her mother, had done. It wasn't just that he'd slimmed up and gotten in shape, which Leah first noticed the very day Noelle moved in, when Franklin—a little muscular in a tank top and shorts, his belly, if still there, more compact and shaped—carried in box after box of her stuff. Nor was it that he was rarely home, only in the mornings and evenings, always occupied, off doing something new, even at his age, forty-seven, and even though he had a grumpy daughter to worry about.

It was all these things together that bothered Leah, and she let her father know it one afternoon, not long after she had damaged Noelle's table and offered only her indifferent apology. He'd come down to her room prepared to accuse her of something, which was obvious to Leah by the way he announced his intention—"We need to talk," he said—then took a book off her shelf and began flipping through its pages without looking at it because he hated conflict so much that he needed to distract himself when he saw it coming. At least, thank God, this had not changed. "I want to say a few things. Just a few things. And then I want a promise from you."

Franklin was wearing a button-up plaid shirt and new penny loafers. Leah knew that he had gotten these clothes with Noelle. Noelle liked plaid, she liked button-up shirts, and didn't much care for middle-aged men who wore T-shirts and jeans all the time. "You're different," Leah said. "Totally different."

"Not really," he said. "I'm just happy."

She smelled something astringent and good on him, and knew at once that this too had been Noelle's influence. "You're wearing cologne."

"So?"

"So you're different."

"I'm going to do the talking, Leah." And even in his ability now to stand up to her, to say what he had just said calmly and with enough force to make Leah's chest constrict and her stomach woozy, he was not the same.

"I'm not different," Leah said. She was sitting on the carpeted floor, her legs akimbo, the headphones of her Walkman resting on her neck, while Franklin stood against her dresser, still playing with the book. "I haven't changed at all." And she hadn't. She was the same girl she'd been three years ago, when her mother had died so quickly it almost seemed that she'd wanted it, that she'd turned over in bed one day, seen the darkness, and chosen it. Never mind that she'd been happy, that she'd enjoyed being a third-grade teacher, enjoyed walking the five minutes down Fifth Street every day to her school, enjoyed going grocery shopping—where, to Leah's embarrassment, she'd hum in the aisles—and enjoyed pulling into the driveway afterwards when, without fail and to Leah's annoyance, she'd always intone, "Home again, home again, jiggety-jig." How simple and irrefutable it had been: Within months of learning of her illness, she was gone and had left Leah and Franklin alone and despairing. And Leah was still despairing while Franklin was not, while Franklin was leaving her behind, dumpy, sullen, unattractive Leah, all things she wanted to be, all things she cultivated by wearing the same pair of frayed, oversized Levi's, the same extra-large white T-shirt for days in a row until they became a loose, unclean second skin, by not wearing makeup or perfume, by letting her long, flat hair remain long and flat, by staying locked inside even in July, when summer had finally come, by saying rudely, bitterly, "It's okay. I like being a cave creature," every time Noelle asked her to come out and do something.

Her father put the book down and seemed about to speak. "She's going to ask you to shave your beard next," Leah said. "I know she is."

"Leah," Franklin said.

"Please don't do it."

"Please stop being a brat," he said with an anger that took her by surprise. Her father never got angry, never raised his voice to her. And now he continued in an overrehearsed, almost mechanical manner, though Leah still heard the most uncharacteristic, barely repressed frustration in his voice. "I came down here to tell you that I am tired of seeing you hurt Noelle every day. I love Noelle. You need to understand that. And so it makes me . . ." He struggled to come out with the word. "Mad, angry to see her get hurt."

"You hate me."

"That's not what I'm saying."

Leah put her headphones on and pressed play, and Franklin came over and removed them from her ears. "I love you," he said as the music continued to issue from the little foam-covered knobs at her neck. "And for your information, I still love your mother. But she's . . ."

"I know," Leah said.

"We know this is difficult for you. It would be difficult for anyone. We understand that. I'd like you to see a therapist."

"That's her idea."

"That's our idea, and it's a good idea. I think it could really help you."

"No."

"It could help you, Leah. It could make you feel better."

"You mean," Leah said, "that it could make *you* feel better."

"Yes," Franklin said. "It might. It just might."

"No."

Franklin nodded and looked down at his new shoes, and remained silent for so long that Leah had to say something. "She's got nicer boobs than Mom had. You must like that." Leah hated the fact that she had more than a few times imagined them together: Noelle, athletic, strong in the hips, on top of the newly buff Franklin, and Franklin, made unrecognizable by sexual frenzy, turning her over, taking her anyway he wanted, sideways, from behind, against a wall.

"I'd rather you not share that sort of thought with me," Franklin said.

"I have to tell someone."

"How about a therapist?"

"Stop asking me that. And please . . . please don't shave your beard off." Because Franklin was clearly more upset now than he'd been since entering her room, Leah said, "I *am* a brat. I know I'm a brat. I don't want to be." And in the abstract, she didn't. But she also knew that she would likely continue to be one.

"I want you to promise me something," Franklin said.

"Maybe."

Franklin gave her a look then that she had seen from him only a few times in her life, a look that would not stand for defiance. "I want you to promise me that you will treat Noelle better. You will treat her with respect."

"Okay," she said. But he didn't leave her room until she said the words he wanted to hear. "I promise."

2

Max had been right about the dogs. They were the real challenge, the harder to watch die. They were mutts and came in all sorts and sizes: small and large, long- and short-haired, spotted, mottled, fat and far too skinny, long-nosed, pug-nosed, beautiful and ugly. As soon as they arrived and settled in their cages, they treated Leah like a mother, a good and caring master. They whimpered and whined; they licked at the thin bars of their cages and at her hands and fingers. At mealtimes, they dove into their bowls, wagging their tails, wagging their entire bodies, until the food and the activity of eating calmed them. Afterwards, when she took the dishes away, they leapt on her, they squealed and yipped and looked into her eyes with something like recognition, something that approached gratitude, that was, in fact, more than gratitude. It took Leah some time to put a word to that look, that recognition, and when the word came to her, she was certain the dogs felt it: trust. As soon as they stepped into her cage, they gave themselves completely over to Leah. The sheep, on the other hand, were indifferent. They hardly made eye contact and remained in their animal world, a stinky dark void without language, without sensations beyond fear and hunger. But the dogs invaded the human realm, leapt over and into Leah's world readily and with the assumption that they belonged there, that their home was with Leah. They trusted her. And what bothered Leah more than the dogs' eventual fate was how terribly misplaced this trust was. "Stupid, stupid dogs," she told them several times a day, and they didn't hear. They continued to depend on her for everything and to seem more than happy to do so.

Unlike the sheep, they didn't resist the short trip from the cages to the operating room. They always competed to be the first out, lunging toward freedom and toward Leah, who delivered a dog to the operating room at least every other day. Leah never chose the animal. There were three to a cage. If she had more than three dogs, she always chose the cage closest to the front of the room, where the most senior dogs, those who had been at the lab longest, stayed. The first out of the cage was the dog she would deliver. In this way, they seemed to choose themselves. To make things worse, they enjoyed the brief trip down the hallway, licking Leah's ankles, diving for her shoelaces, rearing up with excitement. A rubber ball in hand, Max usually made this trip with Leah. At the first sign of apprehension in the animal, he'd let the ball go and the dog would dive for it, focus entirely on the toy and forget everything else.

Leah didn't stay for the operations. Max had already told her more than she'd wanted to know. They were needed to test the utility of a new laser scalpel that might eventually be used on humans for common gallbladder operations. Their gallbladders were cut open, sewn up, and then the whole dog was disposed of. The scalpel cauterized vessels, staunching bleeding, as soon as it cut into the flesh. For certain tissues, such as the gallbladder, this sort of surgical instrument, if it worked, could be very useful. "And how do you know if it works?" Leah asked one afternoon when Max had stopped by her animal basement.

As usual, Max looked sleepy, as if he'd just woken from a nap, his hair tousled, in need of a comb, and his large, drowsy body filling Leah with the urge to grab hold and hug him. "You make sure it cuts effectively. You make sure it causes minimal tissue damage. You make sure it staunches bleeding. In short, you use it."

"Why on dogs?" Leah asked.

"They're similar enough to us, and they're affordable."

"So you cut a few dogs up and see if it works or not. Then you're done."

"I'm afraid we need more than a few dogs. We need a few hundred if we want a statistically significant sample."

"Okay," Leah said. "So why not let them recover?" Leah was sitting at her big, perplexing clerk's desk and listening to the light-rock station turned down low. She'd tried to listen to the jazz station, but the sounds of horns—saxophones, trumpets, trombones—made her dogs (she had five of them now) howl in a forlorn, heartaching way. But harmless old rock songs like "Tie a Yellow Ribbon Round the Old Oak Tree" and "Raindrops Keep Falling on My Head" didn't seem to bother the dogs.

"That would be too expensive," Max said. "Too expensive and too painful for them."

"Don't you think they'd rather live than be spared pain?"

"I'm not sure what they'd prefer," Max said. "I'm not sure they have preferences. They're dogs. We're humans."

"I know that," Leah said, irritated by his insistence on playing the role of the teacher. All the same, Leah knew exactly what the dogs "preferred." She saw it in their every gesture, every bark, howl, and scream. They preferred to live. "We're killing them so that we humans can piss more easily."

Max laughed a little. "You're confusing the gallbladder with the urinary bladder. The gallbladder secretes gall."

"OK," Leah said. "We're killing them so that we can secrete gall."

"Not exactly," Max said. "We're killing them for knowledge."

"And it's worth it?"

"I think so. Eventually. In the long run. Yes." Then he added, "These dogs aren't pets, you know. They're not even strays. They're bred for the lab. No one has trained them. They've never lived in a home."

Leah nodded thoughtfully. "I guess I agree."

And for some stupid reason, Max had to ruin their little discussion of science and ethics by repeating his cautionary note to her. "It's not a good idea to befriend them, Leah."

"No duh," she said. Then she asked an odd question that had been on her mind for some time and that seemed both wrong and necessary to ask. "How much do they cost?"

"Not much," Max said. "They've been donated to us. The transportation, the food, and your services are our main costs."

Leah was surprised to learn that she was part of these costs. "Ten bucks? Twenty bucks?" she asked.

"More or less," Max said.

It was to teach Max a lesson that Leah befriended a dog the next day. It was a medium-sized, long-haired mutt, its white coat spattered with muddy brown spots. He'd been delivered that morning with two other dogs, and Leah had noticed him immediately. He was the calm one, serene almost, amid his barking companions, who would probably spend the next hour jumping and howling at their cage until they discovered that it would not budge. He looked at her in the same moment she looked at him. And when she walked up to him, his companions becoming more frenzied even as he remained calm, she could not help saying, "Sit, boy." Amazingly, the dog sat. "Lie down," she said, and he obeyed. But what excited her most was when she said next, "Roll over," and he did absolutely nothing. That decided it: He would be hers for the day.

As soon as he sauntered out of the cage and calmly plopped himself beside her desk, she sensed that she'd made a mistake. She liked him—liked him a lot—but she didn't want to like him. He edged closer until he was beneath her chair, resting his head on her feet. He licked the rubber toe of her shoe, then closed his eyes, snorted, and all at once fell asleep. Trying not to disturb him, Leah didn't move for nearly an hour. When she did, he followed her everywhere, as if terrified that she might leave him. He wanted to be close. He was at her side as she watered and fed the sheep, as she swept their cages and replaced the wood shavings; then he trailed her back to her desk. He was hungry for her fingers, licking them, nibbling on them whenever they came near. She tried to stop herself from touching him, but he looked at her with a wide, dopey gaze that pulled her in. She wanted to get him back into his cage, get him away from her, but she couldn't make herself do it.

When Max came by that morning to say hi, the dog was still at her feet. "What's he doing out?" Max was angry, and this made Leah angry in turn.

"He's my friend," she said. Max shook his head and seemed too upset to speak. "His name is Ten Bucks." She hadn't intended to name the dog, and as soon as she'd said those words the dog leapt to its feet, seeming to recognize its name, and once again Leah felt that she was wrong. She was making a mistake. And yet she couldn't stop herself. "Watch," she said. She made him sit and lie down. "You said these dogs aren't trained. But he is. Somebody trained him."

"You're playing with him, Leah. He's not to be played with. He's here for a specific reason. He's to be fed. He's to be treated with respect. But he is not a pet. He is the subject of an experiment."

"I know," Leah said.

"He belongs to the lab. We can't let you have him."

"I don't want him," Leah said. She felt something go cold in her. She felt something reckless and compulsive, something she'd felt too often lately, something that made her want to strike quickly and do damage before she could reflect enough to stop herself. Max didn't understand her. He didn't understand her the least bit. "We need a dog this afternoon, don't we?" Leah said. Max nodded. "We can use Ten Bucks. It's fine with me." She looked down at the dog, who was again licking her shoe with that unbearable gaze of affection and dependence trained on her. It angered her. At that moment, everything did.

"Don't call him that, Leah." She thought she saw Max squirm, inwardly shiver. Leah herself felt woozy, off-kilter. *I'm sorry,* she wanted to say. But she was determined not to. "Put him back in his cage now."

She called the dog to the cage, opened it, and he readily—too damn readily—complied, though once she closed and latched the door, he looked at her from the other side with muted injury, with a few simple questions: *Why? What next?*

Max crossed his arms. "I take it you're protesting what we do here. I take it you're not willing to work by our rules. Perhaps you don't really want to be at the lab with us."

"No," Leah said. "That's not it. I want to be at the lab." And she did. She couldn't even begin to imagine the summer without her job. "I want to be here," she said again.

"Then what's the point?"

"The point is," Leah said, "that I'm not a baby. I don't fall in love with dogs and sheep. I can handle it. It doesn't bother me. What you do here doesn't bother me."

Max looked down at his old tennis shoes and seemed to consider Leah's words. From the back of the room, a sheep bleated. The radio began to play an old Chicago tune with a horn section that made the dogs begin to howl and yip so loudly that Leah had to turn the music off. "All right," Max finally said. "You can take it. I get your point. That doesn't mean that you can play with these animals. They're not toys, Leah."

Leah put her head down. "OK," she said.

"The dogs stay in their cages."

She nodded, and Max left her basement.

When he returned that afternoon and asked Leah to bring a dog, something terrible, if not altogether unexpected, happened. Ten Bucks, a name she could not take away, could not now disassociate from him, stepped out of the cage first. She had no one to blame but herself. She'd made herself his master and caretaker, he'd accepted, and now here he was, wagging his tail and wanting—she saw this in his eyes—to be her dog. So he volunteered himself. And when Leah pushed him back into his cage, into safety, the dog lunged forward again and was free. Had Max not been at the door waiting for them, had he not said, in his very concerned way, "Are you sure you don't want to start with one of the others?" Leah might have saved him, at least for a few more days.

"He's got to go eventually, doesn't he?" Leah asked.

She put Ten Bucks on a leash, though it wasn't necessary. He heeled perfectly, his head at her knee all the way down the hall. As usual, Max held the rubber ball and was ready to play with the dog as soon as he saw it become fearful. But Ten Bucks wasn't aware of any danger. It was dumbfounding: the trust of this creature, the strange, boundless faith it placed in Leah, of all people, and in Max and now in Diana, a complete stranger, at the sight of whom Ten Bucks wagged his tail and sat on his haunches. *So happy to meet you,* the dog was saying with his eyes, his open, slack mouth, his whole excited body. Cradling the dog in his arms, Max lifted him to the table.

Most dogs were so frightened of the electric razor that Leah and Max had to hold them down. Not Ten Bucks. He licked Max's palm as Diana stripped his shoulder of hair and exposed a bony, pinkish swath of hide. "He's a sweet one," Max said.

"He sure is." Diana was cooing at him, speaking in a baby voice, which irritated Leah. Once shaved, her dog had lost a subtle measure of dignity, seemed partially naked and skinnier than Leah had guessed, and cooing at him did nothing to compensate for this fact.

"I've got a vein," Diana said, and she sunk a needle into his shoulder. Ten Bucks yelped, but was quickly distracted by the ball that Max now let him mouth. At this point, Leah usually left. But because she had made things difficult that day and because she wanted more than anything to leave now, she felt obligated to stay.

The dog made no protest until the sedation began to take hold and he whimpered. He gazed up at them with a look Leah could not place at first, and then saw that it was fear. Max seemed to sense Leah's need for an explanation. "It's not feeling any pain. It's just a little scary for the animal when the drug begins to take effect."

"Oh," Leah said.

"Such a good boy." Diana was still speaking in that baby voice.

"Please don't talk to him like that," Leah said. Diana gave her a cool look, and Leah understood she'd overstepped her bounds. "Sorry," she added in a quiet voice.

Before Max began to cut, he made Leah wear the same turquoise-blue medical mask over her nose and mouth that Max and Diana wore. What followed was mortifying to watch, though surprisingly bearable. Leah could handle it. She could take it. Ten Bucks was out, his head thrown back on the table, eyes closed, and tongue dangling from his mouth. With his laser scalpel, Max sliced through the soft, white belly, making his incision to the left of the dog's penis. He worked quickly. Following each rapid cut, Leah took in the odor of burnt flesh and something else, something she hadn't experienced before, the earthy, sulfuric scent of the animal's open body, its hot insides. Max described the anatomy as he worked, but Leah could see only a scarlet chaos of blood and flesh. She nodded. She uttered variations of the affirmative—*Yeah, uh-huh, I see*—to Max's instructive comments, even though what she felt was a typical, girlish disgust. She wanted to turn away, throw up, faint even.

When it was over and they had deposited Ten Bucks into a large yellow bag labeled Medical Waste and Diana had rolled the bag on a cart into another room, Max looked at Leah with concern. "How was that?" he asked.

"That was interesting. I've never seen a gallbladder before," Leah said. And Max seemed reassured by her answer.

That evening, Leah allowed herself to be coaxed to the dinner table. She wanted to appease her father, to show him she'd listened to his request of the other day. She was also a little spooked and on edge, and felt relieved to escape the isolation of her room. She couldn't stop thinking about that dog, about the way Ten Bucks had responded to her roll-over command by doing absolutely nothing. By sitting there and looking expectantly, its eyes expressing a terrible eagerness to please. And so Leah found herself at the table hoping she'd be distracted by conversation, by company and good food.

Noelle, who'd changed out of her business suit, looked great in a floral sundress that showed off her toned shoulders and her small waist, a dress that most women in their late forties could never have worn. Noelle was aware of it, too. She was proud of her body—too proud, Leah thought. Nearly every day, Franklin would tell her how great she looked. In fact, he did so now, and his compliment turned on her smile as if he had flipped a switch. Yet as beautiful as Noelle was, she was nervous. She was always nervous around Leah. Dumpy, slovenly, seventeen-year-old Leah, who shouldn't have given this woman a moment's pause, made her clumsy and cautious. And when Leah sensed Noelle's vulnerability, she became all the more hostile. At the moment, for instance, Noelle was watching Leah carefully without seeming to do so. She watched as Leah took a serving of wild rice and a serving of coq au vin—chicken with red Burgundy sauce, Noelle had just explained—and finally a serving of broccoli raab. "With butter and lemon," Noelle said, though Leah hadn't asked. Noelle watched as Leah took a taste of each. She knew exactly what

Noelle wanted from her, and she usually wouldn't have given it. But tonight Leah did. Tonight, she looked up at Noelle and told her her food was delicious, as, in fact, it was. "Even the green stuff tastes good," Leah said.

And though she'd meant it, she saw her father look up at her suspiciously. She'd never freely offered a compliment to Noelle.

"I really do," Leah said. "I like it."

"Thank you," Noelle finally said.

A long silence followed in which the bare sounds of clattering knives and forks, of chewing, swallowing, and drinking, could be heard too loudly. No doubt to put an end to the crude sounds, Noelle asked Leah what she'd done at work that day. "I don't want to talk about it," Leah said. Franklin gave her that look again. "I don't. I'm not just saying that to be a jerk." And now the evening was going wrong, despite the fact that Leah wanted it to go right for once. There was no conversation. Everyone felt awkward and looked down at their plates. So Leah told them the truth. "I demeaned an animal," she said. "I demeaned it and then I killed it."

"That will do," Franklin said, raising his voice.

"I did," Leah said. "I'm just telling you what happened."

"Okay," Franklin said. He clearly didn't believe that she was being honest. "Maybe we could discuss something else."

"I like Noelle's food. I like it a lot," Leah said again. But she was irritated now and couldn't hide it. Noelle smiled, but no one said anything for a while. Because it was clear to Leah that the dinner was ruined, she decided to shut up and let Noelle and Franklin carry on their own conversation about a closing Noelle had completed that day. Leah would have remained silent and that evening would have come to a usual and dull end had Noelle not turned to Leah at the end of dinner with a question. "What do you think your father would look like without his beard?"

Leah had known this was coming. That's all she could think. She had known it and had even warned her father. Noelle had asked the same questions about his clothes, his hair, his shoes, and had, with this kind of rhetorical innocence, changed him completely. "I like his beard. I like it a lot," Leah said too insistently.

"I do too," Noelle said, though she was staring at Franklin now, studying him, imagining him without it.

"He's not shaving it!" Leah hadn't meant to yell, but it was too late. Franklin was upset. She saw it in his face and heard it in his voice.

"I'm not?" he asked her. "Are you sure of that?" He seemed to think that what he was about to do was funny, a simple joke. He put his cloth napkin on the table, excused himself, and headed down the hallway to the bathroom. By the time Leah got there, he was facing himself in the mirror and holding a pair of shearing scissors. Gobs of thick brown beard were falling into the sink. The scissors made a crisp, resolute click and snap. "Daddy," Leah complained. He shut the door and locked it. Leah felt her chest tighten and the tears rise, but she pushed them back. She banged on the door. "Don't do it," she said. He didn't respond, so she charged down to her room and stayed there until she could no longer bear the silence, the cramped aloneness of it. Upstairs, Franklin was still locked in the bathroom and Noelle had not moved from her place at the table. Leah sat back down and said nothing for what seemed a very long time. Finally Noelle said in a voice that was far too sweet, "That was unexpected."

Bitch, Leah thought. And then, without looking at Noelle, she said it, with a deadpan tone that made the word all the more brutish. "Bitch."

When Leah looked up, she saw that word working its effect on Noelle. She saw the shock in Noelle's face, a frozen moment of hurt. Noelle struck Leah then. Not hard, though hard enough for the unexpected blow to sting, hard enough to make Leah scream out, "Noelle hit me! She hit me!"

Franklin came out of the bathroom, one of Noelle's peach-hued towels draped over his shoulder. The evening sun was still out, and he stepped into a spot of it in the hallway as if to show himself more clearly. His beard was entirely gone; only a few bright curls of shaving cream remained at the edges of his face. His brooding scruffiness was gone. His shadowy, deep-set eyes were gone. He seemed to have lost half his age, half his weight. His jaw was surprisingly strong and handsome. A moody graveness had left him. He almost seemed to float down the hall and into the clean whiteness of the kitchen. "She hit me," Leah said again, though without much volume or conviction.

Noelle stood behind her chair at the table, wringing her hands, looking stunned, ashamed. "I'm sorry. I . . ."

Leah felt a flash of sympathy for her, which, thankfully, was replaced by resentment as soon as her strange father looked at Leah. "What happened? What did you do?"

"Me?" Leah said. "I didn't hit anyone."

"Yes, you."

There was exhaustion and frustration in his voice, and Leah couldn't stand there and hear it. She bolted out the front door, slamming it behind her, and stood in the yard beneath the huge maple, its branches fluttering in the light summer breeze. She waited now for her father to run after her, to ask for an explanation of her rude behavior or, better yet, to apologize for what his girlfriend had just done. But the door remained closed. It was quiet, far too quiet. She kicked at the air. She felt that she should have been crying, bawling, but she couldn't summon the energy for an all-out fit. She considered her options. She could walk back into the house and face her father, or she could flee, she could run away, head west, for California, for the beaches and docks, for the deserts and mountains. Or she could head east, for the big cities, for the cramped streets, the bars and clubs with lights and loud music. But she was too old to run away. She didn't even want to run away. She couldn't care less about the West or East or anywhere else. Next year, she'd have to leave for college, which she was hardly looking forward to. What Leah wanted most was to stay home, to sit down in her room, unbothered, lock the door, and smolder there.

Because Leah had no friends and needed to go somewhere that evening, she headed to Max's. Max lived on the other side of Stadium Street, about a twenty-minute walk through parks and quiet neighborhoods. She hadn't been there for years, since before her mother's death, but the house was the same: a simple yellow two-story midwestern Victorian, two windows facing the street downstairs and one sullen window upstairs. A dingy white-picket fence separated the front yard from the sidewalk. Max was out cutting the grass with a push mower. It was mid-evening. The sun edged low on the horizon, just above a storm cloud, from which Leah saw a flash of lightning. But the sun still had heat in it, and the first raindrops were lukewarm and tiny. "Hey," Leah said.

Max wore a floppy straw hat that made him look more folksy than scientific and the same blue scrubs and T-shirt—it said *Take the Pepsi Challenge* and must have been twenty years old—he'd worn at the lab all day. On his feet, as always, were his scruffy tennis shoes, now grass-stained. He greeted her with far more friendliness than she'd expected, waving, then inviting her in. How strange it was to see Max pop his shoes off, the laces still tied, in the linoleum entryway. The sight of him in his white socks felt at once homey and intimate to Leah. Max was a neat freak with absolutely no taste in furniture and interior design. In the living room, Leah walked over an orange shag carpet, then sat in an old, if perfectly preserved, La-Z-Boy, a wooden paddle at its side. Leah gave it a tug, laying herself out flat beneath what she saw now was a thickly textured ceiling. His house was stuck in the seventies. He no doubt owned a waterbed.

Max came out of the kitchen holding a bottle of beer, obviously for himself, and offered Leah a soda pop. "How about a beer for me, too?" Leah said, though she didn't care for the taste of beer.

"That's not going to get me in trouble with Franklin, is it?"

"No," Leah said. "Franklin is pretty cool with that." In fact, he was cool with it; he allowed Leah to have an occasional glass of wine with dinner, in the belief that parents should teach children to drink responsibly.

Max returned with a beer for her, and when he sat down on the couch, Leah noticed something outright grim: two spots of black on Max's scrubs. "Is that blood?" Leah asked.

Max looked at his pant leg. "I'd guess so."

"From the dog?"

Max nodded.

"Oh," Leah said. Outside, the rain was coming down harder now, thumping against the roof, even as the deep orange of twilight poured in through the windows. "I came to apologize for my antics today. For naming the dog and everything."

Max finished taking a swig of beer. "Apology accepted."

"It was an insult to the animal's dignity," Leah continued.

"I'm glad that you see it was problematic."

Leah took a large gulp of her bitter, unpleasant-tasting beverage. "It didn't really hurt him, though, did it? As far as he was concerned, I just let him out of the cage and gave him companionship."

"I see," Max said. "So you did it for him. You did it to make him more comfortable."

"All right," she said. "It was a mistake. I'm sorry. Now I'm going to shut up."

But she couldn't shut up. She was no good at shutting up these days. She gave him a critical look-over. "You're a terrible dresser," she said. "My dad used to be a terrible dresser, before he met his new girlfriend. Before he fell in love. It was because he was depressive. I bet you're depressive. I bet you take Prozac or something."

Max chuckled. "Really? You think so?"

She hadn't expected her words to bounce off him, and the fact that he remained untouched by her sudden honesty made her want to find his soft spots, his vulnerabilities. "I do. I think you're brokenhearted." Leah took another long drink of beer and tried to look mean as she did so. "I think you never got over your wife leaving you. You never even tried to date other women, did you? My dad did. It only took him a few years, and then he was crazy in love. I wish he'd been more like you."

Max put his drink down, and Leah could see that she'd gotten to him this time. He was glaring at her. "You're trying to make trouble, aren't you?"

"Maybe," Leah said. "I guess I sort of do that sometimes."

He studied her for a moment. "Part of me wonders if I shouldn't fire you from the lab right now. Before you do something. I almost did it this afternoon."

"I won't do anything. Not in the lab. I promise. I'm interested in science," she added.

He shook his head. "I'm not so sure you are."

"I am. And I like the animals."

Max sat back, sank into the couch and seemed, for now, satisfied. He was a softie. "I'm a terrible dresser, too," she admitted now. "I know I am. I don't know if I'm depressive. But I know that I don't look so good."

"Nonsense," Max said. "You look fine."

"I don't mind. It doesn't bother me to look this way." She gazed down at her black high-top sneakers. No other girl at her high school dared to wear such unattractive shoes, and Leah couldn't help but be a little proud of their ugliness. When she looked up again, Max was smiling at her. It was a smile of affection and goodwill, and it made her say something she hadn't intended to say. "I sort of have a crush on you. I think about you a lot. I wish I didn't, but I do."

"Hum," Max said. He looked out the window, where the rain had really started to come down now. He smiled. He thought it was cute. He laughed. "You'll get over it, I'm sure." Then he stood up. "I've got to make myself a little dinner. You hungry?"

Because she'd already had dinner, she sat and watched Max eat an odd assortment of food—microwaved hot dogs with mustard, reheated rice and green beans. He ate hungrily, cutting up the hot dogs, slathering them with mustard, and washing each bite down with beer. It felt good to be with him. It felt good just to sit there and watch him eat while it rained outside. Later, Max lent her an umbrella, and during her walk home in the drizzling dark, she thought about them sitting together. She thought about Max, who had no one, no wife and no children. And she thought about how she'd discovered his broken heart, his soft spot that night.

3

The next morning, Leah's father met her in the kitchen dressed in his work suit and surprised her with an offer. "How about breakfast?" he said. The sun was so bright that Leah had to squint as they walked up Washington Street where the noise of traffic mixed oddly with a racket of birdsong.

"I thought you were going to punish me now," she said once they'd been seated at the Broken Egg and Leah's orange juice and Franklin's coffee had been delivered.

Her father nodded. "Yes, I suppose I'm going to." But at the moment he seemed to be stalling. "Noelle told me you two had a talk last night. She told me that you both apologized." Leah nodded. In fact, they had, but the interaction had been brief and uncomfortable. "I know Noelle is sorry. She wishes she hadn't slapped you. I also wish she hadn't. She shouldn't have."

"It's my fault, too," Leah said. "I'm sorry for calling her that."

Franklin put a hand to his bare face. "My prank with the beard didn't help things any, did it? I blew my top. I have to admit I did it to provoke you. Unfortunately it worked." He laughed now and profiled his face for her. "How do you like it?"

"It's strange," Leah said. "You don't look like you."

"You're changing, too, you know." He smiled at her. "You look more and more like your mother, to tell you the truth."

This comment, together with her father's gaze—he was studying her, admiring her—made Leah blush. She grabbed the saltshaker and squeezed it. "You still think about her?" Leah asked.

"Of course, I think about her. You're just as pretty. Maybe even more." He folded his arms then, still looking at her, still smiling. "I wonder," he said, "if you haven't caught the eyes of a few boys. I bet you have."

Leah shrugged. She didn't much want to revisit the boy issue. "I'm not exactly a babe, am I?" She looked down at herself—her T-shirt and loose jeans. "At least, I don't try to be. I don't want to be."

"I think you are. But it might not hurt to try a little harder."

"I don't want to talk about this."

Franklin put his hands up in concession. "All right."

"I bet you forgot what next weekend is," Leah said accusingly. He stared into the air, trying to remember. "It's Mom's birthday. You forgot it."

"Leah." There was a warning in his voice, and the last thing she wanted was to fight now.

"We should do something together, the way we used to," she said. The past two years, Franklin and Leah had spent her mother's birthdays distracting themselves. Last year, just a few weeks before Franklin had met Noelle, they spent the afternoon and evening in the cinema multiplex, walking out of one movie and into another, filling up on popcorn and Cokes, and not leaving until midnight, after which Leah fell asleep on the couch listening to Franklin weep behind his closed bedroom door. The house had been a mess then, dishes stacked in the sink, the floors dirty, their beds unmade, and unfolded clothes from the dryer piled over the living-room chairs. Without Margaret, Franklin and Leah, both bad cooks and natural slobs, had been helpless. Margaret used to institute weekly cleanups, or "dustups," as she'd called them, rallying everyone from bed on Saturdays and cheerfully commanding them, putting brooms and mops in their hands, turning her favorite music up high on the stereo, Johnny Cash or the Doors, so that Leah could remember crouching around the toilet with a sponge of ammonia to "Break on Through" while her mother, scrubbing the countertops, swayed in the kitchen and sang off-key, "You know the day destroys the night." Jim Morrison's drug songs were so not Leah's mother, who was sweet and soft-spoken; she would always counter Leah's assertion that Morrison was all about tripping and getting high by reminding her that the Door's inspiration came from William Blake, from high art. "We're cleaning the house to drug music," Leah would nonetheless say. How this memory could seem pleasant now baffled Leah. At the time she'd resented the chore, resented the interruption of her Saturday-morning sleep, and even found the post-cleanup family breakfast of pancakes or eggs and bacon boring. Now she'd give anything to be scouring that toilet again while her mother danced in the other room.

"Sure," Franklin said cautiously, "we'll do something together."

After they ate, Franklin moved his plate aside. Leah knew her punishment was coming by the way he sat up stiffly. When he spoke now, she could hear that he'd rehearsed his little speech. "It's fairly obvious that you'd rather not make a family with me and Noelle. Not right now, anyway. We both hoped we could persuade you, and we still hope things change soon. In the meantime, we've decided to stop trying to force you into our lives. We won't ask you to eat with us. We won't ask you to go to movies with us. We're happy to let you have your space. If you'd like to do something with us, we'd love the company. We'd love *your* company. But we only want you along if you want to be there. In other words, we want you to make the decision to spend time with us. We can't do that for you."

Franklin placed both hands firmly on the table and let out a long breath as he waited for her response. She felt something very much like the *Oh-well*, the *What-can-be done?* feelings she'd experienced after seeing the first sheep begin to die in the lab: a slight undercurrent of sadness that she could easily hold down and contain. "Okay," she finally said.

Leah did not expect to feel their absence as keenly as she did over the next days. Nor did she expect them to keep their word, to ignore her, to stop extending invitations that she could turn down again and again. They were busy people. When not working, they played. They cooked long, involved dinners, during which Leah made a point of not leaving her room. They spent weekends at bed-and-breakfasts on the coast of Lake Michigan. They attended concerts and theater. Of course, she had not spent much more time with them in the past. What was new and what she noticed now was their lack of interest in her. They too easily got on without her while Leah had very little to do. She had only the lab and Max now, and in some ways she hardly had these. Max had been right; Leah was not interested in science. And Max was not too terribly interested in Leah, save as his student and as an upset young person for whom he might do some good. She had her clarinet and her interest in jazz. But she could stand to play her clarinet no more than an hour each day before the endless scales and dexterity exercises along with her own boundless mediocrity drove her crazy. As for jazz, she could live without it. In fact, the interest was not really her own. She'd picked it up from the first and only guy she'd slept with—an eighteen-year-old drummer named Larry who'd lived across the street from her a few years ago, and with whom she'd slept far too soon after her mother's death. She'd just turned fifteen, and Larry, who was, Leah could tell, a little bored with her, had taught her to like jazz. They had exhaustive sex, in every possible position, for two weeks, after which he'd put his possessions in a duffel bag the size of a human body and left for college.

In short, Leah had, when she thought about it, nothing.

Nonetheless, she liked her work at the lab, where she had become more accustomed to the fate of the dogs. By mid-July, she'd seen scores of them die. While most wagged their tails all the way to the table, a few fought so viciously it took both Leah and Max to hold them down as Diana administered the anesthesia. Weirdly, inappropriately, the fighters were the easiest to help kill; their struggle somehow made the experience more bearable. Leah always chose to stay in the operating room. She stayed because she would rather have left, and her compulsion to avoid this spectacle made her feel equally compelled to do the opposite. At the same time, she had begun to feel that she was more than a spectator, that she was, perhaps, a witness. She saw something that neither Max nor Diana, to whom each dog was a necessary sacrifice, could see. She was watching the animals die without the least bit of certainty that it was worth it. She saw waste and death where they saw anatomy and potential improvements in common gallbladder procedures. And her ability to accept and endure this vision was, as far as Leah could make out, her one accomplishment that summer.

4

It was at the tedious, hot beginning of August that Leah began to visit the properties that Noelle was trying to sell. These were large, beautiful houses in the nicer areas of Ann Arbor—Burns Park and the Old West Side, where Leah lived—green areas with nicely mowed lawns and shady maples spreading their branches over both sides of the street. Noelle kept the keys to the houses she planned to show the next day in separate envelopes, each labeled with an address, on her bedside table. On a sunny evening when Franklin and Noelle had, as usual, gone out, Leah decided to do the same. Why should she remain home when no one else did? And so she borrowed the keys to a few houses that were a short walk away.

At the first, on Green Street, Leah read the name of the realtor on the For Sale sign out front—Noelle Jones. From a plastic folder tacked to the post, Leah took a fact sheet with Noelle's photograph, which captured well, Leah thought, her pleasantness and her highly competent and neat prettiness. This was Noelle's territory, and as Leah turned the key, opened the heavy front door, and set foot on the rich yellow shimmer of wood floors, she was acutely and thrillingly aware of being the intruder, the outsider, the one who could wreck and ruin the careful balance and order of a world to which she had no right of entrance. This home was Leah's. All of it. And when she latched the door behind her and heard the cool and resolute slip and lock of door to jamb, she felt wonderfully transgressive.

This first property she entered happened to be, as most of the houses she would visit over the next days and weeks were not, furnished. Without fear, she switched the lights on and walked from room to room. French doors with beveled glass separated the dining room from the living room, where she turned on the stereo, pressed play, and was happy to hear Freddie Hubbard blasting out "Night in Tunisia," to which she did a brief dance down the hallway. She didn't care if she got caught. Let it happen. Let someone find her and stop her. She took a highball glass from the wet bar, poured herself a bit of brown liquid from a bottle that reeked of adulthood and poison, and felt deflated when she found it undrinkably bad. She lunged onto the king-sized bed in the master bedroom and bounced. She opened the closet, ran her hands over blouses, skirts, dresses, many of them freshly dry-cleaned and wrapped in plastic. Oddly, there were no shoes, but Leah did find a small collection of adult films in a shoebox—*Deep Throat Three, Cock Till You Drop,* and *Analbolic Annabelle.* She pissed in the toilet and left without flushing. She peeked into the children's rooms, one done in blue and the other in pink, as if checking up on the kiddies. She turned on the giant-screen TV and watched twenty minutes of *Friends.* No one came. No one knocked on the door or burst in to stop her. Perhaps the owners had already moved and left behind furniture and clothing, for which they would later return. Or perhaps the owners were still living here and were out for the evening. In any case, Leah was underwhelmed by her first uneventful act of breaking and entering, and so she conducted what Max might have called an experiment. She took a vase from the entryway table and dropped it, watching it shatter and feeling almost nothing. A slight twinge of guilt, a shiver of pettiness and irrelevancy. She hardly knew what she'd expected, but she'd wanted more. She cleaned it up, turned all but a few lights off, left out the shot glass to make a simple statement—"I was here," she wanted it to say, "and had a taste of the porridge."

The second house she visited was empty, and its complete vacancy seemed to watch her and follow her as she invaded each room, opened every door, every cupboard and closet, only to find more emptiness, which entered her as easily as she had entered that house, and left her feeling spooked and agitated, especially when she discovered in an unguarded instant someone else at the end of the dark hall, clearly odious, staring at Leah, poised as if to attack, and who turned out to be, as she saw in the next instant, merely herself in a full-length mirror. Even once she had locked the front door and rounded the corner at the end of the street, Leah couldn't shake the surprise of that odd ambush and the spookiness of that place.

As soon as she opened the door to the next house, she heard a measured, unsettling beeping. Because it sounded like a microwave, she hurried into the kitchen, only to see the blank face of a convection oven, eerily silent and giving her the time—7:38, it said—in green digits. When she discovered the code on a slip of paper in her envelope, the alarm had already begun screaming. Every light seemed to be flashing, and the electric pulsating howl seemed to come from the house itself, the walls, ceilings, stairs, planks, boards, the slow liquid of the windows, the plaster, the wiring hidden beneath it, the electricity that flowed through that wiring. But she didn't feel the thrill, the vigor, the good and vital urgency of panic and danger until she began running, until she fled down the hall, out the entryway, leapt through the front door without closing it, and began her sprint toward home. She sprinted one, two, then three blocks, right past the police department on Huron Street, where a cop car just then pulled out, its lights flashing and siren whirring, and she hoped it was heading to that house. How good it felt to have escaped, to still be fleeing, how good the burn in her legs and lungs, how good—so suddenly and remarkably good—everything had become, everything still was, until she reached her front porch, unlocked then locked the door behind her, and found her own home as strange, empty, and quiet as any she had seen that night.

Leah had not given up on Max—on catching his eye, on showing him she was more than his disturbed young charity case. So she did the obvious: She put an end to her self-imposed ugliness. She dispensed with the baggy boy's jeans and the extra-large T-shirts, which, untucked, reached nearly to her knees and took on a floppy, pajamalike appearance. Franklin too eagerly gave her cash when Leah told him she needed new clothes. "Of course," he said with an enthusiasm and a smile that stung her, that made her feel she had lost a struggle they'd been engaged in for some time.

In less than an hour at the mall, Leah reoutfitted herself with khaki pants, a few blouses, colored T-shirts, a few sundresses and skirts, all of which fit her. In the mirror at J.Crew, she discovered that she was not at all bad-looking. Her hips and thighs were fuller than she might have liked, but her breasts were prominent and shapely, where before, in her frumpy drapes, they had appeared matronly and fat. So surprised was she by her body that it did not seem at all hers. She recognized it, though. It was her mother's. Franklin had been right—Leah did resemble her. Thighs, hips, breasts: all her mother's. Her mother's, that is, before she'd had Leah, before she'd put on what she'd called an extra layer over her hips and tummy. "You don't get rid of that," she'd told Leah. "That's from you. That's what I got for bringing you into the world." It had never been an easy body to have, too pronounced and curvaceous. In the fifties, it would have been fashionable. But not now. And Leah's mother had always treated it as an adversary, glaring at it in the mirror, struggling with diets, losing ten pounds in a few months and gaining it all back in a few weeks. In the end, it had betrayed her. Her blood had turned mean, self-destructive. She lost her appetite. The bones surfaced in her face, her arms and legs. And because the treatment was usually ineffective and often worse than the disease, she just waited for the leukemia to take her. In her overcheerful manner, she tried to be funny about it. "I finally lost that weight, didn't I?" But Leah and Franklin couldn't laugh, and in the final month her mother was frightened. She was afraid to be alone and needed constant company. "Tell me something, anything. Let's talk," she'd say. And when they ran out of things to talk about, Leah read *Gone with the Wind*, her mother's favorite novel, out loud to her. "Scarlett is such a beautiful little bitch, isn't she?" her mother said one day, interrupting Leah's reading. Leah had never heard her mother swear before. She'd been a sweet woman, someone who almost never showed anger, who became quiet when annoyed. "I swore," she said, laughing uncomfortably. "It felt good to swear. I'm going to swear some more, if you don't mind." Leah put the book in her lap. It was late on a cloudy afternoon and white, sunless light fell in through the window. "Goddamn it," she said experimentally. "Shit, shit," she said again. "Bastard, goddamn bastard." Her voice had turned angry now, angrier than Leah had ever heard it. "Fuck, goddamn fuck shit!" Her mother sat up, closed her eyes, and put a hand firmly over her mouth. When she took her hand away, she breathed in deeply. She was crying. "Sorry, sweetheart," she said, her voice warm again, recognizable. "Please read some more."

Standing in front of the mirror at J.Crew, Leah felt a tug of the old grief, the force of which had pulled her under and kept her there for years. But it was only a tug, and it didn't persist as Leah continued to look at herself and as the blond salesgirl, who must have been Leah's age, stood behind Leah, smiled in the mirror, and said, in her bright voice, "That's so cute. I think it's you. I really think it's you." Seeing herself, a pretty, if not quite sexy, young woman, Leah understood that she was no longer mercilessly sad, that she no longer had access to the torrent of loss and rage that had been her absent mother. That had been replaced now by a distant ache, a suppressible grief. And so Leah put her mother out of her mind now, faked a smile, and handed over her father's money.

On the way home, driving by strip malls and the vast parking lots surrounding them, she realized she had let her mother's birthday pass last weekend. She had forgotten it, done nothing to mark it. Leah was suddenly agitated, uncomfortable. Where had that storm of feeling gone? And when? How had she failed to notice its departure? Her grief had simply faded. Yet the world had not changed because of it. She noted the remarkable plainness of everything—the streetlamps, the produce market on the corner, the train tracks and the brown, desiccated weeds growing out beneath them. And when she arrived home, she found Noelle as irritatingly nice and accommodating as ever. Noelle asked to see all her purchases and praised each one, praised Leah's taste. "You look darling," she said as soon as

Leah stepped in the front door. Leah smiled, even as she inwardly cringed. How could she believe this woman? How could she think that Noelle was anything but quietly contemptuous of the dumpy-looking teenage girl who had, for months now, been equally contemptuous of her?

In fact, Leah was sabotaging Noelle. Over the past week, Leah had been the source of numerous client complaints about Noelle's irresponsible treatment of their properties. Leah had left lights on, front doors ajar, dirty drinking glasses out on the counter. She'd even heated a frozen pizza in a microwave, left half the pizza uneaten on the dining-room table, and neglected to clean the dishes she'd used. Noelle was perplexed, worried, and, of course, certain of her innocence. She denied everything and, for now, her realty company and most of her clients remained patient, if also suspicious.

The next day at the lab went poorly. First of all, no one noticed Leah's transformation: her jeans that fit, her bright red T-shirt and bright red tennis shoes, her lipstick and her hint of eyeliner. Max said nothing as he helped her push one more nervous sheep down the hallway. She wanted to bring it up somehow. *Do you notice anything different?* But how could she as she squared off with the backside of a farm animal and pushed until exhausted? Nor could she compete with the video graph of the catheter and with Max's intense focus on the EKG after he'd administered another infarction.

Later that afternoon someone finally noticed her: Jason Clark, the guy who dropped the animals off and took their remains away. Leah had always thought of him as the mortician, the caretaker of the lab, and she shrank from him when he approached her that day, smiling in a way he hadn't before and putting his hand out to introduce himself for the first time. "Jason," he said. "I'm the Sanitary Technician. I'm the guy who brings the animals here alive and takes them back . . ." He'd been about to say dead, but then seemed to realize that he couldn't. Not as part of a flirtation, anyway. "You know," he said.

"I'm Leah. I'm the animal girl," she said, because she couldn't come up with anything better to call herself. "I feed and take care of the animals."

He must have been eighteen or nineteen. He was tan and muscular, wore a Tigers baseball cap backwards and expensive sunglasses. He'd seemed to Leah a perfect jackass—one of those cool guys—before this afternoon, when he first noticed her.

In the uncomfortable silence that followed their introduction, Leah asked Jason something she had not, until now, wanted to know. "Where do the animals go? What happens to them?"

"They go to the incinerator in Detroit."

"Incinerator?"

"A big oven. They burn them there. Dust to dust, you know."

Leah nodded. She knew almost nothing about Detroit, although it was only forty-five minutes east of Ann Arbor. Every time she'd been there, its endless blocks of gutted buildings and gray cityscape had frightened her. It seemed like the appropriate place for the animals to be discarded, thrown away. "It's a bit gloomy there," he warned. "But you're welcome to come, if you want."

Gloom. For some reason, Leah was drawn to it and wanted to know about it. And because there were no procedures scheduled for that afternoon, Leah cleaned her cages, fed and watered the animals a few hours early, then met Jason Clark in his large white truck out back.

This trip to the incinerator was the closest Leah had ever come to a real date. With Larry, it had really just been fucking, fucking and casual companionship. She'd go over there in the morning, hang out, talk about jazz, listen to him practice, bang on his drum set, before they eventually got around to doing it in his soundproof practice room in the basement—one, two, sometimes even three times in one day. They'd been active enough for Leah, only ten days after her mother's death, to suffer her first urinary tract infection. At the time, her house had been full of mourners, friends and relatives, her mother's brothers Tommy and Eric, both of Leah's grandmothers, and her one living grandfather. It was crowded—always someone locked in the bathroom, either pissing, shitting, or weeping, though mostly weeping. They'd tell stories about her mother, start laughing, laughing hard, too hard—it wasn't that damn funny, Leah knew—until everyone was crying. Tommy and Eric had already gotten into a shouting match about which of them had convinced Leah's mother at age five to press her finger against the red-hot coil of a stovetop burner. And every fight had to end in apologies, repetitive and too intensely honest. Leah's grandmother, her mother's mother, cried more than anyone. Every minute of every day, she let you know how unfair it was. Why should she, at seventy, be alive and well and her forty-two-year-old daughter be dead? Why? It was more than a constant irritation. More than too much family in too little space. It was hysteria. It made Leah want to scream.

From this insanity, mild-mannered, sweet, and horny Larry, with his long, narrow face, his beaked nose and dazzling hazel eyes, was her only release. She woke every day around eleven, showered, and went to Larry's for more fucking, though, in truth, mostly they'd just talked and listened to music together, music Leah had never heard before: Miles, Art Tatum, Coltrane, Ellington, Fitzgerald, Sarah Vaughan, Billie Holiday, Jelly Roll Morton, Coleman Hawkins. She'd liked the music more than anything else, more than Larry's company, more even than the sex. She liked it despite the fact that she heard the same emotion in just about everything Larry played for her: anger, laid-back, just behind the beat, dark and seething, pounding, blasting, soft, tender, sad, bluesy, fast and slow, loving, passionate, ecstatic anger. In every note, she heard it. While Larry commented on the phrasing, this or that solo, the allusions, the staccato style of Sonny Rollins, the hypersonic energy of Dizzy Gillespie, Leah was in awe at how much rage this music could convey. How could it possibly hold so much of that one emotion? In song after song, musician after musician, in all volumes and tempos and tonal colors. Anger, wrath, fury. How beautiful that music was, more beautiful than Leah could remember anything ever being.

Larry was nice about it. He kept saying it was his fault that Leah's crotch hurt, which struck Leah as sweet, if somehow cowardly and unfair to her. She wanted it to be her fault. She wanted to feel the burden, the shame. Both of them were sexual dolts and had no idea what could be wrong with her. They assumed it was a venereal disease, never mind that neither of them had had sex before. Leah found the physical pain a relief, real and undeniable. She sat at home crying, and everyone thought she was thinking of her mother when in fact she could think of nothing else than the pain in her crotch. Larry wanted to drive her to Planned Parenthood, but Leah refused. She took the city bus. She sat hunched over while her crotch pounded, while she felt the constant, burning urge to pee and yet could not. In the clinic, surrounded by pamphlets on AIDS, gonorrhea, herpes, and genital warts, Leah felt she was being punished. She had fucked too much and indiscriminately, not more than a week after her mother had died. She was being punished, and the simplicity and rightness of it was satisfying. Then, after she took the prescribed antibiotics, the pain left, as did her relatives and Larry. She was suddenly alone. No longer a virgin, though not diseased, not doomed. And when the grief came, it was more forceful than she had expected. Leah saw quite clearly that it would never leave. It would always be with her. It would always crush her.

But it was no longer what it had been, no longer all-encompassing, as Leah had noticed only yesterday. And now she had caught the eye of another boy, Jason Clark, and was sitting in a big white flatbed truck that carried two dumpsters, a red one and a black one, which held dead animals. On the way out of Ann Arbor, Leah sat up high in the truck, above the small cars and their smaller drivers. She felt the rumble of the engine in her thighs and torso. And she felt surprised to be thinking to herself that this was it—her first real date.

"That's Category One and Two," Jason Clark said as they barreled down 23. He was talking about the dumpsters chained to the flatbed behind them. "It's all regulated by the government, by the USDA. Category One is the classification for the small stuff—rats, mice, bats, birds, reptiles—stuff that's not protected under the Animal Welfare Act. Two is larger mammals—cats, primates, the sheep and dogs you work with. The black container is for One, the red's for Two. We keep them separate—when they're alive and when they're dead. It's all regulated. As is incineration. You can't just dump them in a landfill."

Jason was doing, Leah guessed, what guys did to impress girls. He was telling her what he knew—the facts, the tidbits, the plain, uninteresting stuff in his head. "We pay the incinerator by volume. The university buys the right to dump fifty thousand gallons of medical waste in Detroit every year." Jason drove the huge truck with one hand on the wheel. "Can you imagine?"

"Nope. I can't," Leah said. The truth was she didn't want to know any more about the dead things that were their cargo. What was she to make of what she knew, anyway? She knew, for instance, that the dead sheep behind them had had their hearts removed, cut out of them and refrigerated, and the dogs had had their gallbladders destroyed. Fifty thousand gallons of medical waste per year. She knew that now. Category One and Category Two. Small animals and big animals. It added up to nothing. So why know it? "Let's not talk about this anymore."

He nodded. "No problem." He turned and looked at her then. "You look . . . better . . . different. I mean, you did something to yourself. You look good, really good."

In the instant that he began to appreciate her, Jason Clark became annoying. It wasn't, it seemed, that he was unhandsome (in fact, he was handsome), nor was it that he was a showoff. It was, as near as Leah could tell, that he liked her. Now that she saw this, his sleek, equine face—the long nose and narrow cheekbones—became horsy, just right for a bit and bridal. His ears seemed cartoonishly large. His teeth stuck out too much. His arms and shoulders were too buff. He was all wrong.

Thank goodness, then, that they were arriving in Detroit, which was indeed gloomy. The incinerator was not, as Leah had assumed, on the city's edge, in the shadow of industry, of warehouses and factories, but at its center, just off Cass Street, where only a few years ago, Leah knew, crack cocaine had been bought and sold. A block of concrete supporting two smokestacks, one larger than the other, the incinerator stood just behind a strip of buildings—a diner, a pawn shop, a secondhand store, a bar called I Love Lucy, and a number of boarded-up storefronts. Down the street, a broken fire hydrant spewed torrents of water. A paper bag tumbled across the sidewalk in a gust of hot wind. Shattered glass shimmered in the street gutter. In Detroit almost everyone, it seemed to Leah, was black: the man sitting barefoot against a wall, the boy walking past him wearing sneakers that shone a perfect, unmarked blue, the nicely dressed couple who'd just stepped out of a brand-new Mercedes SUV, the old woman on the opposite side of the street, tapping along on an aluminum cane as she walked her little dog on its leash. This fact scared Leah and made her feel something she rarely felt elsewhere: white. It was one more thing to know, one more thing she couldn't make sense of.

The incinerator was surrounded by a red brick wall, blackened by dirt and exhaust, and a high chain-link fence topped with razor wire. As they turned into this odd-looking fortress, Jason said again, "Fifty thousand gallons of waste." A black man stopped them at the entrance. Jason and he exchanged paperwork, and soon Jason was backing the truck into a port, from where a stationary crane lifted the color-coded dumpsters—Categories One and Two—and delivered them into the incinerator. Leah felt the truck lift and lighten. In a few minutes, the dumpsters were spit back out, empty now, and lowered onto the truck. "That's it," Jason Clark said cheerfully. He was more and more annoying and made Leah appreciate Max, who despite all this grimness believed in knowledge, believed it led to something more than impressing girls, something more than a list of information to be recited.

Leah thought it was disgusting how quickly and neatly the animals had disappeared. And though neither stack of the incinerator was smoking, she rolled down her window, sniffed at the air for burnt flesh, and smelled nothing beyond the exhaust of the truck she sat in.

To enter Noelle's houses, Leah no longer had to borrow the keys. She'd had them duplicated. She had her own keys now.

A few times, she'd almost been caught. Once she'd nearly walked in on a couple making love in the shower, their clothes strewn over the master bedroom and the loud sounds of their sex echoing from the bathroom. She'd quietly backed out of the room and escaped. Another time, she'd just left a house through the back as Noelle and a client came in through the front.

Leah tested the limits of her trespassing. She not only ate meals, peed, and watched TV in these houses, but now and then spent the night.

Her favorite place for a sleepover was the Bradford house, the first house she'd entered that summer. It was fully furnished, its letterbox stuffed with mail that the neighbors would collect every few days.

There was frozen food—pizzas, burritos, Swanson dinners, chicken, steaks, hamburger meat—in a lay-down freezer in the basement. There were twelve-packs of Coke, Sprite, and root beer in the fridge, stores of toilet paper in the laundry room, clean linen and towels in the closets, even movies on DVD, including the small selection of porno films she'd discovered earlier, which she found both thrilling and tedious to watch—all those tits and cocks. Mr. and Mrs. Bradford, with their huge caches of frozen food, their full closets, their beautiful house, their adult films, and even framed pictures of their kids—a girl and boy of grade-school age—poised just so on the bedroom dresser were a mystery to Leah. Why would anybody leave such a life behind, all its trimmings, all its provisions in place? Had one of them died and the other taken the kids and fled? Had one of them left, simply walked out of the house and never turned back? Had their children been brutally murdered, kidnapped? Leah guessed it had been a tragedy. Why else would anyone leave the remnants so obviously in place, so ready for use, for a family to slip into? Everything was there—even a dresser filled with men's socks and underwear, even three different kinds of half-used mustard in the refrigerator, a coffee can of quarters, nickels, and dimes on a table in the entryway, used toothbrushes in the bathrooms. Everything was there save for life itself, the joy and anger, exhaustion and energy, the desire that was needed to do anything, anything at all: eating, fucking, getting out of bed, loving and raising kids, talking, yelling, shouting, spitting, scratching, kissing. Now all of it had been left—tables, chairs, ceilings, windows, room after room; two staircases, one leading to the basement, the other to the second floor, the master bathroom with marble sinks and a whirlpool bathtub, magazine racks filled with *National Geographics* and *New Yorkers*, all of it abandoned, frozen in place. The entire shell locked under one roof, for sale (furniture inclusive, the fact sheet had said), and, as it happened, for Leah's exclusive use, at least while it lasted.

The first time she spent the night in the Bradford house, she arrived home after work the next day, after nearly twenty hours of being away, and discovered that neither Noelle nor Franklin had noticed her absence.

On another occasion, already tucked into the Bradfords' king-sized bed and watching TV on mute, she called home and got Franklin. "Leah, is that you?"

"Hi, Dad."

"We thought you were downstairs in your room."

She could hear music in the background—the Beatles, of which Noelle was, of course, a fan. They were one of the easiest possible bands to like, one of the bands that everybody, no matter what their ages, adored, and so they seemed just right for Noelle's good, if conventional, taste. At the same time, Leah had to admit that Noelle's affection for the music was genuine. She had once seen Franklin and Noelle, in the kitchen, wineglasses in hand, boogying to this music, moving their hips and arms and legs. She imagined them now, even as her father talked to her, dancing, swinging an arm, kicking a leg in an awkward, middle-aged style of dance that was nonetheless joyous. They loved each other. They loved each other so much they wanted to dance together in the kitchen. "Nope," Leah said. "I'm at a friend's house. I thought I should call and tell you I'd be staying over here tonight."

"A friend's house," Franklin said in a tone of surprise. "She's at a friend's house," he said now to Noelle, as if boasting.

"I do have friends, Dad." It stung to say this, since Leah and Franklin both knew she didn't have friends.

"Of course," he said. "Which friend's house are you at?"

"Michelle's. I'm at Michelle's house." Leah felt a shiver of fear and anticipation because she had just decided to confess, or at least sort of confess. "Michelle Bradford. I'm at the Bradford house."

"Great," he said. "Enjoy yourself, then."

"Dad," Leah said, irritated now. "I'm at the Bradford house." She clenched her eyes shut and waited for her father to realize what she was saying. But he didn't. The stupid man simply hadn't heard her.

"Okay," he said, becoming a little irritated himself.

"Don't you want the number over here?" she asked.

"Oh," he said, "yes. That might be a good idea."

She gave it to him, and then he hung up.

The next day, instead of going home, she entered another house, an "armed" house, as the security stickers on its front window called it. Though she knew the code and could have disarmed the security system, she sat down on the living-room carpet and waited for the cops. The alarm was deafening. Its scream and the pulsating lights of the house seemed to mark the end of everything. She thought about what to say and how to explain herself to Franklin and Noelle, the scene of anger and tears that would soon come. Outside, another beautiful, hot sunny day was in its slow, late-afternoon progression. Five minutes passed, and no cops arrived. It was a Saturday, and the neighbors were either not home or had decided to stay in their houses. Every man for himself. She could destroy the entire house, and no one would come. She could burn it to the ground, take a hammer to its walls, smash its windows. And as she sat in the middle of the empty living room, she felt sleepy, exhausted. She wanted to curl up and shut her eyes, and might have if not for the terrible electrical shrieking of the house.

After ten minutes, Leah gave up. She walked outside and had already crossed the street when the officers finally arrived. One talked into the radio while the other, a young Asian woman, came for her. She hardly knew how to be arrested, how to present herself to be "taken in," and so she'd been about to raise her hands above her head when the cop said, "You see anybody enter that house?"

"No," Leah said.

"Did you see anybody leave?"

Leah shook her head.

"Did you see anything?"

"Nope." And that was that. The cop left her standing there, on the loose, and she walked down the street now, lacking the courage to turn herself in.

5

At the end of the summer, the lab had a barbecue and softball game, to which everyone—Leah, the security guard, Diana, Jason Clark, and people from different departments whom Leah had never met—was invited. The diamond was in a park across from Max's house, where people hung out in the backyard drinking beer and waiting for hot dogs, chicken breasts, and hamburgers to come off the grill. It was Leah's last chance, before leaving the lab and returning to school, to impress Max, to show him who she was and what she was capable of, and to make a claim on him greater than that of a student and dullard adolescent. And so, naturally, she did nothing. She froze and felt painfully shy, holding an illegal beer, the taste of which she did not at all like, while jolly and collegial adults told jokes, conversed, drank a little too much and gossiped all around her. "What?" Jason Clark asked in mock surprise as he looked at the selection of grilled meats. "No lamb chops. Why on earth not?" Leah, Max, and Diana all laughed. Other researchers joked about the animals they worked with. Someone giggled at the gruesome thought of rabbit stew. "I sometimes dream about mice. I see nothing but mice," a woman said and began to laugh uneasily.

Meanwhile, Leah wasn't having a good time and wasn't laughing.

Max tapped her shoulder at one point. "You seem quiet, kiddo. You all right?"

"Of course," Leah said. "I'm fine."

Always oblivious to fashion, Max wore shorts that were just a little too short and an old pair of leather cleats. He held a worn baseball glove in one hand and a bat in the other, and Leah saw in his soft burliness something she hadn't anticipated: the eager physicality of an athlete. "Let's go play," he said. Then he began following the other research scientists and laboratory employees across the street to the baseball diamond when he surprised Leah again by turning around and saying, "By the way, you look great today. You really do." It was the first time he'd noticed, and though his tone suggested nothing more than friendliness, and seemed to reflect more his good mood than anything he saw in her, Leah felt a distinct lifting of spirits. She'd taken pains that day to look her best; she wore eye makeup, lipstick, a jean skirt and white tank top, through which showed, very faintly, the red lace of her bra.

Because she had taken extra care in her appearance and felt that it could easily crumble, that she could lose all her elegance in one wild swing of a bat, she refrained from playing and stood behind the high chain-link backstop and watched. It was a mild day in late August with a light breeze, a seamless blue sky, and a full, if not quite hot, sun, a day in which the chill of autumn, still distant, could nonetheless be felt. The great maples that bordered the park lifted countless pale green leaves that shimmered in the light. Tree cotton whirled through the air. In the distance Leah heard a siren, but it was faint compared to the urgent calls from the infield of "Hey, batter. Hey, batter, batter, batter."

Leah was surprised by the competitiveness of these scientists. They wanted to win, none more than Max, who turned out to be a powerhouse. When he stepped to the plate, the outfielders stood farther back. And though Diana threw a fierce underhand pitch, winding up and throwing strike after strike, she couldn't keep her boss from hitting a three-base grounder and a home run in the first inning. Max ran like a tank, not fast but with a scary momentum and force, his entire body leaning forward and the muscles in his thighs quivering with power. After the first hour of play, he was drenched and his T-shirt was heavy with sweat. And though Max hit another homer with the bases full in the final inning, and jogged over each base with the confident swagger and ease of the victor, his team finally lost, overpowered by Jason Clark and a skinny, pale research scientist with long, braided hippie hair, who despite his sticklike frame matched Max in strength and competitiveness. As much as he wanted to win, Max didn't seem to mind losing, shook hands, and said, "Next year. There's always next year."

Leah never would have guessed at this happy, vigorous, physical side of Max had she not seen it. And now that she had, now that she knew more about him, she was thrilled. He kept surprising her. She wished it wasn't true, but it evidently was: She loved him. She loved him despite—or even because of—something else she'd discovered during the game when she'd gone in to use the bathroom in Max's empty house. She couldn't resist searching his medicine cabinet and was saddened to see that her guess had been right. He did take Prozac. She'd been stupid to hurl her reckless guess at him a few weeks ago, to say something so intentionally hurtful. Nonetheless, after she'd made this discovery, she searched for more secrets. Having invaded several homes that summer, she knew right where to look, right where people kept the things they wanted no one else to see. She could hear the distant noise of the game still in progress—the cheers and boos—as she sifted through Max's closet, looked through a few boxes and bags, and found nothing more than dozens of pairs of old sneakers of the sort he wore every day, photos of him and his ex-wife on various vacations, shoehorns, and bottles of athlete's-foot powder. Just before giving up and leaving his room, she bent down and saw the box under his bed, which was not, she was surprised to discover, a waterbed. He'd hardly hidden the stuff. He had no one to hide it from. The two magazines showed typical images—women with fake boobs engorging themselves on cocks, men with multiple women climbing over them and serving them in every conceivable manner. There was a bottle of lubricant called Sex Silk and a well-worn paperback entitled *Stories of Eden: Real Erotica Written by Women.* Leah was angry at first, jealous. She might have thought he was a creep had she not already known him and had she not seen that some married couples kept this sort of thing stashed away. And so her jealousy was tinged with curiosity and sympathy. He was needy, vulnerable. He wasn't just a scientist, a careful and brilliant man. He wanted what most men wanted. He wanted women and didn't have them. He wanted sex and didn't get it. He no doubt wanted companionship. And unlike the married couples who—or so Leah imagined—used this stuff together, Max had to look at it alone, locked in his house, and this sad thought made Leah want him more.

She stayed late that night, after everyone else had left, helping clear the plastic cups and empty bottles from the porch while Max scrubbed grill utensils and silverware in the sink, soapsuds sticking to his hairy forearms. *Kind of Blue* played on the stereo, a sliver of bright moon hovered in the corner of the kitchen window, and Leah hummed to the music as she wiped down the counters and put a few dishes away. As she worked she felt that she and Max made something like a family, something that felt comfortable and maybe even permanent.

Afterwards, they sat on the couch in the living room, where Max offered her a second beer—"As long as you think Franklin won't mind"—and she took it, though she had no intention of drinking it. Max sat back into the puffy couch and smiled at her. "You've changed your look, haven't you?"

He'd now noticed her for the second time that day, and Leah felt things begin to shift between them, begin to feel different, slightly uncomfortable and tense in a good way. "A little," she said.

"I noticed that Jason Clark has taken an interest. He tries hard whenever you're around." Max was smiling. He thought it amusing, this romantic tension between two young people in his lab.

"I could care less about Jason Clark."

"Poor Jason," Max said, with far too much sympathy. Then, in the dim puddle of light cast by a dinky side-table lamp, Max reached over, leaning in close to Leah, so close that Leah almost lifted her face to his, almost presented herself to him, just when he clinked his beer with hers and ruined everything by sitting back into the couch and saying, "We're going to miss you. I have no idea how we're going to replace you at the lab. Thanks for your good work this summer." And that was it: good-bye with a simple clink of beer bottles.

"I think Jason Clark is an asshole," Leah said, unable to suppress the tremor of something like tears and rage that made Max sit up then. "And I like you. I still like you a lot."

"I like you, too," Max said.

"Don't say that." She grabbed his arm, unsuspectingly draped across the couch, then his shoulder, gripping onto his cotton sweatshirt, and pulled him toward her with more force than she'd thought herself capable of. Their lips did not meet so much as collide, and when she kissed him she felt both teeth and mouth and smelled the surprising salty warmth of him.

"No, Leah." He started to push her away, then recoiled when he realized that his hands were on her breasts. He relented then, and for a moment that Leah might have imagined, he started to kiss her, really kiss her, before he dug his fingers into her shoulders and threw her back against the couch.

"Stop that. Jesus."

"Let's just kiss."

"Leah," he said, half shouting now. "I don't want to kiss you." And then, obviously out of discomfort and completely without humor, he began to laugh and shake his head.

Why did he have to laugh? Any other response would have been better. "You *do* want to kiss," Leah said. "I know all about what you want. I looked under your bed. I saw the stuff you have there, the stuff you get off to."

"Leah," he said.

"You're depressed, too. I looked in your medicine cabinet. I was right about you being depressed. You're perverted and depressed."

"Jesus, kid," he said. For a moment he put his head down, and Leah saw something in him she hadn't seen before. The loose neckline of his sweatshirt had been pulled down over his shoulder, where Leah's fingernails had left three red trails, and half his belly, soft and full, was showing. In this disheveled state, he was vulnerable, childish. Leah thought he might start crying. But he didn't. He was blushing. He was ashamed and humiliated. And as if just then realizing what Leah had seen, he straightened his sweatshirt and covered himself. "That's private, Leah. That is my . . ." He looked at her now and, in a voice neither loud nor angry, in a voice that left Leah feeling utterly irrelevant, he said, "Get out of my house now." When she didn't move, he said in that same calm voice, "Now. I mean it."

The next day, Leah knew she couldn't go in to work. Nor could she stay at home, lest Franklin and Noelle suspected that she'd once again done something wrong. So she left in the morning and loitered around town. She sat on the corner of State and North University where the dispossessed teenagers and homeless adults, most vaguely insane or very drunk, hung out, asking for money or playing old instruments, guitars or harmonicas, badly. A kid who wore a ripped T-shirt and something that looked like a dog collar kept asking her for a cigarette, and she kept saying she didn't smoke, until he started to freak her out and she left. She had a coffee at the Starbucks on Liberty Street, where she couldn't help overhearing a woman two tables away talking on her cell phone about the sex she'd been having with someone she'd just met. "It was a wonderful oral experience." She actually said that, whispered it, with Leah sitting right in front of her. To get through the afternoon, Leah perused the used bookstores on Liberty. She found herself picking up book after book, but not really looking at them, not even reading their titles. What was she doing? Why was she even in this place?

She had keys to eight homes in her pocket. But when she walked into the quiet, green neighborhoods and faced these houses, she couldn't enter them. Each confronted her with its vacancy, its quietness. When she stood in front of the Bradford house, where she was surprised to see a "Sale Pending" sticker over the sign, she wanted a child, a little girl to rush out the front door, leap onto the lawn, and begin jumping rope over the grass. A little girl to dispossess it of emptiness. And a man pulling weeds in the front yard, a dog in the backyard barking, a neighbor crossing the grass to get to the front door and knock on it. So she was all the more startled to see that someone was, in fact, home. Through the glare of sunlight on the kitchen window, Leah could see the arms and torso of a woman standing at the sink. Leah glanced behind her, saw that no one was looking, and approached. The woman wore a simple white blouse, and as Leah came closer she heard her humming a childish, frivolous song. She was happy, and this thought made Leah smile, made Leah step closer until she saw that the woman was Noelle. She was looking down, wiping the counter or maybe cleaning a dish, with a nonchalance, a girlish, simple pleasure in her face that Leah hadn't expected and that made her pause. She didn't know this woman, the one who stood at this sink and hummed this random song. She didn't know her at all, had never known her. Leah stepped forward, stepped directly in front of the window, not more than a few feet away. Had Noelle glanced up then, what would Leah have said? "Hi." Or: "I saw you in the window. I was just passing by." Or, for the umpteenth time, "I'm sorry for being a brat." Or: "I was just thinking how beautiful and happy you look." That last one—that's what she would have said, what her best self would have said. But without so much as glancing up, Noelle turned and walked out of the kitchen. It was a sudden turn, unexpected, just like another slap across the face.

* * *

On her way home that afternoon, Leah passed the police department. What she did next, she hadn't planned. It simply occurred to her when she saw three uniformed cops exit through a side door. She did not give herself time to reflect, to imagine what might happen, to foresee the consequences—a word Franklin might have used—of her actions. She simply did it. She walked in the door she'd seen the cops come out of and found her way to a thick glass window, obviously bulletproof, where an officer sat hunched over a microphone. He was reading something that was out of Leah's view. On the glass, just above eye level, a plastic sign read, "Pay fines here." When he finally looked up, Leah had just begun to sense the words she would use. She spoke through a microphone on her side of the glass and could hear her voice amplified on his side. "To whom," she said, "do I talk about having been raped?" The archaic construction of that sentence came right out of her Latin III class, in which, last semester, she'd received a B-, her lowest grade ever.

The cop didn't seem to understand. "Excuse me?" he said.

"I've been raped," she said this time.

"I just do traffic tickets." For a moment he looked helpless in the face of what Leah had just said. But then he was on the phone, and shortly after he hung up, a plainclothes officer, a young woman, appeared, escorted Leah down a brightly lit hallway and into an office that reminded her of the principal's office at her high school. An American flag stood in the corner and a few framed diplomas hung on the wall.

"You've been sexually assaulted?" the woman asked. Beneath a short haircut, her face was square and solid. And though her simple gray slacks made her appear mannish, her face expressed a great deal of sympathy when Leah nodded. "I'm sorry that happened to you. Are you hurt?" Leah couldn't remember the last time someone had asked her this question, and she liked hearing it now. "Do you need to see a doctor?"

"I don't think so," Leah said.

The door opened then, and a balding man poked his head in. "You got a minute?" he asked, and the woman gave him a severe look that made her colleague immediately retreat, closing the door behind him.

"I'm seventeen," Leah blurted out. This seemed necessary to say, though she hardly knew why and realized then that she was on the verge of panicking, that she was visibly trembling; her arms, her legs, her hands wouldn't stay still.

"It's all right," the woman said. "You're all right now." She offered Leah a cup of water, and Leah drank it down. "We should call your parents. I'm sure they'd like to know you're safe."

Leah shook her head. "You can't call my mom. She's dead."

It was a relief to have said this and a relief to see the woman nod. "Okay," the cop said, expressing less sympathy than simple acknowledgment. It was, after all, simply so. It had happened. It was one more thing to know and not question. And this remedial gesture, this "Okay," left Leah feeling calmer. "How about your father? Could we call him?"

Leah nodded, and soon the woman officer had reached him at work. "Your daughter is here in my office, Mr. Mitchell. She's just told me that she's been sexually assaulted." How easily—as if it were straightforward information—the woman had said this sentence. And now, reassuringly and repeatedly, she was saying, "She's safe, Mr. Mitchell. She's right here with me. She'll stay here until you arrive."

After the lady cop hung up, Leah told her story about how Max had raped her: first the picnic and softball game, the departure of all the guests but Leah, the cleaning up afterwards, the beers he had given her, the conversation on the couch about how sorry he was to see her go, followed by him reaching over and kissing her, then the struggle Leah had lost. Leah was struck by how easily she began to lie, and by how, without contempt for Max, without much feeling at all for Max, she continued to lie. The woman nodded. She said, "I see. I understand." She gave every possible sign of listening and taking it all in, and this encouraged Leah and kept her talking. There were more difficult questions, questions Leah hadn't expected and didn't want to hear. "Did he penetrate you, Leah? Did he ejaculate inside you?"

Leah shook her head. "I don't know," she said. "I mean, maybe not. I don't think he did."

"Okay," the woman said gently. "You'll need to see a doctor."

"Not now," Leah said.

"The sooner the better."

"But not immediately. Not this minute."

"No," the officer said. "Not right now, but soon."

It was not until her father arrived that Leah wanted to take back everything she had said and realized that she could not—not with the woman officer sitting across from her. Franklin was oddly shy when he entered the room and saw her. He wore a suit and floral-pattern necktie that Noelle had recently given him. "Leah," he said. His beardless face, thin and clean, still seemed unfamiliar to her. How strange it was to see him in the middle of a workday. There was something—not quite pain—in his face as he looked at her. As if he were trying to see the ruin and suffering she'd undergone. As if he were trying to imagine what had happened to her. He hesitated before touching her, placing a hand cautiously on her shoulder.

"I'm okay, Daddy," she said. It was unbearable, looking out at the nightmare she was creating. She closed her eyes then and heard Franklin make a sound, a brief sigh, a sign that he, too, couldn't bear this scene. His hand left her shoulder. Leah opened her eyes.

"My God," he said. And though he was usually calm, mild, slow to react and feel things, he became suddenly fidgety, nervous. He thrust his hands in his pockets and paced. He looked frightened now. He looked impulsive and uncertain. "What do we do?" he asked the officer. "What next?"

She said something that Leah couldn't listen to about a doctor, about filing criminal charges. "I need to leave now," Leah said. "I need to go home. Please. Now."

Soon Leah was following her father down the hallway and out the station, knowing she'd have to return later that afternoon, though she wasn't thinking about that. She just wanted to move, get out and away, forestall and put everything behind her. Acceleration and velocity. That's what she needed now.

But the world outside the police station was slow. It seethed with humidity and a dull, fleshy layer of midafternoon sun. Franklin's forehead broke out with sweat as soon as they hit the air. The green on the trees seemed unctuous, seemed to weigh them down and sadden them. There was no breeze, no motion. As they crossed the street, Leah felt the sticky asphalt burn through her soles and bake her ankles. And everywhere she looked, Leah saw terror thinly veiled. A small, shirtless boy on the other side of the street, his chin smeared with something like ice cream, held onto a bike and quietly sobbed. Where were his parents, his brothers and sisters, his friends? A large truck backing out of a driveway, its bed filled with layers of ripped-up sod, made that insistent bleating sound that was supposed to warn pedestrians away. Franklin was walking too fast across the street, and though no cars were in sight, Leah felt the threat of being hit, crushed in a moment too sudden to anticipate. Before getting in her father's car, she looked for the truck. It was gone. Suddenly nowhere. As was the child. Gone. Snatched up. Stolen. "I'm sorry," Franklin was saying. Inside the car, the heat became viscous, as if the air would gather and begin to boil. The leather seats stuck to Leah's legs, sucking on the backs of her thighs. Her skin—her face, her arms, her chest—stung with sweat. "Daddy," she said.

"It's going to be all right," he said. And then: "I'm sorry. So sorry. I can't believe Max would do this. I can't believe anyone would. He's a little funny, a little lonely. But that's all I thought he was."

Leah's window came down. Air rushed in. One tree, then another and another, passed by. They were driving. "But you're okay, aren't you? You're fine. You're safe. I can see that. Thank God. Anything could have happened. We just need to go home now." But home was just down the street from the station, and they had already passed it. He looked at either side of the street. "We drove right by our house, didn't we? We'll have to turn around. We'll go home and rest. And then we'll see what has to be done." He let out a sigh. "Bad things. First your mother and now this. We were okay before. We survived. We'll be okay again."

"Daddy," Leah said.

He didn't look at her. He just kept driving.

"I lied," she said.

He was trying to find a place to turn around, his eyes searching the road, attempting to focus, to concentrate.

"I made it up." She wanted him to stop the car now and listen, but he didn't. "Max didn't rape me. Nobody did. Max didn't even touch me. He didn't do anything. I made it up. I did it because I hate people. I hate everyone."

He slowed down now. He stopped, pulled the keys out of the ignition, let his head drop to the steering wheel, and began to sob, at first quietly and then more loudly. This was him. The man she recognized as her father: small, hurt, weak, overcome by grief. Not happy, not vigorous, not in love. He lifted a fist, the keys clenched in his fingers. "Daddy," Leah said.

He stepped out of the car then and, without shutting his door, began to walk. They were on the edge of West Park, a place her parents had often taken her as a little girl. Leah's mother had been alive then, and everything had been fine. When Leah walked after him now, he left the sidewalk and started moving faster over the grass. "Daddy," she said again. He began to jog, and so did Leah. And then, his suit tail flapping behind him, he was running. Leah ran after him, but he was fast and thin, in better shape than ever. He lengthened his stride, leaned forward, and broke into a sprint, losing a black leather shoe in the grass. Leah ran until her lungs burnt. Then she stopped and watched her father run over a hill and disappear on the other side.

When Leah arrived home with her father's shoe, a police car was parked at the curb. Inside, Franklin stood in the entryway. "Here's your shoe." Leah held it up. That shoe, the largeness of it, the empty, clunky presence of it in her hand as she had walked through the park, then around and around the same block, wanting never to go home, never to face her father again, haunted her, reminded her of the times as a little girl that she'd put on his buckskin house slippers and been consumed up to her ankles by animal hide as she tromped through the house, imagining and visualizing his gargantuan strangeness, the simple mystery of his size in comparison to hers, all the while overjoyed by the fact that this alien giant was hers, all hers. And now he wouldn't take it, wouldn't even look at it. Leah put the shoe down. His necktie was undone, and his face showed an exhaustion Leah had not seen since her mother's death. Two cops sat at the kitchen table, obviously waiting for her. "They're going to arrest you," Franklin said. "I called them."

"I don't suppose we'll need to use handcuffs," one of the cops said.

Franklin was looking at Leah when he said, "I'd like to request that you do use them."

She turned and put her hands out behind her. "I don't mind," she said. The younger cop, a boy with a crew cut who seemed only a few years older than Leah, stood up and began taking the cuffs from their container at his waist. With her head down, she could see where the bulky black pistol sat in its holster on the boy's hip. "You have a gun," she said. Then she began to cry.

Still holding the handcuffs, the boy looked over at Franklin. "All right," Franklin said. "I guess she doesn't need those." The boy put them away.

Leah truly did not know how to be arrested. It was awkward and humiliating. The young cop, no doubt new to his work and seeming anxious, gripped her arm too tightly while the other read her rights. Her father said and did nothing. From the curb outside, Leah looked back for him, but the front door was already shut. "Thank you," she sobbed when the boy lowered her cautiously into the backseat, making sure her head did not hit the car. It wasn't right. She wasn't right. Criminals didn't say thank you. At the station, the cops gently—too gently—searched her with a metal detector, took her mug shot, then left her in her own private cell that nonetheless had real bars and a door that slid heavily into place. Later she would hear from both her father and Jason Clark how four uniformed cops had gone into the lab and compelled Max to accompany them to the station for questioning. They'd visited him at his workplace without warning because such visits intimidated criminals and because, Franklin explained, intimidation often led to confessions. In front of Jason, Diana, and others, the cops told Max he was suspected of criminal activity. They offered no more explanation, and Max had been too terrified to ask for more. "You should have seen his face," Jason Clark would later tell her. "He couldn't speak. He just followed them. He got into a car, and they drove him off."

But in her cell Leah wasn't thinking of Max. She was too terrified to think of Max. It wasn't the handcuffs, the Miranda rights, the body search, or even the mug shot that scared her. It was the numbing aloneness of incarceration, the lack of detail, the simple repetition of bars, the orphaned bareness of the single toilet in the corner of her cell, the bland white of the concrete wall at her back, the drain—not unlike the drain in her animal basement—in the concrete floor, the weird echo of someone whistling somewhere down the corridor of cages. She'd expected the place to be teeming with prisoners, with bad men and women. But across from her and next to her, the cells lay vacant. There were no sounds of talk, of laughter. No screams, no sighs, no grunting. She half expected to hear her dogs and sheep, and she thought of them now, thought of them in the basement of the lab, in their cages as she was now in hers. She wanted some sign of them: a bark, the bleat of a stupid sheep. But she heard only the weird whistling and her own unsettling breathing, heavy and too fast and snotty because she couldn't stop crying. She felt the thud of her heart. She wanted someone—her father, Noelle, even a criminal, a real criminal—to be in the cage across from her.

Finally, Leah heard footsteps approaching. It was the woman cop who had questioned her. She was gruff and unkind and disgusted with Leah. "I'd like to know why the hell you did that," she said. "You had me convinced. You really did."

Leah shook her head. "I hate people," Leah said. But she'd already said that, and it didn't seem entirely true. "I don't know. I don't know anything. I'm stupid."

"You are," the cop said. "Stupid."

She left Leah alone again. At some point she fell asleep, and woke when her cell door opened and a cop took her to her father. Franklin was in his white shirt and suit pants, and seemed diminished without his jacket and tie. His face did not greet her. It told her nothing. When she embraced him, he did not receive her for a few terrible moments. And then she felt his arms lift and hold her.

That night Leah and her father said very little. They sat down at the kitchen table without Noelle present. She was down the hall in the

TV room, keeping a low profile so that Franklin could, Leah imagined, discipline his delinquent daughter. "I have two things to tell you," Franklin said. "I called Max. I apologized for you. He doesn't want to see you. He doesn't want you near his house. He doesn't want you near the lab." Franklin paused and Leah nodded. "The other thing is this: I can't forgive you quite yet. I don't understand you, Leah. I'd even say I'm afraid of you. I don't know when I'll be able to forgive you. I just know I can't tell you that it's all right. It's *not* all right. It won't be all right for some time."

Leah nodded again and Franklin stood up and left her at the table.

6

That season ended with rain. Day after day of rain, preceded and followed by a mist that rose in sheets from the grass and trees and left the sky white and featureless. At times, thunder would accompany the storms, and black weather rolled across the lush flatness. But mostly the rain was a quiet, constant drizzle, and the days were blank and colorless. Leah stayed inside and waited, for what she wasn't sure. Perhaps for the weather to pass. Perhaps for her final year of high school to commence and for what seemed an endless stampede of stupid classes, inane teachers, and even more inane classmates to end forever so that finally—thank God—something else could begin. College. University. Without anticipating it, Leah felt something like optimism: She entertained the thought that these future four years might be better than the years before. How could they possibly be worse?

As she waited, as she lay on her bed and stared at the ceiling, as she read one silly paperback mystery after another, as she walked down the hallway to piss, as she napped and woke in the middle of another white rainy day, she felt it distinctly. A weight in her chest that needed to be relieved. She wasn't exactly sorry. It was more than that, since she knew apologies would fix nothing. It was remorse. And the demands of remorse, she was now discovering, were nearly as impossible as those of grief. She wanted simply to undo what she had done. She saw her father bent over in the front seat of his car and willed him to sit upright, willed his sobs, his fear, and shock to be undone. All of it needed to be erased in a series of simple reverse gestures. She saw Max looking up at the cops in his office, his face blue from the glow of the computer screen and all his scientific intensity, his passion for knowledge arrested by fear and humiliation. And again she willed the cops to return from Max's office, walk backwards toe to heel down the hallway, up the stairs, and out the lab until their car doors had closed them off from what they'd long ago done, until their patrol car drove off in a backwards enactment of all that had happened, of which every event, every action, even the smallest of them, Leah saw now, was done and would not be undone.

The demands of remorse were impossible. Nonetheless, Leah gained some relief when she stood before the district juvenile court, which was no more than a small office with two chairs, one for Leah and one for Franklin, facing the judge's desk. "Have you gained any insights into your actions, and do you wish to share them with the court?" The judge was a thin, middle-aged woman with elegantly graying hair, a judge's hammer and gavel at one end of her desk and a fancy aluminum travel mug at the other. She wore a black gown, though a fringe of white blouse showed at the garment's loose neckline. Leah recognized this woman. She'd seen her going in and out of the shops at Kerrytown, seen her in the cafés on Main Street. It seemed that Ann Arbor was so small that a criminal could not escape her accusers. No doubt this woman, the Honorable Mary Shreve, recognized her, too, and this fact put Leah to shame. "I'm not sure," Leah said. But when she saw the judge's face respond with disapproval, Leah was afraid and began to speak of her mother's death, of her changing home situation, and again of her ignorance. "I didn't know what I was doing. I do now. I wish I'd never done it."

"You're sorry, then?" the judge asked.

"I am," Leah said, and she was relieved to say so, especially knowing that Franklin, who sat stiffly beside her, had heard those words.

Leah was charged with making false accusations, with intentionally deceiving an officer of the law. As a first-time juvenile offender, she was sentenced to eight hundred hours of community service at a nearby homeless shelter, an assignment she had chosen because she had wanted to work with lots of people. She was tired of being alone, and whenever she walked by the shelter there were hordes of homeless loitering outside or lining up for a meal. Giving to others for something that she'd taken away. It seemed too simple, too cliché to work, but perhaps it would. Perhaps it would reform her.

Leah did not like Noelle any more than she ever had. She wished it were otherwise. She wished she could see in her some of what her father did. And when Franklin announced to Leah that they planned to marry in the fall, she acted jubilant. She hugged him. She lied and told him she was happy. She waited until she could lock her bedroom door behind her to cry, to beat her pillows with fists, to act like the brat she still was on occasion.

Twice she tried to see Max. One afternoon she waited outside the lab, standing across the street so as to abide, technically, by her promise to Franklin not to go near, or at least *too* near, her former workplace. But when Max exited, he saw her waiting and retreated into the building. For several days, she wandered into Max's neighborhood. When she saw him on a Saturday morning pushing what appeared to be a new gasoline mower, she stood across from his yellow house and waved. He refused to acknowledge her as he cut the grass in neat rows. She said it anyway. She shouted it over the roar of the mower. "I'm sorry. I'm sorry." She yelled the words repeatedly until she was sure he had heard them. And when he still did not acknowledge her, she walked away.

He hated her. He hated and feared her, and the injury she had done him was irreparable.

Finally, almost a month after her trial and sentencing, she confessed to Franklin. She told him she'd broken into Noelle's houses. She'd tried to sabotage Noelle. She'd committed minor acts of vandalism. Once again she saw her father close his eyes and put his head down. "If you chase her away from me now," he said, "if you take her out of my life . . ."

Because Leah could not hear what he might have said next, she interrupted him. "I'm done. I finished with that weeks ago. Never again."

"Okay," Franklin said. "We're not going to tell her. I want you to promise me that you won't tell her."

Leah promised, though part of her was tempted to do otherwise.

Part of her still wanted to hurt Noelle. And in the wake of this impulse, Leah realized she had something else to confess. "I no longer cry over her. Mom, I mean. I can't even picture her that well. I guess she's been gone too long. I can't hear her voice. Not exactly. Not the way it was. I can't hear the way she used to laugh. Thinking about her dead, gone, used to be unbearable. Now I don't think about it so much. And when I do, I can make myself think about something else." Leah shook her head. "I actually forgot her birthday a few weeks ago. We were supposed to do something, remember?" Franklin nodded. "But I forgot. I let it go. It feels wrong. It feels like she's getting farther and farther away."

Franklin nodded. "I know," he said. "I know what you mean."

In the last week of summer, Leah discovered that she wanted less than ever to be alone. Though she still shied away from the dinner table, she ate with Franklin and Noelle a few times a week. And to guard against loneliness, she got to know Jason Clark, the only person who would still be her friend. In truth, he wanted more than friendship. He wanted to get laid while Leah wanted to hear about the lab—the dogs, the sheep, and Max. "Max is Max, you know," Jason Clark said when Leah asked repeatedly how he was. Jason wasn't nearly as bad as Leah had assumed. She kind of liked him. They made out sometimes and she was surprised by his adeptness, his tender, fine kisses. Jason talked about the books he was reading, most recently a history of salt. "The staff of life," he said. "It was the currency, the most precious substance in the ancient world. They traded slaves, tracts of land for a few pounds of it." He loved facts. He thought they meant something, and Leah was both amazed and bored by his hoarding and reciting of them. She made him listen to jazz. She struggled through a few Mozart études on her clarinet for him. "Cool," he said. But he wanted more than jazz and kisses, and sometimes, when they were making out, she had to push his hand away from her breasts. "You're in love with Max," he said once, discouraged. "You're stuck on him."

Leah shrugged. "Maybe so." But she told him it was kissing or nothing, and she was glad when Jason decided that he would settle for kissing.

Franklin and Noelle were married in the backyard of Leah's childhood home on a sunny afternoon in late September. Noelle chose a dress for Leah to wear, and though she didn't care for the Victorian sleeves and its particular shade of pink, she wore it. When she cried at the end of the service, Leah did so quietly and with a smile, so that the small group of attending friends might think she was happy. And maybe she was. Just slightly happy, if not about the marriage, then about her departed grief, about her remorse, which was going to be, in the end, bearable, about the simple fact that she regretted having hurt people, and no longer wanted to do so.

And yet, she was still uncertain, still puzzled, still frustrated by how little she knew. A few days before the wedding, Leah dreamt of Ten Bucks in his cage, wagging his tail. That desk was there, behind her. "Rain Drops Keep Falling on My Head" was playing, and Leah had wanted to change the channel, but she couldn't find the radio. Slabs of flesh lay in the industrial sink. The stink of chemicals was in the air. But there was Ten Bucks in his cage. And while the other dogs yipped and leapt all around him, he remained calm and focused on her. He sat when Leah commanded it. Then he lay down. How real he seemed. He'd been restored to her. Her good dog. This time, she knew, she wouldn't have to lead him down the hall. She knew, too, that anything could be restored: the lab, Max, her father. And she'd been so satisfied, so happy. Nothing seemed doubtful or small about that happiness. And then that dog rolled over. She hadn't even asked him to. "You can't do that," Leah told him. She woke up, angry, still feeling the authenticity and nearness of Ten Bucks, as if he had just sat at her bedside, just looked at her with that open, needy gaze, just nibbled at her fingers.

A SMALL MATTER

When Martin and Nancy took a weekend trip in late March to Florence, escaping their home in Basel, Switzerland, they hoped to reintroduce some romance and excitement into their marriage of three years. Not that their lives together were unsuccessful. Martin and Nancy both had high-paying jobs at a large American pharmaceutical company and were living the lives of well-heeled expatriates. They had friends from Turkey, France, Germany, Latin America, and of course Switzerland. They were gradually mastering German and even beginning to understand the funny dialect the Swiss spoke. Martin could now politely request anything he wanted. *Ich möchte die Butter, bitte. Ich möchte das Brot, bitte. Ich hätte gern ein Schinkensandwich, bitte.* Bread, butter, sandwiches. Situations hardly ever arose in which he could not express his wants and needs. All the same, a certain compulsion had gone out of Martin and Nancy's sex life, and they would have liked some of that back.

Their Swiss friends, Beat and Nina, recommended Italy. "When we go to Florence, I always fall in love with Beat again," Nina had said. Nina was in the last stages of pregnancy. Her ankles were fat and red, and her upper body had taken on a slow and bulky eminence. But she claimed to enjoy pregnancy. "I feel powerful," she said. "I like being this size for now. People notice you. They get out of your way." Nancy was always touching Nina's large stomach, and Nina had once invited Martin to touch it. "Go on," Nancy had said when he hesitated. She had even taken him by the wrist and placed his hand on Nina, right where she had lifted her maternity blouse. He was shocked to find that Nina's stomach was leathery and as tight as a drum. He had always imagined that pregnant women would be soft. But in fact Nina was sturdy, durable. "God," Martin said when he felt the baby move, "it's alive." The women laughed at him, and he began to laugh at himself, too. "Of course it is," he said. But he could not deny that the miracle of Nina's baby had startled him. The movement inside her—the life—had been bony and sudden and unexpected.

Martin and Nancy were thinking of beginning their own family soon. They had achieved success in their professions and were now ready to focus their energy elsewhere. Martin was a widely published research chemist, and Nancy, a translator of medical texts, often marveled at how oblivious to his own accomplishments Martin remained. "You're only thirty," she said. "People in your field look to you as some sort of chemistry god, and you don't seem to care. You seem bored."

"I'm not bored," Martin told her.

"I admire you for it. You know that, don't you?"

"Thank you," Martin said.

"Don't thank me, Martin. It's not a favor. You're always thanking me for things that aren't about gratitude."

Nancy was at times so forthright that Martin hardly knew what to say. In fact, on their early dates, Martin had often been tongue-tied. Nancy was slim, with small breasts and long, unruly hair she often wore up in a tempestuous ball. Martin had never imagined he would end up with such an attractive woman and occasionally he wondered what she saw in him.

They made the decision to go to Florence on a whim the Thursday night before their departure. Nancy had just turned away from Martin's reading lamp, pulled the covers over her, and seemed about to fall asleep when she sat up and proposed the weekend escape. Martin had been proofing an article of his that would soon be published—checking the spelling and keeping his eyes out for misplaced commas—when she said, "For once I want us just to do something. Spontaneity, you know."

"Spontaneity," Martin repeated. "We have to work tomorrow."

"We can call in sick."

"I would feel wrong about that," Martin said. Martin was terrible at deception. It made him feel uncomfortable and guilty.

"I'll do it for you," Nancy said. "I'll call tomorrow and tell them my husband, the famous chemist, came down with a twenty-four-hour bug. Then we get on the morning train and go, just like that. We'll be back by Monday. Okay?"

Martin put his manuscript down and looked at the wall in front of him. He meant to be considering it—the options, the pros and cons, this and that side of the issue—but instead he drew a blank, a void of will and impulse, so that when he finally said, "OK," it did not seem like a decision at all.

"OK," Nancy said.

On the train they sat with a nun and her two Latin pupils, who conjugated a few basic verbs of that ancient language—*to love* and *to make war* and *to conquer*. The boys were dressed in dark, formal clothing, their hair neatly combed and pomaded. They had for the most part mastered these verbs, and Martin felt a sense of triumph for them. He had also been schooled in parochial institutions, where Latin had tormented him. He had failed at it miserably, and his own Latin teacher, a chalky and withered Sister who wore eyeglasses of a plasmalike thickness, had often made him stand before the class and demonstrate his incompetence. The language of politics and passion, she had called it. He could not speak that language. Nor could he afford public displays of incompetence in high school, where he was not particularly well liked. His one talent—this was before he discovered his passion for the sciences—was his mediocre ability to play the trumpet, an instrument he carried daily to school in a square box. Others in his high school had not carried around the one thing they could do, a clunky accessory in a box. It made him feel morbid, as if he were hauling around a small death, a bit of his own cold self, while his peers were simply capable in and of themselves. They were handsome or athletic or charming or all these things.

"Excuse me," Nancy said. Martin looked up from his book and saw that his wife was addressing the sixth passenger in their compartment, an Italian businessman who had just lit a cigarette.

"Yes," the man said.

"This is a nonsmoking compartment," Nancy said.

"Please," he said in quite good English. "I will be done in a moment." He smiled pleasantly at Nancy and tapped some ash into a handheld ashtray. His teeth were large and his left upper canine was solid, yellow gold. His thick rings, bulky wristwatch, and copper bracelet gave his hands a heavy, substantial presence. The smoke came from his mouth in flutes and slowly settled in the air above them. It was perfumed, rich, nauseating smoke. European smoke, Martin imagined. The man held the cigarette elegantly, pinched between his massive fingers.

Nancy pointed to the symbols on the compartment walls. "This is a nonsmoking compartment, sir."

"I will be done in a moment," he said.

The nun turned to him and spoke a rapid sentence of Italian, to which he did not respond. "Americans," he said, "are so sensitive about a little smoke, no?"

Martin now closed the book he had been reading. Nancy's face was red. She was furious. Nancy responded extremely in cases of small injustice, especially cases of rudeness. Martin had always admired her passion, but she could be uncontainable, too. Once, when she had accompanied him to a conference in New York City, she had charged up to the open window of a cab and shouted at the driver—who'd been honking for no apparent reason—to lay off the horn. "There are other people in this city, too!" she yelled in the man's face. Martin warned her later that she could get them hurt like that someday. She'd just shook her head and said, "I have to vent, Martin. I don't know how you stay so quiet all the time. But I can't do that." He wished she weren't venting now. He did, it was true, like to stay quiet. Martin crossed his legs. Then he recrossed them the other way, which felt more solid. Something needed to be said. Nancy, of course, was in the right. It was a nonsmoking compartment. Martin held on to his knee with both hands. "Sir," Martin said, "smoking is not allowed in this compartment."

"It is raining now," the man said, gesturing toward the rain-speckled window. Outside, a mist rose from the black mud of farms where cows looked indifferently on at the speeding train. "But later the sun will come out. Then we will have that smell of rain in the air. I love our weather in Italy in the springtime."

"We're not talking about the weather," Nancy said. She turned to

Martin and said, "This guy is a genuine idiot."

"Nancy," Martin said, in a scolding tone.

"Nancy what?" Nancy said. "Don't you Nancy me."

"Excuse me," the man said. He was not smiling now. "Did your wife call me an idiot?"

Martin felt his body temperature rise sharply. He noticed for the first time the thickness of the man's midsection, his girth, his solidity. He noticed a turquoise-colored vein that pulsed now in the man's forehead. He noticed the man's dark pork-chop sideburns, his large mouth, his nicotine-yellow teeth, and again the one gold canine. The boys had abandoned their Latin lesson to look first at the larger man and then at Martin. The pupils seemed to sense, looking back at Martin a second time, what would happen to him in this exchange. "This is a small matter," Martin said, uncomfortably aware of his sudden retreat. The man smiled again, as if appeased.

"Put your cigarette out," Nancy said, almost yelling. "This is a nonsmoking compartment."

"Maybe it is not so small," the man said. He was done with his cigarette now and snubbed it out with what seemed to Martin like repressed rage.

"I," Martin said, hesitating. "I don't know. But I think it is small."

"I don't think so," the man said. "I think it is big. I think I would like it if your wife apologized for calling me what she called me. I think also that I will have another cigarette." He lit the cigarette.

"For Christ's sake," Nancy said.

"Nancy," Martin scolded.

"You're letting him bully you."

Martin looked at the man and then at his wife. They were both waiting for him to speak now. The nun had forced the boys to resume their lesson; they were nervously conjugating a word unknown to Martin. "Please," Martin said as forcefully as possible. "Please put out your cigarette. This is a nonsmoking compartment."

The man laughed a little. "And if I don't put it out?" he asked. He tipped his head back and blew a great deal of smoke from both his mouth and his nostrils. One of the boys stopped in mid-conjugation and began to cough loudly. "Are we going to . . . How do you say it?"

The man looked up and seemed to see the words now in the silky gauze of smoke. "Come to blows?"

Martin stood up and took their luggage from the overhead rack. "Excuse me," he said. "I am going to find us another compartment." He nodded at Nancy, who had remained seated.

"I'm staying here," Nancy said.

"I'm sorry you have to go," the man said. He was smiling again. "It was nice talking."

"Nancy," Martin said. "Please come." Nancy didn't respond. She batted at the smoke with a hand and looked out the window.

"Your wife seems to like it here," the Italian said.

With the two bags in hand, Martin barely fit into the narrow passageway down which he struggled now, peeking into compartments crowded with weekend travelers. He found no vacancies. The occupants looked back at him with the contempt of those who had seats on a crowded train. Other passengers squeezed past him and his heavy baggage, which made Martin think again of his trumpet case and his morbid little talent. And yet he was now a moderately well-known chemist. If not as famous as Nancy liked to believe he was, he was nonetheless accomplished in his field. He was a person of importance: recognized, esteemed, respected. He stared out the window at the blur of fence posts in the gray air, the weird and rhythmic rise and fall of telephone wires, and the greens and tans and muddy blacks of the Italian landscape to which a thick mist, white as cheese mold, clung. Important or not, he had to endure the shouts of children playing in the corridor and climbing over his luggage. Beads of rainwater rushed down the glass. Martin imagined himself back in his compartment, where, with sudden skill, he lunged at his antagonist with a shiny knife and sliced open his chest, creating a sucking wound that suffocated the large Italian. These bloody urges nauseated Martin, who pushed the violent thoughts away, turned, and headed back. He had no choice.

"You have returned," the man said. He pulled his legs in, making way for Martin. "Please come in and join us." Nancy was knitting on a small square of baby-blue fabric and did not look up at him.

"There are no empty seats," Martin said. "I am afraid the train is full."

"That is too bad," the man said. "But I am done smoking now, and I am sorry about our unpleasant exchange. I am not always a nice man." The man chuckled at his earlier, inconsiderate behavior, then took out a large apple, the polished redness of which seemed almost to glow in the gray compartment.

"I am sorry, too," Martin said. Martin's response was automatic. He had not meant to be polite or express real regret. But for some reason and for something he was truly sorry.

The nun and her pupils, Martin noticed, had gone. The man must have read Martin's mind just then. "They did not like me much, I guess. I scared them away. I don't understand what is so scary about me. Do you?"

Nancy ignored the man's comments. Martin could hear the clicking of her knitting needles beside him. The Italian produced a small nickel-plated penknife, the sort of knife Martin had used in his violent fantasy, and cut the apple into slices. "This is not, I trust, a non-apple-eating compartment." He got a good laugh out of his own joke before rapidly consuming the fruit. He clapped his hands as if breaking a spell and said, "If you will excuse me now, I am going to leave you." He gathered his things. "I am going to the bar car, where perhaps I will meet other devils like myself."

A while after he left, the nun and her pupils returned, no doubt having also failed to find empty seats. Though Nancy remained cold and distant, Martin ventured to ask what she was knitting. "A sweater for Nina's baby," Nancy said. But those words—*sweater* and *baby*—were full of her bad mood, so Martin sat back. The silence settled around him for an hour until the air became visually thick and slow like water.

When Martin woke, they were just outside Florence, and he could not remember having fallen asleep. He was trying to reconstruct a dream—a head injury, a slab of black liver, the laughter of a man dressed entirely in white—but these images were rapidly swallowed up in the dusky space of sleep that was behind him now. "You were screaming," Nancy said. "You had another nightmare. I had to wake you up."

"Oh," Martin said. The nun looked at him with great concern and said something in Italian. She had no doubt heard his screams. Had she known him, she would have shrugged it off. He had always had disturbing dreams.

As they walked from the station through the narrow, wet streets, Nancy still refused to talk. Out of nervousness, Martin began to speak for both of them. "Florence," he said. "The cultural capital of Tuscany, home of the Medicis. There's the Duomo." He motioned toward the marble cathedral with his head—a heavy suitcase pinned down each hand—but Nancy did not look. Speedy motor scooters dominated the narrow streets and forced Martin and Nancy to stick close to the dripping walls of buildings; rainwater draining from rooftop gutters pelted Martin. The sun broke through the clouds then—a solid white beam—and the air filled with the fresh smell of rain, just as the man had said it would. Martin felt troubled that the stranger's weather report had come to pass.

Nancy was still not talking when they reached Le Hotel Tinto Bianco—The White Hotel—an unsettling name, Martin thought, though Nina and Beat had recommended it to them. The lobby was huge, with twenty-foot ceilings and a number of windows twice Martin's height whose old glass dripped and gathered and bent the light into an aquatic blur. The floors were polished stone, and the aroma of new shoe leather was in the air. Nancy's continued silence forced Martin to deal with the overfriendly clerk, a smallish, rotund man who pounded away at the few English words he knew—*Thank you* and *Very nice* and *Welcome, welcome, welcome*—before speaking ribbons of his own language that Martin, smiling and nodding, pretended to understand. Finally, after Martin signed something, the man handed him an old-fashioned key that felt as heavy as a small pistol.

Their bed was huge, as Nina, smiling suggestively, had told them it would be. It came up to Martin's waist. Its four black posts were made of a dark wood that seemed to emit the smell, both fresh and damp, of a forest. Multiple layers of white sheets gave off a precious, mother-of-pearl glow in the dim room. Martin had the urge to cajole Nancy into the depths of those sheets, where they would cuddle and perhaps make urgent, restorative love. But when he kissed her neck, she quickly moved to the other side of the hulking bed and sat in a stiff-backed medieval-looking chair. "Nancy," Martin said.

"You left me with that man. Why did you do that?"

"I asked you to come."

"I know. But I was too proud to do that, and I didn't know what would happen while you were gone."

"What happened?" Martin asked.

"Nothing really. He just said things."

"What things?"

"You know." She was looking at the floor. "Things."

"I want to know what he said. Exactly what he said." Martin stood and paced, rifled his hands deep into his pockets, then sat down again. "Every word of it."

Nancy began to laugh, but it was not a laugh Martin recognized. It was deep and uncertain and humorless. Then she stopped. "He scared me, Martin. He frightened me."

"Why didn't you leave when he started"—Martin could barely say it—"started saying things?"

"He put his hand up to the door. He put his feet across the aisle. The nun and the boys had already left. He said something to them in Italian, and I guess they didn't want to be in there with him. I would have had to walk right through him, and he was saying things the whole time. He didn't touch me, but he wasn't just going to let me go."

"Why didn't you tell me when I came back? Why didn't you say something then?"

"He scared me, Martin," she said.

Martin stood up from his chair. "I don't understand that. How could you be so scared that you couldn't talk to me?"

"I guess you've never been afraid, right, Martin?"

"I would have done something." Martin sat back down.

"Oh, really?" Nancy said. "You actually *apologized* to him. You told him you were sorry." Nancy began to cry. Martin sat in the purplish dim of the room, saying nothing and watching the minute digit change twice on the bedside clock before walking over to Nancy and cautiously touching her back. Her skin felt surprisingly hot. "What would you have done," she asked, "if we'd had a baby? Would you still have left?"

"We don't have a baby."

"But if we had?" she asked. When he did not answer, she said bitterly, "You ran away. You left me."

"I'm a chemist," Martin said. "I'm not a . . ."—but he didn't know what he wasn't. He didn't have a word for it. A courageous man, a hero, or just a man of average instincts who would have had the proper animal sense to protect his wife. If that were so, he couldn't say it. "I'm sorry," he said.

"Don't apologize," she said. "It makes you sound weak." Then she said, "God," as if she were frightened again. "You couldn't even make that bastard put out a cigarette."

"I could have." He hated the sound of his voice just then—the small stubbornness of it, like a child demanding something it knew it couldn't have.

"When I married you, I thought I would at least be safe. I thought you were a safe man. I thought you guaranteed me at least that much."

Martin left the room then and walked the huge halls of the old hotel, listening to the squish-squish of his thick-soled tennis shoes echo and die. A trickle of water began somewhere behind the stone walls, followed by the asthmatic respiration of pipes. It was early evening, and molten slabs of late sunlight fell through the towering windows and across the corridor. Martin would just have to wait. Nancy was headstrong, could hold a grudge, could even be vindictive. But with time, she softened and saw how unreasonable and demanding she could be. Sometimes it took her only an afternoon, other times longer, as when Martin had thrown her a surprise birthday party four days early—on the date, Nancy knew, of his first girlfriend's birthday. Martin had been sorry and extremely embarrassed. She had seen his slip as a sign of an unfaithful heart still in the grasp of an old love. He had denied it vehemently, pleaded, even written her a love note belittling himself as an absentminded fool. It had taken her two full days to speak to him kindly again, three to accept his apologies. Once she had held a grudge against her mother for three weeks before breaking down on the phone and reconciling. But she always forgave.

When he returned to his room, Nancy was asleep. He undressed, climbed onto the vast bed, and cuddled into her. He remembered warmer times when he had rested in his wife's arms and she had eagerly given him all sensual comforts. They often made love in the mornings with the sun falling over them through their window. "My chemist," she would call him afterward. Martin was erect now. He hooked his arm around Nancy, slipped his fingers beneath the lace border of her bra and found her nipple. This was not usually Martin's way: to disturb her sleep, her peace, for the sake of his urges. But for the moment, he felt the blood flow through him. He was acting according to a natural right. An appetite. He held her breast firmly. A deep, muscular spasm shivered through her. In a surprising display of somnambulant force, she clamped onto his wrist, removed his arm, turned away from him more completely and continued to sleep.

The two days that followed were tainted and sour. Martin and Nancy ate in many of the restaurants Nina and Beat had recommended, but Nancy showed no signs of enjoying the food. They saw the Uffizi and the Palacio Medici. Martin, who had read a great deal on the subject, lectured Nancy about these intellectual princes, and she nodded the whole time, though he suspected that his acumen was no longer attractive to her. He felt her repulsion, her new belief that his intelligence was a sign of weakness. A hired guide explained Michelangelo's *David,* its odd proportions, the principles of perspective underlying its design. Nancy nonetheless concluded that David's oversized head looked somehow wrong and obscene. They climbed the bell tower of the Duomo and were told by an androgynous-looking stranger—he or she looked starved and gasped for air at the top of the climb—that the tower ledge was the city's most popular site for suicides. They walked over the Ponte Vecchio, the only ancient bridge in Florence to survive the Nazis' bombs. There they looked down on the brown water of the Arno that seeped with mud and chemical sludge, and Martin purchased a handsome gold necklace from one of the many jewelers on the bridge. Nancy thanked him, but did not try it on.

Later that afternoon, Nancy bought a piece of citrus from a street market. They sat on the steps of a cathedral in the sun to eat it. It was egg-shaped and green, larger and sweeter than a grapefruit, and its unfamiliarity surprised Martin, who had assumed citrus fruit was a known quantity to him. He would like to learn its name and where it grew, he told Nancy. "That's typical Martin," Nancy said. "Why can't you just eat it? Why can't you just enjoy it?"

"I'm a scientist, all right?" Martin said, sucking the sticky sugar from his fingers. He was surprised by his angry tone. "I like to name things, and I like to know things." He then took out a map and began to plan their way back to the hotel. When she asked him to please take his face out of the map and enjoy the city around him, he ignored her. Martin felt pleasantly addicted to his bit of anger. He would keep it. She tugged at his map then. He ignored her again. She tugged a second time and then, more sternly, a third. When he finally moved it aside, he looked down and saw that it had not been Nancy but a monkey dressed in a sky-blue tuxedo jacket and a French beret of the same color. He jumped to his feet. "Jesus!" he shouted. His heart was racing. The animal had given him a shock. It advanced a step and held out its furry, oddly human hand.

"It's just an organ-grinder's monkey," Nancy said. "It wants money." Martin heard the tinkling music in the distance. A yellow smiley-face button on the creature's tuxedo jacket said in English, "Hi! I'm Mario the monkey. Please don't feed me and please don't hold me." So naturally Nancy knelt and put her arms out to it. "Oh my," she said, lifting it, "you're heavy, aren't you?"

"The button says not to do that," Martin said. Nancy was sometimes too unafraid, especially when it came to any creature she found cute. The monkey looked uncertain, fearful, as if it had come to a place in Nancy's embrace where its choices had run out. It began to poke her with a hand. It reached in her breast pocket and gouged at her ribcage, then thrust its hand in her crotch pocket. With its other arm, it held on to Nancy. She let out a quick sound—something between a laugh and a scream. The animal seemed to be attacking her, and Martin grasped its midsection with both hands and began to tug until he yanked the monkey loose and found himself in a near panic, with this warm-bodied creature clinging to him and shrieking in his ear. "Jesus!" he shouted. He swung around twice and launched the animal into the air. It landed squarely on its four limbs and ran in a circle, performing somersaults and making a series of spastic primate sounds before it faced him, beat its hairy chest, and seemed to scream with laughter in his face. The organ grinder was shouting across the square, "No touch the monkey! No touch the monkey!"

"What were you doing, Martin?" Nancy asked.

"I thought it was trying to hurt you," he said. He was out of breath and trembling. He knew now that he might have overreacted.

"It was just tickling me or something! I was fine!"

Nancy was yelling at him, and a small crowd had gathered. A little boy, who was maybe five and had a choke hold on a plastic replica of the Leaning Tower of Pisa and purple lips from eating too much of some candy, asked his father in a British accent, "Why'd that man try to hurt the monkey?"

"I thought you needed to be protected," Martin said as Nancy and he hurried away from the scene.

"It was a harmless animal," she whispered fiercely. When he started to reply, she interrupted him. "You're trying too hard, Martin."

He reached out, wanting to put his hand on her back as they walked through the streets, but she kept herself just far enough ahead of him, just out of reach.

Over lunch the next day, their last in Florence, Nancy apologized. It shouldn't have come as a surprise to Martin, who had seen her work through anger and disappointment numerous times, but it did. She looked up from her plate of linguini and clam sauce and said, "I guess I have been . . . bull-headed. I ruined our vacation."

"I thought I was the one who ruined things," Martin said.

"And I'm sorry I did it," she said. She reached across the table and took his hand, and Martin was stunned by the utter lack of relief he felt. He'd been waiting all weekend for a small portion of forgiveness; now it had come, and he felt nothing. "I knew who you were when I married you. I knew you were no bar fighter. I married a sensitive and thoughtful man."

Martin sensed a hesitance in her voice, as if she were still convincing herself that he was not at fault. "You still wish I had fought him."

Martin looked down. "You wish I had stood up to him."

"I don't," Nancy said. "Not really."

"Not really?"

"You did the smart thing." She was making an effort to be logical and reasonable now. "I should have been as smart. I'm the one who was determined to stay in that cabin, even once I saw that we were dealing with a real bastard. That was a stupid, stubborn thing to do."

"I should have done something," Martin insisted.

"Would you please let me apologize?" Nancy said, a little irritated.

"He said things."

"And that's all he did. It wasn't your fault."

On the train back to Basel, Martin wanted to talk about what he thought of now as his failure, an event for which he blamed himself more and more now that Nancy did not. Her releasing him from responsibility had only made him clench up with self-recrimination. She insisted that they leave it behind. "That's over. That's in the past." She knew how he could obsess over a misplaced comma or a typo that a copy editor had failed to catch in one of his articles—the smallest of mistakes could fill him with regret—and she was not going to let him obsess over this. "Let it go," she said. "You did the right thing. Period end." Nancy could become combative so quickly, and Martin did not want a fight, so he backed down and stayed quiet until she fell asleep.

Out in the corridor, where he had gone to think, Martin felt his chest tighten and a ball of hot fear rise into his throat when he saw a man dressed in a dark business suit, as the Italian had been, walking away from him and into the next car. But this man was smaller than the Italian, another man altogether. Martin locked himself into the tiny train lavatory, where he sat on the toilet seat with his pants on, his knees pushed against the sink. In front of him, he read in four languages a brief sentence forbidding the disposal of sanitary napkins in the toilet. *Amore, amamus, amare.* He tried his old Latin out, though he was certain that he had declined the verb wrong. He punched at the air with a fist. Had he just stayed in his seat four days ago, just exercised a little courage, no doubt the Italian would have conceded, extinguished his cigarette, and Martin would not have to sit now looking back on the event with the hopeless need to alter it. Pushing his face against the tiny lavatory window behind which the green Tuscan landscape now glowed lavender with sunset, Martin tried to release himself into the spacious beauty of the view and gain a larger perspective from which he could see how silly and small his regrets about this weekend were. But he could only feel the chilliness of the glass against his chin and take in, with every breath, the harsh floral scent of the ammonia-chloride tablet in the toilet bowl beneath him.

That night, Nancy made love to him with rare passion. She straddled him in the dark, a sheet of moonlight throwing her gigantic shadow over the wall, and gripped his shoulders with a force that left red welts the next day. She called out his name repeatedly, and Martin tried to grasp her shoulders and arms with a tenacity and strength to equal hers, but he couldn't seem to hold on. So he lay there and let himself be taken. Afterwards, she spooned him and whispered into his ear, "My dear little chemist," once comforting words that made him recoil now and move to his side of the bed as Nancy drifted into sleep.

He woke too early that morning, as he would the next and two or three mornings each week during that spring, from nightmares, and Nancy cuddled him back to sleep. If he had always had bad dreams, they had never occurred with the frequency, darkness, and confusion of the dreams that came to him now. As weeks passed, Martin felt he was gaining a comfortable distance from the event. Nina had her baby, and Nancy and he began talking about having their own family. Twice, however, as spring turned to summer, Martin believed he saw the Italian rounding a street corner in Basel. He cautiously eyed men who wore jewelry. Once, in a small bar, he smelled a certain perfumed tobacco and became distracted from the conversation of his colleagues. On a Saturday afternoon in late fall, the chill of coming winter in the air and the narrow brick path that passed the animal cages crinkling beneath them with leaves, Nancy and he accompanied Beat, Nina, and their baby to the zoo. When Nancy stopped in front of the monkeys, she began laughing. "Did I ever tell you about the time Martin attacked the monkey?" she said. The look Martin gave her then took the smile from her face. "Never mind," she said, and their friends, seeming to sense his discomfort, did not press the issue.

Time would make this memory fade, of course. It was, Martin knew, a small, unsubstantial thing. Better thoughts would crowd this incident out, would drive it from his sleep. Nancy loved him, and his future children, he was certain, would love him, too, and feel safe with him. He *was* a safe man, even if he was a quiet one. And if he remained quiet about this, too, if he did not speak of it or think of it, this small matter would dwindle in memory so that in the years to come Martin would no longer have to recall what he had failed to do in a few moments on a train one afternoon, in his youth, in the early years of his marriage.

THE SLEEPING WOMAN

Evelyn met Russell one afternoon in a neighborhood café so full that she had no choice—or so she told herself then—but to sit down in an empty chair across from him. He was not at all bad looking, in his mid-forties perhaps, and had always sat alone when Evelyn had seen him at this café in the past. He wore a thick, grandfatherly beard that was graying, in contrast to his dark hair; and his full, soft face and hazel eyes seemed to promise, at the very least, kindness and intelligence. But she was getting ahead of herself, as was her tendency with men. In the four years since her divorce, she'd gone through several relationships—so promising in their first weeks and months of dinners out, of movies and drinks, and finally, in the case of a few men she'd decided she liked a great deal, never mind that she'd only known them a few weeks, lovemaking and the languorous conversations afterwards, during which she knew she talked too much. She talked on and on—about the weather, the quality of the light in the room, the color of the curtains she hated in her living room, the light fixture and rug that weren't quite right and for which, after months of looking, she'd failed to find adequate replacements, her Zodiac sign (she was a Cancer and, as such, a natural homemaker), her mother, her father, her siblings, none of whom she was particularly close to. On and on, she'd talk. And soon after this phase of lovemaking and naked conversation began, her relationship would crash. The man would neither call nor return her calls. She would sleep alone and fully clothed in flannel pajamas and socks. She would consider the grim facts again and again: She was forty-three, divorced, childless, if nonetheless a successful professional, a woman techie, cofounder of her own small firm, Websmith Design. And then, after some months, two, three, six, even a year, as was the case on the afternoon she met Russell, she'd try again.

"I hope you don't mind me sitting here," she said. "I'm afraid I have nowhere else to go." She looked over the crowded, sun-filled café, the tables around them occupied by young couples and mothers weighed down by infants—infants in high-tech slings, infants in strollers, in laps, in arms, infants toddling, falling, crying. This first sunny warm day in early April had made Ann Arbor into a noisy playground of mothers and loud, shrill children, all of whom had come out, it seemed, to mark the end of the cold weather. "My goodness, the young hordes have been set free, haven't they?" Evelyn said, realizing too late that her comment sounded snide.

Russell peeked over his paper and gave a polite, drowsy, yet unmistakably warm smile that suggested a great deal of dormant benevolence in him and made Evelyn all the more determined to wake him, to make him see her, even though he had just raised his paper again and gone back to reading. She had no paper to read, after all; she had only her steeping cup of tea. "I'm Evelyn," she told him, holding out her hand toward the mostly gruesome screen of front-page news, a photo of children squatting in dirt, the muzzles of machine guns trained on a group of dark-eyed young men, a lapdog dressed in a tuxedo. In the next moment, he folded his paper into a baton and was smiling at her again. "Russell," he said, taking her hand.

"I'm sorry if I've invaded your privacy." Evelyn felt momentarily helpless against her impulse—an impulse she acted on far too often—to demean herself in front of those she meant to impress. "I can be impulsive and pushy. If you'd rather read your paper, please do."

Evelyn observed his face turning red. A man who blushed. Why should this draw her to him still more? He wore khakis and a baby-blue Oxford shirt, the sleeves rolled up to the thick middles of his forearms. "Talking would be nice," he said.

"You don't have to."

"Well," he said, slowly, calmly now, "I'd like to."

"All right, then," Evelyn said, and she launched into what she feared might be a frantic monologue since she tended to run on even more than usual when she was nervous. She made herself pause and let him speak as they talked about the weather, life in a midwestern university town, and, finally, about themselves. Spring seemed to have arrived, Evelyn declared, and she looked at her bare arms—they were nice arms, thin and shapely, she knew—and told him that she felt half-naked. "It's the first time I've worn short sleeves in seven months."

Russell smiled, reached out, and dipped his fingers into a small square of sunlight on their table. "Sun," he said. "Light. I don't think I've had a good look around for a long time. Winter does that to me. Today on my walk up here I noticed things—houses, trees, squirrels, cars. I mean I really looked at them." He looked at her then with a flicker of appreciation in his eyes that Evelyn hoped she wasn't imagining. And now that he smiled, glanced down, and took a sip of his coffee before meeting her gaze again, she thought she'd been right.

They talked on an hour, ranting against the current Republican administration, the man in the White House, the useless war he'd dragged the country into. Evelyn was pleased to note their common ground on these matters, though she realized she wasn't making herself attractive by announcing that even darker times loomed ahead and calling the president a tyrant and a criminal in a rabid voice, after which she held forth on the hate the rest of the world felt for their country in a long-winded speech that Russell countered with a single, tempered comment: "We've survived bullies and unfit men in the White House before, and I'm sure we'll survive this one." He cradled the bottom of his thick beard in a hand, a gesture Evelyn found wonderfully paternal, and nodded, as if to give closure to his optimistic prediction.

"Yes," Evelyn said. "Yes, we will." She liked him. Better yet, she liked herself with him. "What about you?" she said. "What do you like to do? You know . . . just for fun?"

"Fix things," he said. He picked up what seemed to be an invisible hammer and pretended to balance it. "Build. Make furniture. I do a little gardening, too. Flowers, not vegetables. And I like to fish. Fly fish. I like to walk in the woods. It gets me out. Otherwise, I'm an accountant. I do people's taxes. I help them give unto Caesar what is Caesar's."

"Well, then," Evelyn said, "you'll have to take me fishing sometime."

Russell sat up stiffly, as if he'd just been pinched. "I'm not sure that I'm entirely available right now."

"Of course," Evelyn said, feeling she'd already made a mistake, been too forward, too stupidly fast. She looked down, regarding his large foot peeking from beneath the table and shod in an ancient penny loafer, the leather cracked and the heel ground flat. "I like your shoes," she said. "They've got character. You should get them fixed, though." Moodiness tended to make Evelyn bossy.

"Thank you," Russell said, smiling, seeming to appreciate her compliment while ignoring her advice.

"You're with someone, I suppose."

He shrugged and glanced at his coffee mug. "I guess the timing isn't quite right. I'm just not . . . ready."

Once again she'd managed, in only a few minutes of conversation, to make a man flee, and now she was sitting across from him and struggling with the simple adolescent feelings of rejection and humiliation, which she, at forty-three, should have long ago left behind. Now *she* was blushing. Sweat beaded across her forehead. She scratched her scalp, after which she immediately regretted this crude, unattractive gesture. She was nervous. Her armpits were wet. She wanted to escape, to stand up and walk away.

And yet he did not seem at all awkward, at all in retreat. She sipped her tea and looked out the window at a young man speeding down the street on a bicycle, his long blond hair trailing in the wind as he turned the corner and disappeared. And Evelyn's nervousness seemed to go with the cyclist, to vanish with the same grace and speed, so that she was calm when she faced Russell again. "Sure," she said, smiling. "I understand."

"It's not you. I've been enjoying our conversation. I'd like to keep talking if you would."

How could Evelyn have possibly believed this cliché that meant that it was her—her pushiness, her unfeminine forthrightness? But he did, in fact, seem to be enjoying their conversation, and so they kept talking, this time about Evelyn; about her childhood in Fort Wayne, Indiana—a red state if ever there was one, though her parents had been hippies, radical lefties; about how she'd come to Ann Arbor to study library science at the University of Michigan, had always intended to be a librarian, but had found her first year at a small branch in a suburb of Detroit boring, and so had started a small web-design firm that had miraculously survived the tech bubble. She talked about her love of mountain biking and cross-country skiing, and finally her divorce four years ago and her recent resolve simply to meet men, to get out and take risks, as she admitted to doing with him that very afternoon. "I could have skulked away, after all," she said. "I've seen you several times before, have wanted to meet you, and simply lacked the courage. This time I just did it."

"I'm glad you did," he said.

Evelyn couldn't help smiling, couldn't help marveling at how easily they talked, at how undaunted by her honesty this man was. They soon discovered that they were almost neighbors, and because they lived only blocks apart, they left together and walked down Washington Street.

They stopped in front of Evelyn's home, where Russell seemed suddenly nervous, looking down, then over his shoulder, anywhere but at her, a fact that thrilled Evelyn. In the distance, the melodious, pied-piper call of an ice cream truck floated through the neighborhood and mixed oddly with the harder sounds of rock music coming from a nearby house. "I should really get back to Tessa," he said.

"Tessa?" All at once her excitement was gone.

"She's my daughter. She turned six last month."

"Wonderful . . . wonderful," she said, guessing now why he was so cautious and hesitant with her. He'd been left alone with a daughter. He'd been rejected by his wife. Or worse yet, he'd been widowed. "Could I ask you why you aren't ready?"

He looked up and let out a breath. "I'm afraid I'd rather not say right now."

"Sure," she said. And then she added, "I'd like to talk again sometime."

He took a few steps backwards. "All right," he said, smiling. He waved at her, and with what she thought was a bounce in his step, a subtle, joyful maneuver, he turned and walked down the street.

Over the next week, Evelyn looked for Russell in the café and along the streets of their neighborhood, where she walked more often than she otherwise would have. Lilacs were blooming and the evening light lingered and the walks, Evelyn told herself, did her good, though she didn't once run into him. She hauled her mountain bike out of the garage, filled the tires, lubed the chain, and took long afternoon rides along Huron River Drive, the high, muddy river just visible through the trees along the roadside. She felt at once lighter and stronger, as she often did in spring, as if she were shedding pounds of winter flesh, though she was slight and didn't have much flesh to shed. And yet, at the same time, she felt a tightness in her chest, something coiled and prepared for disappointment. She was acting girlish, thinking of Russell too much, too often, a man she didn't even know. His beard, his soft face, his large hazel eyes, his thoughtful, even-keeled temperament, his lanky, awkward body. She was careful to remind herself as she pedaled through the Huron River valley that she knew nothing about him, that he couldn't matter to her, certainly could not hurt her, that she simply had a crush and should savor the sweet irrational longing for this stranger while it lasted, the enjoyment of which, after all, was made keener by his absence. She could enjoy that, she decided. She could enjoy not having him.

And then he appeared one afternoon during a storm, the sort of downpour, immediate and powerful, accompanied by lightning and an eerie purple darkening of the sky, that happened only this time of year. The streetlights flickered on in the sudden dark, and the trees bent in the wind. Phosphorescent flashes lit the sky, and thunderclaps rattled the windows of Evelyn's house. She had poured herself a glass of chardonnay and was sitting out on her screened-in porch, the air fresh with the smell of rain, to watch the streets flood and ropes of water fall from her gutters when she saw him, a tall, lumbering man running through the storm, and called out to him. "Please," she said, holding her screen door open, "come in." He stopped for a moment and looked through the downpour in her direction. "It's Evelyn," she said.

Soon he was standing on her porch, dripping puddles onto her tile floor. "I got caught in this," he said. His shirt was plastered over his bony shoulders. His beard dripped, and Evelyn could see the fragile shape of his skull, its slight dorsal rise, through his matted hair. He wore a tool belt, a hammer and screwdrivers holstered at his sides. "I was on my way home from helping a friend." He shook his arms, and water came running off him.

"I haven't seen you anywhere," Evelyn said.

He smiled. "I should go." He seemed pleased to see her, even if he was trying to escape.

"Stay right there," Evelyn demanded. She came back with a stack of towels, an extra-large T-shirt she sometimes slept in, and a bathrobe. "You should get out of those clothes. I'll pop them in the dryer, and in a few minutes you'll be as good as new."

"I really should . . ."

"I'm not going to let you go out in that." Evelyn thrust the towel into his hand and turned around. The thunder clapped, and the lights of the house flickered off and on again.

"This is a bit funny," he said.

"Tell me when it's safe to look."

"Not yet," he said. She heard the racket of the tool belt come off, then his zipper, followed by the watery flop of his pants hitting the floor. She laughed at the thought of a man undressing in her house.

"OK," he said.

When she faced him again, he stood in her peach-colored robe, his thick shoulders pulling at the terrycloth and too much pale thigh showing. At the bottom fringe of her robe, a half-inch of damp, baby-blue boxer shorts peeked out. "Lovely," she said. "Nice and leggy."

As a joke, he fastened his tool belt around the robe, and they both laughed. She put her house slippers down and he stepped into them, though only half of his pale feet fit inside. He was so good-natured, so willing, that she felt she could ask him just about anything then. "You said you liked to fix things," she said. She walked him through her kitchen and into the garage, where she showed him the damage she'd done a few weeks earlier with her Subaru. "I sort of hit the side of the garage. I popped the clutch. It was very stupid of me."

He surveyed the damage, the smashed clapboards, the splintered two-by-fours, and the garage-door track so badly bent that the door closed only halfway. He nodded, seeming to understand what was needed. "I think we could do some of this now," he said, looking around the garage at the odd assortment of old tools and wood scraps left behind by the previous owner.

Soon Evelyn was watching this man, in her robe and house slippers, swing his hammer at the side of her garage with an expertise she found attractive. Wood splintered as he pried it away. The rain fell more gently now, drumming the roof above them. He measured a two-by-four that had leaned against the wall of Evelyn's garage for years, marked it with a pencil, laid it over a wooden horse—another item Evelyn had never used—and began sawing it.

In the kitchen an hour later, she watched him drink down the glass of water she'd just handed him. Outside, the rain had settled into a drizzle and the beaded windows cast mottled shadows across the floor. When he stepped toward her to return the empty glass, they stood so close that Evelyn took in the smells of rain and wood on him. She leaned in and kissed his cheek, then his lips, after which he said, "Oh," in a breezy, startled voice. She'd been about to retreat when she felt the weight of his hand on her shoulder. In a flurry of pecks that missed her mouth and fell over her chin and cheeks, he began kissing her. He was trembling, and to calm him Evelyn held him close.

"I'm sorry."

"Why would you apologize?" Evelyn asked.

"I'm not good at this, not good at all."

"Of course you are," Evelyn said, wanting above all to encourage him, though clearly he wasn't good at it. She began kissing him gently now and felt his breathing grow steadier, his wide upper body rising and falling against her, as he began to return her kisses. She wouldn't dare put her hand down and open his robe, but she wanted to. And when, in the next moment, she changed her mind only to find the thick leather of his tool belt in her way, she laughed. "I've never dealt with one of these before."

"I don't think we should . . ." He stepped away from her.

"I'm being pushy," she said. "I told you I could be pushy."

Russell tightened his robe. "I need to tell you about my wife."

"Oh," Evelyn said.

"It's not what you're thinking."

"I don't even know you," she said, suddenly angry, "and you're standing in my kitchen, you're wearing my robe, you're kissing me and telling me you're married."

Russell looked down, and Evelyn noticed his huge feet again, their long, pale, tendon-streaked boniness crushing her little slippers. "I don't quite know how to explain this. I haven't had to until now."

"But you're married."

"Are my clothes ready? I'd like to put on my clothes." He looked helpless, grasping at Evelyn's too-small peach-colored robe for cover.

"All right," Evelyn said. She pulled his clothes out of the dryer and left him to dress in the kitchen while she sat on the porch. The rain had given way to a white haze. When he stepped through the screen door, he looked larger in his own clothes. His thick hair was a mess where she'd run her hands only moments before, and despite her best efforts, she found the boyish unkemptness of him attractive.

"You were going to tell me something," Evelyn said.

He sat down and put his hands on the table. "I'm not used to talking about this." He smiled briefly, as if to say, "Oh, well," as if to surrender. "My daughter, Tessa, and I have had a tragedy. My wife had an accident. We all had an accident, but she was hurt badly. We weren't. We were fine. She's been in a persistent . . . she's been unresponsive . . . in a vegetative state for almost three years."

Evelyn felt her throat tighten. "Oh," she said. She should have offered condolences. But she didn't feel sorry for him. She felt surprised, disoriented, and, as usual, she said exactly the wrong thing. "Couldn't she still come out of it? Couldn't she wake up?"

He shook his head. "It's more or less impossible. As far as the doctors can tell, her brain stem is alive. The rest is gone. She's there, but she's not there. We took her off a respirator some time back and assumed she would go. But she didn't. I'm recovering. Tessa is too. Fortunately, my daughter was young when it happened, too young to remember everything. But it's been slow for me, and I'm not sure I'm ready yet. I'm not sure that this"—he looked at her and smiled—"is a good idea."

Evelyn could see that he had rehearsed this speech. He'd said it to himself in an empty room, in front of a mirror. Or he'd just imagined himself saying the words as he'd worked on her garage. All the same, she felt stung by how quickly her anger had been countered by his careful hesitation. "Of course," she said. "I understand."

He stood and pushed his chair in. "You know," he said, "I've been purposely avoiding you all week. I've stayed out of the café. I've made sure not to walk down your street. And I've tried not to think about you. It hasn't been easy."

Evelyn smiled. "Thank you for saying so." She stood up and they shook hands.

After he left, Evelyn walked into the kitchen and saw his tool belt on the counter next to her robe, which he'd folded carefully, and the thought that she'd see him again soon pleased her.

Two days later, Russell came for his tools and ended up staying to work on her garage. "I'd like to finish the job for you," he said. With a crowbar, he ripped out more damaged clapboards. She brought him a beer while he worked and felt an unanticipated moment of pleasure in opening it and handing it to him: He wanted to be in her home, drinking her beer. She was so used to quiet afternoons, sitting out on the porch or in the living room. And now a man was here, determined to do her a favor.

At the same time, his particular situation was weird, unsettling. When she'd told the story to her business partner, Heidi, her friend first expressed sympathy for him. "That's tragic," she'd said. Heidi had a husband and two young boys and couldn't imagine the suffering her family would endure were she in such a condition. "But it's sort of freaky, isn't it?" she said, pushing her wire glasses up. Heidi was a plump woman with short, mousy blond hair and wide hips, and Evelyn had always felt tinges of jealousy that her business partner, so obviously unbeautiful, should have a husband and family while Evelyn remained alone. All the same, the thought that Heidi gave voice to then had occurred to Evelyn, too. "I mean, it really is freaky. She could wake up years from now and he'd have a wife again."

"She can't wake up," Evelyn said. "He said it was impossible."

"But it is possible, isn't it? I mean, she's alive."

"Maybe," Evelyn had said.

As Russell worked on her garage and Evelyn retreated inside, where she kept herself busy by cleaning the already clean counters and reorganizing the already tidy cupboards, she couldn't stop herself from contemplating the morbid possibility her friend had entertained. Nonetheless, the noise he made all afternoon, the hammering and sawing, reminded her of the pleasant fact that a man was in her house, and she hummed as she performed her unnecessary cleaning. "You need anything?" she yelled from the kitchen.

The racket from his work stopped. "I'm fine," he answered.

An hour after he'd begun, he walked into the kitchen, sweaty, a blond stain of sawdust in his beard. "We're going to have to take a trip to the lumberyard," he said. "We need a few pieces of wood."

When Evelyn offered to drive, he shook his head. "I try to avoid cars whenever possible. I'll carry the wood back, of course. We just need two pieces."

"That's how it happened, then," she said, announcing what she had gleaned from his hesitation. "It was in a car."

He nodded. "Yes, that's how it happened. In any case, I like to walk. I walk wherever I can, which is just about everywhere in this town."

There was a lumberyard off South Division, about a twenty-minute walk from Evelyn's place. Though it was early evening, the sky was clear and the sun was still high and would be, it seemed, for hours more. Home from school, children screamed and shouted from the backyards of the small Victorian houses Russell and Evelyn passed. An old woman dressed all in white and wearing a wide-brimmed, floppy straw hat cut enormous lilac blossoms from a bush and placed them in a bucket. A fat yellow lab ran past them followed by a slim girl jogging in short shorts. At the curb opposite them, a mother was taking her little girl's hand and instructing her to look both ways when Evelyn felt Russell's hand sweep over hers and take hold, then fasten on to her so securely that she understood he was walking her across the street. When they reached the other side, he didn't let go. "Is this OK?" she asked.

"I think so," he said.

People on porches waved as they strolled by, and Evelyn felt the pleasant sensation of being seen with this man, of being mistaken for his middle-aged wife of many years. At each intersection, his grip tightened. He made them stop as he looked both ways and did not relax his grip until they had reached the opposite curb. "You're afraid," Evelyn said. "You're afraid of crossing the street."

"No," he said a little defensively. "I'm just cautious. I'm used to walking with Tessa. It's probably become a reflex."

A monarch butterfly the size of Evelyn's palm flitted in front of them and was gone. "What does Tessa do when you're not home?"

"She goes to her grandmother's. She lives about a block away."

"Your mother?" Evelyn asked.

He shook his head. "Jenny's mother. She's been great. She's been a large part of our lives."

"Wonderful," Evelyn said, though in truth hearing his wife's name conjured that strange woman to life, made her seem youthful and girlish, as Evelyn imagined a typical "Jenny" to be. It was once again, as Heidi had said, freaky.

At the lumberyard, they strolled beneath a fiberglass overhang among large flats of cut wood. The bleat of a forklift backing up startled Evelyn, but Russell was happy here and no more capable of hiding it than a kid. He brushed his hand over the boards and lectured Evelyn about oak and mahogany and kiln-baked pine. Though the former were stronger, harder woods, the pine, he explained, would hold up just fine and was far more affordable. "This is very solid stuff. No knots," he said, rapping his knuckles over a plank.

On the trip back, Russell offered to take both planks, but Evelyn insisted on doing her part. The two-by-four that she carried was taller than she but surprisingly light. As they walked past yards and gardens with their strange cargo, people noticed them and nodded. One man stopped working, leaned on his shovel, and tipped his baseball cap at her.

"We're building," Evelyn replied.

The fact that Russell seemed to be repairing her garage more slowly than necessary was, Evelyn thought, a good sign. They took two more trips to the lumberyard, buying another piece of wood and some new clapboard. He would come by a few times a week to continue the project. At work, Evelyn and Heidi had just finished redesigning a local news station's weather page, "Weather Watch Five," and were just beginning work on a Web site for a family-owned photo shop on State Street. Over lunch, Heidi prodded Evelyn for details about Russell. "Have you kissed again? Has anything happened?"

"He's rebuilding my garage," Evelyn said.

"That's something," Heidi said. "That's romantic in a way."

"We hold hands," Evelyn said.

"One step at a time," Heidi teased. And then, in a tone of illicit fascination, she asked, "Any more news about the wife?"

"No. We don't talk about her."

They didn't talk about her, but Evelyn felt the strange presence of this woman whenever she and Russell spent time together. She was the reason Russell's hand tightened on hers whenever they crossed the street. She was the reason they walked and didn't drive. She was the reason he kept his distance, working out in the garage, clearly wanting to spend time around Evelyn but not *with* her. And though Evelyn had never seen this woman, had only vaguely imagined her as a figure made gorgeous by years of sleep, by the pervasive stillness of a hospital room—the sheets, the walls, the frozen block of sunlight issuing through a single window—she was the reason Evelyn finally led Russell, smelling of sweat and paint after a long afternoon of work, from the kitchen, where he'd been guzzling his second or third glass of water, to the living room and sat down with him on the couch. "I'll get paint on the cushions," he said nervously.

She pressed her open hand into his, the width of his palm dwarfing her own. His size, the clumsy scale of him—she'd seen him nearly trip over his own long legs a few days before in the garage—continued to strike her with an amazed tenderness, a feeling that threatened to break her open. She touched his thumb, gloved to the first knuckle in the radiant yellow—Pale Orchid, it was called—that he'd been painting with. "It's dry," she said.

"The garage is almost done."

"I'll be gentle. I won't bite." She kissed him now, neither quickly nor slowly, but with precision, on the cheek, and after a short pause he smiled and kissed her back, also on the cheek. "See," she said.

He nodded. "One more," she added, kissing him lightly on the lips, without passion, and though his large hand was trembling in hers, he once again returned her kiss with the same deliberateness.

"That's nice," she said. Again she kissed him and he kissed her, and now they began giggling, returning one simple kiss after another with a metronomic gracelessness, their lips meeting and parting and meeting and parting, that gradually gave way to earnest, reckless, blustering kisses, long and deep and finally, it seemed, too much for Russell, who pushed Evelyn away, sat up on the couch, and gasped for air, as if he'd been drowning. "I'm sorry," he said. And, of course, this woman whom Evelyn had never met and never would meet was the reason he stood up from the couch then and hurried home.

She was also the reason Evelyn took her old mountain bike down from the garage wall, wiped the cobwebs from the handlebars, oiled the chain, and pumped air into the tires. They needed to get away from that stupid garage and do something, anything, together. And so she put the seat up high and presented the bike to him just after he'd applied the third and ultimate coat of paint to the new clapboards, finally completing the project. "How about a spin?" she said. Her biking shorts gripped her hips and butt; she looked good in them, she knew, and was pleased to see that he'd noticed, looking away from the garage and at her for a change. "Not bad for a woman of forty-three, am I?"

He smiled. "I'm afraid I don't bike."

"Of course you bike."

He shook his head, bent and hammered the lid back on the paint can and began gathering up the drop cloth. "No," he said. "I didn't even bike much as a kid, and I don't bike now. I walk. I'll walk anywhere. But I won't bike."

"You mean, you're afraid to bike," Evelyn said.

He kept clearing up, placing a can of paint on the shelf and tossing a stirring stick in the garbage. "I need to get back to Tessa," he said.

"Not just yet," Evelyn said. "We're going to walk these bikes to West Park. There's grass there and I've got a helmet for you. If you fall, it won't hurt. There's nothing to worry about. And once you get going, we'll head down Main Street and onto Huron River Way. It's beautiful there. You'll love it. It's a wonderful feeling speeding along next to the river."

He kept shaking his head, but when she wheeled the bike over to him, he reached out slowly and took the handlebars. "I don't know," he said, squeezing the handbrake.

At West Park, a few kids threw a baseball and practiced batting in a distant corner. The air shimmered with late-afternoon sun, and a light breeze blew through the huge maples that bordered the park and made the empty rubber saddles of the swing set in the sandpit behind them rock gently on their chains. Evelyn had chosen a sheltered spot of grass far from the road where no one could see her holding Russell up and coaching him. "I won't let go until you get some momentum. Once you get going, pedal."

His lanky body fit awkwardly over her small bike. Nonetheless, he was afraid; his shoulders and arms shook. "This is embarrassing," he said.

"It's easy," she said. "It's as easy as riding a bike."

"I wish I weren't like this. You must think I'm . . ."

"I think you're charming and honest and good."

He shook his head, as if trying to ward off a thought. "I worry," he said. "I worry far too much that something will happen and nothing will be the same afterwards."

"The worst that can happen here is that you fall and skin a knee."

He tightened his grip on the handlebars now and took in a deep breath. They heard the crack of a bat and saw in the distance one of the boys sprint to a fly ball and catch it effortlessly in his mitt. "I'm ready," Russell said. And though Evelyn felt a wave of anxiety that something terrible might happen, she counted to three, dug into the soft grass, and heaved this heavy man forward. "Lift your feet," she said.

"Oh, God," he said.

"You're dragging your feet. You need to lift them."

"OK, OK," he said. But he kept dragging his feet over the ground while Evelyn pushed.

"Up," she said. He lifted his feet now and shot forward, out of her reach, his shoulders wobbling as he struggled to hold the wheel straight. He put a foot down, then pulled it up again, holding it away from the bike, like a broken wing. "Pedal!" Evelyn shouted. "Put your feet on the pedals and crank." He swerved right, then left, seeming about to fall over just when he found the pedals and launched himself over the grass. Evelyn applauded as he completed one and then another unsteady lap around the park, his arms flexed and tense and his face red with terror. "Wonderful," Evelyn said. But he didn't reply. He stayed focused and quiet, his eyes fixed ahead of him.

On her bike now, Evelyn followed as he completed another circuit of the park, then pulled in front and led him out on the sidewalk, up East Ann Street, and into the quiet neighborhoods. On Main Street, the pavement ended, and they rode over the narrow gravel shoulder, cars and semis ripping past them. Looking back occasionally to check on Russell, who dwarfed her bike, his knees sticking out with each pump, Evelyn imagined the worst: Russell, in a moment of fear, swerving wide and falling beneath the flow of traffic. But they both reached Huron River Way, where only a few cars cautiously passed them. Beside them, the river, wide and slow, glimmered in evening sun as they sped through the shadows cast by hemlocks and aspen on either side. Evelyn was surprised when Russell, cranking hard, pulled up beside her, his gray beard thrust forward by the helmet buckle at his chin, and shouted out, "Hi."

"Look at you," Evelyn said.

He was still afraid, his eyes fixed on the road as he laughed and said, "I don't do this. I don't ride bikes."

"You do now," Evelyn said.

Two days later, after their second ride, Russell surprised Evelyn with a blunt question. "Do you think we could have sex now? I mean," he said, "I'm ready if you're ready." They were sitting on Evelyn's porch, and he was tearing a paper napkin into tiny scraps.

"My God," Evelyn said, laughing. "That's not very romantic."

"I don't think I can be romantic. Not at first."

"Why not?" When he lifted his glass of water, she saw his hand trembling. How long, she wondered, would she have to attend to this man's fear?

"Maybe we could just make it something we do. Something that doesn't have to be great or wonderful. Just a thing."

Evelyn shook her head. "I'd like it to be at least a nice thing. It doesn't have to be great. But it does have to be warm. It has to be tender."

He nodded, seeming to agree. All the same, Evelyn had to seize the initiative, had to broach the subject of birth control (the IUD she used was 98 percent effective), had to take his hand, lead him upstairs to her room, pull the blinds (because dimness felt more comfortable), sit him down on her bed, and undress him methodically, as she might a child, removing first his shoes and socks, then his T-shirt, which he seemed reluctant to let her pull over his head, and finally his shorts, until he was naked, save for his gray boxers. "I have a little belly," he admitted.

In fact, he did—pale, distinct, and, as he had said, little. "I like it," Evelyn said.

He crossed his arms over his naked chest. "All your clothes are on."

Indeed they were, and she didn't discover her own fear, a warm, unsettling rush of nerves in her stomach and chest, until she'd also undressed, folding her tank top and cycling shorts and placing them neatly over the floor. Despite the warmth of the room, Evelyn shivered now as she sat on the edge of the bed and kissed Russell. He kissed her back. Their lips met again, this time too quickly, so that their teeth clattered together. In the next moment, when Evelyn took hold of his hard penis, he jolted upright, elbowing her in the chin. "I'm sorry," he said, panicky.

Evelyn leaned back against the headboard. "Why don't we take a break?" Outside, a child was yelling the name of a friend or a lost pet. Yelling and yelling that name. And then, all at once, stopped.

"We can always try this again another time," Russell said.

"Of course," Evelyn said.

But moments later, Russell took her in what felt more like a wrestling hold than an embrace, kissing her frantically and pinning her shoulders over the bed with his weight. "Slow," Evelyn said. "Slow." He thrust his knee between her legs and parted her thighs. In the dimness, Evelyn recognized on Russell's face the same expression of concentration and concern he got when cycling, as if, even now, as he entered her too quickly, he were urging himself to keep his eyes on the road and to remain cautious. "Ouch," she let out.

He froze above her. "Are you all right?"

"I'm fine," she said.

"Really? Should I stop?"

She laughed. How could she not laugh? "No," she said, "don't stop." He began moving again, and in the next moment it was over and he'd already rolled off her and retreated to the other side of the bed. "I go too fast," he whispered. "It's a problem I've always had."

"It was just fine," Evelyn said.

"It was?"

"Yes," she said.

He drew close now and curled into her, his slack, damp penis against her thigh. "It will get better," he said.

And, as Russell had promised, it did get better. They made love in the late afternoons after cycling along the river or, on some days, instead of cycling. They drew the curtains against the increasingly bright late-April sun, in which the dogwood and magnolia trees had bloomed purple and white along Washington Street, stripped down, and made more patient and skillful love. Because Russell, as he had admitted, lacked endurance, he indulged her beforehand, taking his time, caressing her, kissing her, performing an act that she enjoyed more than she liked to admit and that most men she'd been with performed only cursorily and out of a sense of fairness. She closed her eyes, giggling at times because his beard could tickle, while he made her come. Then he mounted her, and she made him come.

In the lulls after lovemaking, they talked for hours, Evelyn counting fourteen past lovers and recalling in painful detail how her possessiveness had aggravated and been aggravated by her ex-husband's grumpy independence and inwardness. "Ed": she couldn't say her ex-husband's name without recalling the exhaustion and frustration she'd lived with during their six years together. Silent, removed, cryptic Ed, who'd sat there nodding, agreeing or very quietly disagreeing, never granting her the satisfaction of a good, honest, full-throttle fight, who'd said one thing and done another, who'd punished her for years by showing up late—ten, fifteen, twenty minutes—for every dinner or coffee date they ever made. "I always go for quiet, unhappy guys. Aggressively passive-aggressive guys. And I'm possessive—pushy and possessive. What do you think about that?"

Russell laughed. "You're a force," he said.

Evelyn liked being called a force. What she liked less was the revelation that, aside from Jenny, she, Evelyn, was Russell's only other lover.

"You're forty-four," Evelyn said, "and you've only ever been with your wife and me?"

He nodded.

Evelyn didn't know that men who'd had sex with one woman still existed—or had ever existed, for that matter. And while it was sweet and astounding, she would have preferred a few other women in his past, if only to rob his sleeping wife of some influence.

For the most part, Evelyn avoided the subject of Jenny, though at times she had to know more, as on the afternoon in early May when, back from a long ride, sweaty and hot, they rushed upstairs and made frantic love, first against the wall, then on the bed, and finally on the floor. He lasted longer than usual, and, miraculously, they came together. As they cuddled in the dark, she asked, "Were you able to do that with her?"

"Sometimes," he said, giving her the exact answer she had feared. He continued to answer Evelyn's questions, telling how he had met his wife in high school in Plymouth, Michigan, where Russell had been a shy trombonist in the marching band and Jenny had been the school's first female drum major. "She liked giving orders," he said. "She was bossy and sweet and pretty all at the same time. She was, I guess, a little like you. I'd say that would be my type."

Evelyn felt herself uncomfortably suspended in the dim light of her bedroom, lying naked beside this naked man who, in a half-whisper, his hand holding Evelyn's, had just compared her to a woman who was alive and dead at the same time, a woman who, like Evelyn, had been bossy and pretty, a woman who had commanded a timid, lanky young trombone player. How easily Evelyn pictured him as a boy dressed in an ill-fitting faux-silk costume and toting around a large instrument case, and how easily she became jealous of this woman who had ordered him about, controlled him, told him where and when to march, and later dealt with his incapacity as a lover and schooled him in how to compensate for it. And because Evelyn felt his wife's eerie presence more strongly now than ever, she asked, "Do you still visit her?" He removed his hand from hers. "Please hold my hand," she said. She was bossy. She couldn't help being bossy. At least it worked. He gave her his hand back, and she held on to it.

"Sometimes."

"How often is sometimes?"

"Once a week. Once every two weeks. Sometimes less. Sometimes more."

"But she can't talk," Evelyn said. "She isn't at all conscious or aware, right?"

"That's right."

"And she won't come back? She won't wake up?"

"The chances of her coming back are, more or less, a million to one."

Evelyn closed her eyes. She was surrounded by darkness now, just as Russell's wife was. She felt herself breathing, the air rushing in, expanding through her chest and ribcage, then out again. She tried to imagine it—sleeping through one's life, sleeping when everyone else hurried on with things, went to work and school, ate and biked and drove, loved and was loved, married and divorced, lived and died. Evelyn heard the gentle rush of a car passing outside. She felt the chill of the air on her nipples, her stomach, her thighs. She could feel and hear and think, unlike Russell's wife, of whom, ridiculously, stupidly, she was jealous. Or perhaps haunted. She was *haunted* by her, aware of her presence only because she was so conspicuously, strangely absent.

"I tried to stop going once," Russell said. "But it didn't feel right. She's there, after all. I mean her body is there. In that room."

Evelyn opened her eyes. "Where?" she asked, wanting to know even the irrelevant details.

"She's in a full-care facility attached to the university hospital. It's only a fifteen-minute walk from home. It would feel wrong not to see her."

Evelyn took in a long, slow breath. "Is she blond?"

"What?"

She heard the irritation in his voice. "I'm sorry. I guess I'm jealous. I shouldn't be. I wish I weren't. But I am. And it feels better just to tell you that I am."

"Yes," he said. "She's blond."

Evelyn, a brunette, had hoped this fact might put her at ease, but it didn't.

She felt him shudder, his hand holding more tightly to hers. "Tessa no longer visits Jenny. It's been easier for her that way. When I told her she had to stop visiting the hospital last year, she didn't put up a fight, and it was pretty clear that she had wanted to stay away even before then and had just been waiting for my permission. She doesn't talk about it. But I'd guess that she stopped seeing her mother in that bed some time ago. When I visit, I make sure things look nice. I put flowers on her bedside table. I check that the nurses are doing what needs to be done—keeping her clean, moving her from time to time."

"Oh," Evelyn said, picturing Russell as he arranged a vase of flowers, of tulips or orchids, or perhaps roses, since those would last longer, with his large hands, which were better suited to a hammer and had worked on her house and had touched her body.

"What do you do then?" Evelyn asked. "I mean, after you've made things nice?"

Russell released her hand, and this time Evelyn let him go. "I just sit there. I sit there and look at her. Sometimes I say a few things. I tell her how Tessa is doing. I give her news about her mother. For five minutes. Ten minutes, maybe. Then I go."

Every few weeks, Heidi and her husband, Michael, invited Evelyn over for dinner, the first half-hour of which she'd spend with their boys, ages six and eight, while her hosts finished preparing the food. A loud pair, sandy-haired and soft-faced, the boys startled Evelyn with their barely containable wildness, their yells and yips, their fights and violent affections. They called her Aunt Evelyn, though around them she felt more like an unwanted grandma. Dennis, the younger one, had once complained about her perfume. "It stinks," he said, holding his nose. Chad, the eight-year-old, liked to give her bear hugs that often left sticky food—honey or jam—on her clothes and face. Yet Evelyn, who suspected that these dinners were charity, Heidi and Michael's attempt to help a single, middle-aged woman escape the overcontrolled confines of her neat world, enjoyed this household: the pieces of an obliterated train set, a red caboose with its roof torn off, a Union Pacific freight car loaded with Cheerios, Tonka trucks, wood blocks, and strange-looking action figures, among other toys scattered across the living-room and dining-room floors. Evelyn had always assumed she'd have kids, especially by this time in her life, and these dinners at Heidi's often left her feeling regretful, even if she was happy to return to her quiet home at the end of the evening.

That night the boys, already in their orange tiger-striped pajamas when she arrived, were especially loud and giggly, and it continued after Michael, who was conscientious about cleaning up around the house and sharing parenting duties, went upstairs to put Chad and Dennis to bed. "It's the light," Heidi complained. "It's almost impossible to get them to settle down before eight when the sun is still shining." In fact, it was a few minutes after eight, and burnished sheets of sun poured in through the windows. Evelyn heard Michael's voice intone from above, "I'll count to ten, and if you're not in bed . . ." Evelyn did not particularly crave the company of Chad and Dennis, nor was she attracted to Michael, a thin man with a beaked nose and curly hair, but she nonetheless felt slightly envious of Heidi's disorderly and lively household.

"We've been having sex," Evelyn whispered across the table to Heidi, who let out a laugh and clapped her hands.

"Tell me all about it," she said. "Everything."

Evelyn felt a sudden tenderness and yearning for him when she said, still whispering, "He doesn't last long, but he takes his time beforehand."

Heidi giggled. "Michael has a bit of the same. You might tell Russell to practice."

"Practice?"

"Masturbate," Heidi said. "Only slowly. He should take twenty, thirty minutes or so. That will build up his endurance."

"I don't think I could tell him that," Evelyn said. "Not yet." But she looked forward to a deeper intimacy that would allow her to give this sort of instruction. "You might try masturbating," she imagined herself telling him.

Evelyn enjoyed talking about Russell and went on now about his newfound love of biking, his deep concern for Tessa, his gardening and fishing, his handiness with a hammer.

"You're glowing," Heidi said then. "You're as happy as I've ever seen you."

In mid-May, after nearly five weeks of cycling and good sex with Russell, Evelyn grew tired of the pattern they'd fallen into—bike rides two or three times a week, followed by early-evening lovemaking, after which Russell would hurry home. One afternoon, groggy from sex, Evelyn lay over her bed and listened to the funny splash of Russell urinating in the hallway bathroom. That sound filled her with tenderness and an equally powerful irritation at the fact that he would soon be rushing off. When he stepped back in her room, naked save for his boxer shorts, and began riffling through the bed sheets, where his T-shirt had been lost during their lovemaking, she said, "This feels like an affair. You come over to my house every other afternoon. We close the blinds and we . . . we fuck." That word made him stop and look up at her. "Then you go home to your family."

"You're angry," he said, sitting down on a chair across the room.

"No," she said. "I'm frustrated. Don't you think it would be nice to make love at other times? In the morning or evening, for instance. It would maybe even be nice to spend the night together once."

"I have a family, Evelyn," Russell said. "I can't just disappear for whole nights at a time." He stood up and grabbed his T-shirt from the foot of the bed, where he'd evidently just seen it, and pulled it on.

"Please," Evelyn said, "please stop getting dressed." He sat back down. "Maybe I want to meet your family now."

He nodded slowly and cradled his beard in a hand, a gesture that she'd come to recognize and adore and that meant he was thinking. "Not yet," he finally said.

She hadn't expected his resoluteness, his certainty on this point.

She'd expected fear and hesitation. She'd expected him to be the Russell she'd come to know. "Why not?"

"I'm not sure."

"You can't just say that. You have to give me an answer." And when he didn't, when he just sat there in his T-shirt and boxer shorts, she said, "You still love your wife. She's asleep and won't ever wake up and you still love her."

Russell glared at her. "Please don't speak about her in that tone."

"I'm sorry," she said.

He nodded, seeming to accept her apology. "I do still love her. I may always love her. But I think I'm getting better . . . slowly. And she's only part of it. Tessa's been through a lot. I'm not sure how she'd take this. And then there's her grandmother. She knows about you. She understands that things may change. In the past years, we've all managed to make a family together. Maybe you'll want to be a part of that family. But maybe you won't. I don't think I want to try it out just yet. I have to be more certain about us. I have to know that we're more than just dating."

"Are we just dating?" Evelyn asked. "Aren't we together? Aren't we a couple?"

Russell shrugged. "I don't know. I've only ever been with Jenny and now with you. I don't have much experience here. Maybe it's just a matter of more time. I think we have to wait."

Evelyn nodded. She wanted them to be a couple now, but in the past she had moved too fast, she'd been pushy, and her relationships of weeks and months had crumbled in days. "OK," she conceded. "We'll wait."

Nonetheless, over the next weeks, Evelyn resented the fact that Russell's house remained off limits to her. She was neither invited as a guest nor was she free (though he'd never said as much) to walk casually down his street and past his small house, as any pedestrian might do without thinking twice.

And so she did. She made a habit of it, in fact, strolling by two or three times a week, overcome by an embarrassing, adolescent urge to be closer to him, to know more about him. Murray Avenue was a quiet side street with small, identical Victorians huddled close together and painted variously in cheerful bright yellows, blues, oranges, and purples. Each house presented a compact, nicely groomed square of yard to the street and a porch just large enough for a small family to lounge on. One afternoon, when Evelyn saw them, Russell and a blond little girl out in the front yard, she could have stopped and turned around. Instead, staying on the opposite side of the street, she kept walking. Surrounded by tulips and begonias, they were kneeling in a rich, dark bed of garden dirt, digging and planting seedlings. The girl wore a red sports jersey, baggy shorts, and what appeared to be black soccer cleats. Tessa did not notice Evelyn, but Russell, a trowel in one hand and a small flowering plant in the other, caught sight of her. For a moment, she stopped and registered the look of confusion on Russell's face. He mouthed a word at her, a single syllable, "go" or "no," followed by a harried and angry wave of his garden tool. Then he turned and sunk the little plant into the dirt as Evelyn, feeling like a stalker, stood still for a moment before hurrying down the sidewalk.

An hour later, wearing the same Levi's cutoffs he'd been working in, Russell was at her front door. His fingernails and bare knees stained with earth, he smelled of sweat and the rich, organic odor of the garden. "I can't come in," he said. He crossed his arms and then uncrossed them. "I like you, Evelyn," he said in a voice that was both determined and hesitant.

Evelyn despised the half-measure of that word. "You *like* me. I want you to more than *like* me."

"I like you a lot," he said, though there was a fierceness in his voice.

"It was nice to see you in your garden," she said now, because, in fact, it had been nice and she wanted him to know it. "It was nice to see Tessa. Does she play soccer? She seemed to be wearing a uniform. She looked darling."

He shook his head. "I have to just say this. I like you, Evelyn, but please don't ever do that again. If you do that again, if you come without being asked, I don't know that I can be with you."

Evelyn felt a rush of hopelessness that turned, with some relief, into anger. "For Christ's sake," she said. "You shook that little shovel at me. You shooed me away." And then: "I don't know that I can be with you either."

He looked at her for a moment, as if trying to make a decision. "All right." He let his arms fall to his side. He stepped off her porch.

"I didn't mean . . . ," she began to say.

"I should go now." He retreated a few more paces, seemed about to say something, and then turned and walked away.

After Russell had stayed away for several days, Evelyn called Heidi and cried. "The situation *was* a little weird," her friend said, trying to comfort her. "You might be better off looking for someone whose wife . . . you know. . . isn't a vegetable." Evelyn had to laugh at this, laugh and weep at the same time.

She was determined to be happy on her own. She had friends, hobbies, and a career, after all. At work, she was in the midst of negotiating what would be her largest contract ever, with Detroit Edison, a deal that looked likely to come through. She would meet other men, she told herself. Yet while she might, after weeks or months, achieve partial happiness alone—she always had in the past—she would have been happier, she was sure, with Russell, with that physically awkward, frightened, emotionally damaged man who could not last ten minutes in intercourse, who would not get in a car, who had been afraid, before meeting Evelyn, of bicycles, for God's sake, but who was good with a hammer, generous, attentive, and tolerant, up to a point, of Evelyn's forcefulness, her inappropriate and inelegant honesty. He'd even rebuilt her garage, the newly painted perfection of which she'd glared at a number of times since he'd stopped coming.

To distract herself from heartbreak, Evelyn biked, took long walks, sipped wine alone on her porch, read, now and then masturbated in the dark of her bedroom, called Heidi in the evenings and talked far too much about Russell until her friend found some excuse to get off the phone. It was late May. The rain had given way to long sunny days, and at the height of afternoon, Evelyn felt the heat of the coming summer. In the parks and the front yards of neighbors, lilac blossoms drooped, wasting away in the heat and saturating the air with a sweet, overripe mustiness.

During the worst of these slow afternoons, Evelyn thought about the last months of her marriage, how Ed had told little lies to explain his increasingly long days at work. He'd had a meeting, or fallen behind on a project and had to stay a few extra hours; he'd been caught up in his workout routine at the gym, or stuck in traffic. She'd been convinced that he'd been having an affair until she ambushed him at his office one night and found him surfing the Web for nothing, not even porn. He had just been reading basketball scores, stats and news, passing time away from her, and in the exchange that followed he had finally told her the truth with a shockingly uncharacteristic directness. "I don't like being around you. I don't *like* you anymore." The fact that her passive, quiet, sad husband, a man who had retreated from her and let her bully him for five years, had been the one to go, to pack his things up, to hire a lawyer and take a job in North Carolina, surprised and infuriated Evelyn even now. She had been incapable of stopping him, of making him like her again. Still more painful, if sadly predictable, witnessing his unlikely forcefulness, his determination to leave her, had made her want him more than ever, had made her want him the way she wanted Russell now.

After a week without Russell, seven days that dragged on because heartbreak was not only painful but boring and laborious, all that time with one stupid, unsophisticated feeling of rejection and hurt, she ran into him at noon on Washington Street. He waved from the opposite curb, and though Evelyn was wearing heels, she trotted over the crosswalk to reach him. He had trimmed his beard and gotten a haircut, but otherwise looked unwell, too thin, pallid and generally diminished in his dark suit, and the overall impression of misery he made left Evelyn feeling overjoyed. "How are you?" he asked with enthusiasm.

"Not well," Evelyn said, though she was smiling and laughed now. "Wretched, in fact."

He nodded. "Yes."

"Yes what?" Evelyn asked.

"Me too." And then, after this wonderful confession, he looked nervously around. "Would you like to walk with me?"

Fortunately, Evelyn had a meeting in a few minutes and was obliged to say no, an answer she could not have otherwise given. He took it badly, nodding too rapidly and seeming to force a smile. "Maybe later this afternoon," she said.

"Good. Excellent." And then an idea came to him, something exciting, she saw, by the way he stood up straight. How much taller he seemed when he felt well. "Would you like to go fly-fishing on the Huron with me this afternoon? The weather is right for it. There should be a hatch this evening, and I can almost guarantee you a fish."

"A hatch?" Evelyn asked.

"Lots of bugs," he said. "The more bugs, the better the fishing."

And though Evelyn had never been fishing, had never particularly wanted to go fishing, and did not like bugs, she accepted.

He dropped by her place later that afternoon on a used, hunter's-orange mountain bike he must have bought over the last week. He wore a shiny turquoise-colored helmet, aviator sunglasses, and a backpack stuffed with gear, and presented a bunch of red and yellow tulips to Evelyn. "From our garden," he said. He was excited and eager to get on the river before twilight, when the mayflies, he explained, would hatch and send the otherwise lethargic bass into a feeding frenzy.

At a small sporting goods shop at the end of Main Street, Russell bought her a fishing license and, as a joke, a baseball hat that read "Kiss My Bass" on the front. Soon they were on the water, where Russell couldn't stop talking about fish and fishing, about how Evelyn was to cast and "present" her fly, allowing it to drift with the current. It was a cloudless, windless day, as hot as any yet that spring, though the river cooled Evelyn down when she stepped into it wearing waist-high waders. In the evening sun, the water took on an otherworldly molten glow marred only by the flotsam of twigs and dead insects. Pairs of bright blue dragonflies—strange, alien creatures—shot through the still air while clouds of tiny bugs circled just above the water in a haze of light and wings. Evelyn was surprised and a little frightened by the force of the current, its slow tug on her legs. Russell stood about five yards downriver, coaching her on her cast. "Use a little wrist and a little elbow. It's just like painting the ceiling," he said. "Imagine you're holding a paintbrush above your head. Now stroke." He threw one elegant cast after another while Evelyn's efforts produced an awkward splash of fly and line that was all wrong, though Russell kept encouraging her—"That's close. Now use a little more wrist"—until she finally managed to lob her fly into the current.

Slowly they worked upstream, casting as they went. Now and then, Evelyn looked over at him, poised above the water, staring intensely at his leader as it drifted with the current, then lifting his line into the air in a backwards arch, gorgeous and seeming for a moment to hover, before he tossed his fly upstream again. He was utterly absorbed by this activity that Evelyn found, in all truth, after only half an hour, tedious. Nonetheless, it was clear to her then—she experienced the unannounced suddenness and simplicity of the feeling even as she teetered in the cumbersome rubber suit and pushed through the water—that she loved him.

"Are you enjoying yourself?" he called over to her.

"Yes," she lied. It was thrilling to see him now, with his floppy green hat, his sunglasses, his graceful command of the rod, and know that she loved him, never mind the fact that above the thick canopy of trees on the opposite bank she could make out in the distance a battery of high buildings that she knew to be part of the huge university hospital where, in one room among thousands, Russell's wife had slept for three years. Was still sleeping now, at this moment.

To avoid this thought, she kept her eyes on the river and struggled to cast her fly into the current. Just as she was settling into a fishing torpor, struggling to appear absorbed, Russell let out a loud, wild call. "This is it," he said. Evelyn shrieked now as a snowy flurry of bugs lifted and fled from the dark glass of the water and fell over her, soft as spider web. Silky multitudes were in her hair, on her arms and bare neck, so fragile and tiny that they seemed to die as soon as they landed on her. She might have stopped, swatted at them, even cried for help had Russell not yelled at her. "Get your fly in the water! This will only last a few minutes longer." The river boiled with fish breaking the surface, their muddy bodies flopping and roiling.

Russell had already caught and released one fish and had another on the line when Evelyn looked up at the blue sky, cloudless, immaculately clear, and, absurdly, imagined herself painting a ceiling; with a simple flick of her wrist, she finally cast her fly into the middle of the frenzy. "You're going to get a hit," Russell said.

And Evelyn felt exactly that—one and then another hit—and now the end of her rod bent low. "Shit! Shit!" She backed up, lost her balance, and nearly fell before she felt her rubber boots sink into the river bottom and grip. She half wanted to let go of the pole and allow whatever was fighting her to win.

"Keep your tip up! Don't let any slack into the line!" Russell was shouting at her now, not with anger but with rough, urgent excitement. "Great. You're doing great." The fish ran upstream, then down, the reel whining like a buzz saw as the line fed out. "Let it go. Let it get tired," he told her. When she finally pulled it in, Russell crouched below her and netted a large, thick-bodied bass, viscous yellow, ugly, bleeding at the mouth and gills, and, as Russell announced, nearly dead. "We'll have to keep this one," he said, taking a good-sized rock from the bank and killing it swiftly with a blow to the head.

"My goodness," she said.

"Congratulations," Russell said. "This will be dinner."

That night, he called from Evelyn's kitchen phone to tell Tessa's grandmother he'd be staying later than expected. Evelyn opened a fine bottle of white wine, and they ate her fish fried in a batter of cornmeal, buttermilk, and eggs with a batch of what Russell called, in a clownish French accent, *pommes frites*, thickly sliced potatoes, pan-fried and seasoned with herbs and salt. After weeks of lovemaking, this was the first meal they'd shared together. They were hungry and ate their greasy, delicious food quickly, though Russell's good manners, the way he had set the table, the cutlery correctly placed and the cloth napkins folded into tents over their salad plates, the way he waited for her to lift her fork before beginning to eat, the way he looked her in the eye when they toasted to more fishing trips, were not lost on Evelyn, who could be picky when it came to small matters of etiquette.

After they made love that night, the first time they'd done so in darkness, Evelyn, resting in his arms, listening to the hushed and constant working of his heart beneath her, had to ask a question. "Did she fish with you?"

"No," Russell said. "Jenny didn't much like that sort of thing."

Evelyn squeezed him tightly and held him like this for a moment. "I do," she said. "I like it a lot."

"Good," he said.

Some hours later, Evelyn woke when she heard Russell getting dressed. "I love you," she said in a dark so thick that she could see nothing.

"Yes," he said.

"Yes, what?"

"I love you, too." She heard him walk over to the bed. He bent down and whispered, "Would you like to meet my family next week?"

Evelyn smiled, thankful that he couldn't see her obvious happiness in this dark. "I would."

And then she heard her bedroom door open and close, and she knew, before falling asleep again, that he was gone.

Three days later, Evelyn met Tessa and Margaret at the house on Murray Avenue for an early dinner. Heidi had warned her to prepare for the worst. "I'm sure the little girl still hopes her mother will come back. She might not be welcoming. And you might want to think about dressing down a little—not looking too pretty." Instead, Evelyn wore her nicest blue sundress, blue being the color that complemented her most, brought a bottle of wine and a dozen orchids, which turned out to be unnecessary in this house surrounded by garden beds of irises, tulips, daisies, and other flowering plants and bushes that Evelyn could not name.

"This is my good friend Evelyn," Russell said, introducing her to his family on the front porch. They'd all dressed nicely, too: the grandmother in a white blouse and yellow skirt, a surprisingly youthful outfit for this woman who wore her gray hair in a tight coil, and the girl in a green dress with a lace collar. The girl's long blond hair had been fussed over, pulled into a braid held together by brightly colored barrettes. They all shook hands, after which Tessa stepped back, behind her father, from where she stared at Evelyn with obvious perplexity. Evelyn had never felt comfortable around children—their high volume, their fierce likes and dislikes, their blatant honesty and unchecked emotions—even if she'd always wanted to have at least one child of her own. In the last weeks, she'd caught herself wondering what it might be like to assume a maternal role toward another woman's child. But now that she stood before the girl, she was surprised by a rush of anxiety, even as she forced herself to bend down, smile, and say, in her sweetest voice, "I've heard a lot about you, Tessa." The girl stepped out from behind the shelter of her father now and twirled, her dress flaring out. When she faced Evelyn again, Tessa was smiling, and Evelyn felt relieved; for whatever reason, this gorgeous little girl seemed to like her, at least for the moment.

"Welcome," Margaret said in a voice that was polite, if not entirely warm.

Out back, Russell donned an apron and presided over the fire with an easy authority, a large grill fork in one hand and a spatula in the other, while Tessa took Evelyn on a tour of the flowerbeds. "I'm responsible for the backyard," she said. "I water twice a day, in the morning and evening. It's better to water when it's cooler. And earlier in the spring, I keep the squirrels away from the tulip bulbs; they like to dig them up and bury them at the neighbor's so that next spring our tulips come up in someone else's yard." After telling Evelyn of the thieving squirrels, Tessa smiled mischievously. "You're my dad's girlfriend, aren't you?" she whispered.

"Well," Evelyn said, flustered.

Tessa nodded. "I thought so."

They sat out on the back porch for dinner and talked about harmless topics—the cold, long winter that had recently ended, Tessa's soccer league, and Russell's latest project, a stone path through the flowerbeds, which he'd start on next week. In the shallow darkness lightning bugs drifted by, and Russell lit citronella candles to keep the mosquitoes away. Now and then, the rattle of locusts began in the distance, crescendoed, and all at once ceased. While Tessa remained talkative, if increasingly tired, sprawled in her father's lap, Margaret was reserved, listening too carefully to Evelyn, nodding at her every word, and seeming to watch her so closely that Evelyn became self-conscious whenever she looked at Russell and made sure she did so without obvious affection.

It was not until Russell had gone upstairs to put Tessa to bed that the two women, Margaret at the kitchen sink rinsing wineglasses and Evelyn loading the dishwasher, talked more openly. "Tessa's wonderful," Evelyn said, wanting to break the silence of the last few moments. "In fact, to tell you the truth, I was worried that Tessa, for obvious reasons, wouldn't much like me."

Margaret had just turned the water off and faced Evelyn now. "Yes, she is a wonderful girl. And it's more than clear that she likes you."

"But you don't like me," Evelyn said, responding to the elderly woman's chilly tone.

"No," Margaret said, "it's not that. It's that I don't know you yet. I'm sure you're lovely. Russell is very taken with you. Of course, you're aware of his feelings." Margaret smiled briefly, but her tone remained guarded. "I should tell you that I have no illusions about my daughter. She is not at all likely to return to us. At the same time, I still struggle with wanting things to be otherwise. I still hope. And I think I can say for Russell that he still hopes, too. It is not impossible, you know, that she could return. It is only nearly impossible." Margaret took a dishcloth from the counter and began drying her hands vigorously.

"Russell tells me the chances are a million to one."

To this, Margaret snapped back, "There is a chance, isn't there?"

"Perhaps I should go," Evelyn said.

Margaret shook her head. "I'm sorry. I've been rude. But you'll understand, won't you, that it's different: the way a mother sees her daughter and the way a husband sees his wife? A man can always go out and find someone else. My daughter will always be my daughter, no matter what happens." Her voice had become angry, and she paused, surveying the wiped surfaces of the kitchen, before looking at Evelyn again. When she spoke now, her anger was gone. "Russell has been without a companion for years. I can certainly understand that he'd want . . . that he has his needs. In any case, he tells me that you're serious about him."

"Yes."

Margaret nodded, not to approve but merely to register Evelyn's brief answer. "I should tell you, if Russell has not already, that we've considered letting her go. We've considered stopping food and water, but I haven't been able to reconcile myself to taking an active role in terminating her life. I think Russell might do so if it were just his decision to make."

"I'm not sure why you're telling me this," Evelyn said, noting how practiced and calculated Margaret's speech had seemed.

"With you," Margaret said, "there might be added pressure."

"There won't be added pressure." Evelyn felt her voice rise, but Margaret did not seem at all ruffled.

"Good," she said, folding the dishcloth, placing it resolutely on the countertop, and making it clear with this gesture that they could move on to other topics of conversation.

By early June the thunderstorm season had ended and left the river level high and its waters full of debris and insects, so that the fish, Russell claimed, were more eager to feed on the surface. Evelyn's cast improved and Russell became more at ease on his bike, though he was cautious in ways that irritated Evelyn and, at times, drove her to provoke him. Russell would never, for instance, run a red light, even if no cars were visible for blocks in either direction. He cycled on the sidewalks whenever possible while Evelyn, not about to satisfy his paranoia and avoid the traffic with him, especially when there was no traffic, rode beside him in the street. She even made a show of it. "Look," she'd say, lifting her arms into the air, "no hands." During breaks in traffic, she ran red lights and waited for him on the other side of the intersection until the light turned green.

On a breezy, sunny afternoon, at the end of a long ride, Evelyn, fed up with Russell, who was waiting at the crosswalk, shot into the intersection of Huron and Main just as a Ford Explorer had been about to take a left turn on a green light. Though Evelyn and the Explorer stopped, easily avoiding a collision, Russell began shouting at her from the corner. "Get off!"

"What?" Evelyn was still in the middle of the intersection, and a car behind the Explorer began honking.

"I said to get off. We're walking." The anger in his voice made Evelyn comply.

Without talking, they walked their bikes down Huron, passing the meager oak saplings that the city had just planted at intervals along the pavement. "I don't understand why you're so upset," Evelyn finally said. "That wasn't even close." He just kept walking, determined, it seemed, to remain silent, and Evelyn mounted her bike and rode into the street again. "I won't let you bully me. I won't."

He stopped then, and so did Evelyn. A car whipped past her. His face was red and streaked with sweat. "Please get out of the road."

"No," she said.

"You do this on purpose," Russell said. "You run red lights, you ride too fast. And I don't know why you do it."

"I can't always be afraid."

"You almost . . . you almost got," he began to say.

"I didn't almost get anything."

Russell shook his head and let out a long breath, after which his shoulders seemed to collapse, as if he were conceding the point. "Please," he said. "Please just walk with me for now. Tomorrow you can ride in the streets. You can do whatever you want."

And because he was pleading with her, Evelyn got off and walked beside him on the sidewalk.

Minutes later, after they had closed Evelyn's front door behind them, Russell surprised her by removing the keys from her hand, kissing her rapidly, without tenderness or passion, and lowering her to the dining room floor. He stripped her tight biking pants off, pulling her panties with them and yanking them over her shoes. "I'm all sweaty, Russell," she said, wanting to slow him down. His hand was on her crotch and he was kissing her mouth forcefully. The throw rug dug into the skin over her tailbone; she yelled out for a pillow, and he grabbed one from a chair and shoved it beneath her. She grasped onto a table leg while he entered her, moving with enough force to make the ceiling light fixture sway. His hands gripped her shoulders, holding her down, in place, while he came, after which he lifted himself off her and rolled onto his back.

Evelyn lay quietly, looking at the myriad legs of the table and chairs rising above her and the jigsaw scraps of early evening light scattered over the floor. "I didn't like that," she said. It wasn't that she'd felt coerced or violated. It was the fact that what he'd done had been all for himself. The way he'd held her, the way he'd moved, finished, then retreated. She hadn't been necessary. She'd felt like anyone, any woman being fucked too quickly. "You seemed far away," she said.

"There are worse things, Evelyn, than death." He was still breathing hard from his exertion, and there was an edge of meanness in his voice. It occurred to Evelyn that he'd been furious with her the whole time he'd been inside her. "I know that firsthand. Most people don't. Most people never even think about it."

"Don't, please, bring her up after we've just had . . ."

"I know it," he said. "I know it firsthand." He stopped himself and let out a breath. "I'm sorry."

But he didn't sound sorry, and Evelyn felt even angrier at the thought of how he'd treated her, how he'd taken her on the floor just now, how he'd been thinking of his wife, of his tragedy. He must have thought of her constantly, every minute of the day, every time he saw a car drive past, every time he mounted his bike, every time he fucked Evelyn. "I want to know something," she said. "What would you do if she woke up one day and was herself again?"

"That's not possible," Russell said.

"I'm asking it anyway."

"I'm not answering it." They were lying side by side, not looking at each other and not touching.

"Margaret had a talk with me last week," Evelyn said. "She told me that you still hoped Jenny would come back."

"Do you want me to say that I don't?"

"She told me that you two had considered letting her go, but decided against it. Margaret worries that our relationship might influence you, might pressure you into reconsidering."

"Is that what you're doing now?" Russell said, calmly, as if he'd just understood something. "Are you pressuring me?"

"If it's really impossible for her to wake up," Evelyn asked, "if she's really gone forever, why don't you let her go?"

"I see." There was a fierce tremor in his voice now.

"While you fuck me, you think of her," Evelyn said. "You think of her the whole time. What would you do? What if she woke up tomorrow and asked for you?"

"All right," he said, sitting up on his elbows. "I'd go with her. I'd leave whomever I was with, and I'd go with her. She was Tessa's mother. She was my wife for nearly twenty years."

He had raised his voice. He'd spoken out of anger. But Evelyn understood that he had also spoken honestly, and for that she was both furious and grateful. "Thank you for answering my question," she said. "I'd like you to go now. Please."

The next afternoon, Russell showed up at her front door, his shoulders slouched in a posture of exhaustion and defeat that Evelyn recognized now and that made him seem, despite his size, small. "I didn't sleep much last night," he said. "I owe you an apology. I'm sorry. I really am."

"Me, too," Evelyn said. She had planned on delivering a speech about taking a few weeks apart, a small break from each other. But she hesitated now. His hair was uncombed, his face drawn and bloodless, and seeing him in despair made Evelyn want to stay with him until he felt better.

He shrugged. "I'm no good to anyone, I'm afraid."

"I'm not perfect either." And then Evelyn added, "This might not work. I'm not saying we shouldn't keep trying. I'm just saying that we might not want to get our hopes up."

Russell put his hands in his pockets, took a deep breath, and nodded. "I won't hope too much, and I'll keep trying."

"Me, too," Evelyn said, feeling relieved and already too hopeful.

That weekend she and Russell went out on the river again. It was a windy afternoon, and the water rippled with the changing directions of sudden gusts. Wind-torn branches and maple leaves floated by. Drifting with the current, canoers—a father and son, a girlfriend and boyfriend—waved at Russell and Evelyn. Russell had already pulled in two small-mouth bass while Evelyn struggled more than ever to control her casts in the wind. She caught her line three times in the thick growth on the riverbank before giving up and retreating to a patch of grass, where she sat and watched Russell, up to his thighs in water, gracefully lobbing his line into a ripple.

She'd wanted so much to like fishing, because Jenny had not, and because this shared activity might somehow sustain them, keep them going despite an ornery mother-in-law and Russell's maddening fear. But Evelyn was tired of her jealousy and didn't much like the person she was becoming under its influence. Even as she sat back and admired this lanky, tall, surprisingly agile man, she imagined how they'd eventually ask each other for space. She wanted to be the first to do it, to have at least that little bit of satisfaction and power, and to avoid the familiar humiliation of rejection, of all those men who'd never called her back and, even more urgently, the helplessness she'd felt when her ex-husband had left, had ceased to like her, and nothing—not begging, not threatening, not crying, not yelling, not even feigning indifference—would change his mind.

No doubt Russell, gentle, lovely Russell, would let her end it without trying to seize the initiative, to hurt her back. He'd likely apologize, say how sorry he was for them to come to this. Then he would leave her alone. This thought made her want him more; and so, sitting on the grass in a patch of warm sun, the breeze on her face, she saw that she was already hopeless, that she wanted him and could not be with him. Nonetheless, on the long, slow bike ride into town, she behaved herself, staying behind him on the sidewalk. At the busy intersection of Ashley and Huron, where she'd come to a stop ahead of him, her front tire sticking out into the street just a little, and perhaps, she had to admit to herself, intentionally, as a test for Russell, she felt the bike go rigid beneath her. When she turned, she saw that Russell had grabbed her seat post. "What?" she said. "Let go."

"You were about to . . ."

"I'm not going out into that," she said, gesturing at the traffic rushing by and feeling more upset than she wanted to be.

Russell looked down at his hand and let go. "I can't help myself, can I?" he said, his voice frustrated and angry. He shrugged now, as if he too had given up.

And, of course, he was right. They couldn't help themselves. He'd continue to irritate her and she'd continue to provoke him. They'd push each other until they had nothing but aggravation between them. And so she'd ride, she told herself now, however the hell she wanted to. At the next intersection, against a red light but with no cars in sight, she sped through, glancing back at Russell's terrified face so that she didn't see the car until it struck her. She felt the incredible lightness of her body hurtling forward, the air sucked from her lungs, the impact against the hood, a thud so deep, so all-encompassing, thrumming through her thighs, her torso, her ribs, her head, that it seemed to come from inside Evelyn. Her bike was gone, nowhere to be seen. A girl—the driver, perhaps—stood out of the car. "The light was green. The light was green. I didn't see her," she was saying. Russell, in his silly helmet, was galloping toward them and yelling, "Help us! Help us!" Evelyn stood up and saw flecks of blood and smudges of road tar on her hands. Her helmet—somehow it had come off—lay in the asphalt gutter. Very slowly she lowered herself back down to the street. People at a sidewalk café abandoned their tables, rushing toward her, and a man in a tank top—the words "Peace Despite Everything!" emblazoned over the chest—spoke loudly on his cell phone. Bending over her now, Russell said, "You're OK. You're OK," and she knew, from the expression on his face, that she couldn't have been.

Evelyn was in the hallway of a hospital, ceiling tiles and rectangular fluorescent lights in their silver ice-cube trays above her. There was the sound of a child crying somewhere, and she was trying to remember how she'd gotten here and was able to piece together images of a fire truck, an ambulance, a man's steel-toed boot, a woman with a pie-shaped face and a reassuring smile saying, "How are you, Evelyn? Can you move your fingers for us? Your legs? Good. That's very good." And now, in the hallway, a young male doctor asked her to count backwards from twenty and then to recite her home phone number and her address, and in the middle of this recitation Evelyn began to cry, tears taking her over, their force mysterious and irresistible. And then she understood why she was crying. "Russell," she said. "Where is Russell?" Finally, pale-faced, his eyes frantic, he stood over her and took her hand. His thick hair was smashed and lopsided the way it got after he'd worn his bike helmet. "I'm here," he said. "Right here."

Then it was dark, it was nighttime, and Evelyn saw white butterflies flitting above the thick, molten river, swirling with eddies and undertows. Russell was casting and casting, and the shadowy form of a fish rose to his fly, then folded into the dark river again. She slipped under the water with the fish and couldn't seem to struggle back to the surface again. And because it was easier, she allowed the cold current to take her. "They don't want you to sleep for more than a few hours at a time," Russell said now. She realized that she was awake and he was sitting beside her, a blue curtain at his back. "It's important that we make sure you're OK. You have a concussion." He asked her a series of remedial questions. "What's your name? Can you say your name for me?"

"Evelyn," she said, smiling. "You're here," she said. "You're here."

"And my name? Who am I?"

"You're Russell." And then: "Am I hurt badly?"

"No," he said, and despite the trembling in his voice, she believed him. "They just want to watch you for a day or so. They had to give you stitches. You cut your head."

She sat up. "I feel good. I feel . . ." But she felt a heavy ache behind her eyes, and when she put her hand to her chin it felt at once too close and too far away. She lay back down.

"You'll be fine," he said. "You'll be as good as new in a day or two." His hand was shaking in hers, and she understood then that he was the frightened one. She understood how hard it must have been for him to return to this place, the beds and stretchers and wheelchairs terribly familiar from the hours and weeks and months he'd passed in waiting rooms, wanting everything to be all right when nothing was.

"I did it on purpose," she said. "I rode out into the intersection. I wanted you to see that there was nothing to be afraid of." She shook her head. "More than anything, I did it to piss you off. But I didn't see that car. I didn't see anything. I know you're always thinking about what happened to her. And I just wanted to make you forget it. I'm sorry. You must be furious with me."

He closed his eyes and squeezed her hand more tightly. "Later," he said. "I'll be furious later. You can sleep again if you like."

When she woke next, it was daylight, and Russell, eyes puffy and ringed with purple, sat beside her with a cup of coffee in hand and a copy of *Newsweek* in his lap. He was still wearing the clothes he had fished in—his Levi's torn out in the knees and his Michigan Wilderness T-shirt. He hadn't showered, hadn't even gone home, Evelyn guessed. On her bedside table sat a vase of red and yellow tulips. "Those are from the garden," Russell said. "Margaret brought them over earlier this morning."

Evelyn felt surprisingly well. She sat up and stretched her arms above her head. "That was nice of her," Evelyn said. Then she laughed. "Margaret doesn't think much of me."

"She brought you flowers, didn't she?"

She passed her hand over her head, discovering the wiry lattice of stitches in her scalp. "Fifteen," Russell said.

"She's right, you know. She's absolutely right not to like me." She gestured at the tulips. "They're beautiful, but I bet she brought them for you. I bet she feels terrible that I'm putting you through something like this all over again." Russell shook his head and tried to smile, but there was a blankness, a helpless exhaustion in his face that told her the truth. "You didn't go home last night. You probably didn't even sleep. And I did that to you."

"I'm fine," he said.

"I put you through hell."

He looked away, toward the TV on the wall opposite her, and nodded. "Yes," he said, "you did."

Later that morning, she was taken in a wheelchair to radiology and learned that she had sustained a minor fracture in her left fibula. They put her in a bulky plastic boot, which she'd have to wear only a few weeks and in which she could walk without the aid of crutches. Otherwise she was fine, and her doctors told her she'd be released that evening. Though she insisted that Russell go to work, he stayed through the day and they played game after game of checkers, between which she rose from bed and practiced hobbling around the room in her plastic cast. After picking over a terrible lunch, they switched from checkers to chess, and just when Evelyn had been about to seize his queen with her knight, she looked up to find that Russell's head was down and that he was sleeping.

When he woke a few hours later, she greeted him with a kiss and then had a question. "She's here, isn't she? In another room somewhere?"

"Yes," he said, "she's here."

"Can I ask you something . . . something you can say no to?"

He nodded.

"Could we visit her before we leave?"

He pulled away from her then, sitting back in his chair. "I don't understand. Why would you want to do that?"

"It's all so unreal," she said. "Your past and everything that's happened to you . . . Maybe I'd just like to know more, to understand more. You can say no. I won't mind at all."

He looked away, out the window, and after a moment shook his head in a gesture that seemed to mean no. But he stood up now and rolled the wheelchair over to her bed. "You have to realize," Russell said, "that she's not herself anymore. She doesn't even look like herself."

"I understand," Evelyn said.

After asking a nurse for permission to take Evelyn off the ward, Russell rolled her down the hall, into the deep vault of an elevator meant to hold several hospital beds, down another hall, and over a sky bridge alit with an orange evening sunlight so effusive and luminous that Evelyn had to squint. Finally they came to a reception desk, in front of which a corkboard, set on an easel, announced, "Arboretum Summer Outing This Saturday" and "Mrs. Harriet Becker celebrates her birthday tonight in the Events Room. She invites one and all to join her for cake and ice cream." A skinny male nurse sitting at the desk greeted Russell by his first name, and an awkward moment, in which the nurse noticed Evelyn and seemed to stop himself from asking Russell about her, hovered in the air. "She's a friend," Russell said quickly, and the nurse nodded.

Russell wheeled her down the hall and stopped in front of what must have been the door to his wife's room. "I've never done this before," he said. "I've never brought anyone to see her. I want to check on her first. I want to make sure she looks . . . she looks presentable."

"Of course," Evelyn said. He opened the door quietly and closed it behind him just as quietly, as if not to wake a sleeper. During his absence, a very old woman dressed in what seemed to be several layers of pajamas and robes took impossibly tiny steps behind her aluminum walker as she passed Evelyn and made her way down the hall. When Russell opened the door again, she saw, just behind him, a wedge of evening light coloring the air a soft burgundy. "OK," he said, and he wheeled her inside.

The room held a bed, a normal bed with a headboard that might have been in any bedroom or hotel, and a side table on which sat a small digital clock, one hour fast, and a vase of freshly cut flowers, red and yellow tulips, so that Evelyn knew immediately that Margaret had also visited her daughter that day. A plastic chair sat at the bedside, and from a west-facing window light fell into the room. The woman, Russell's wife, her arms at her sides, wore a yellow terrycloth house robe that any healthy woman might wear. Evelyn noticed purple bruising just above the ankles. "Bedsores," Russell told her, and he arranged the robe to cover them.

He pulled Evelyn's chair up to the bed and sat down next to her; she took his hand, felt him stiffen, and so let go again. "We might have to leave soon."

"Of course," Evelyn said.

"It doesn't feel right—letting you see her like this. She cared a great deal about how she looked, and she used to be so much more . . . more beautiful."

"She still is beautiful," Evelyn said. In fact, she wasn't. She was hard in some ways to see at all. Her hair was cut short, like a boy's, and her head seemed too large for the small body beneath the sheets. The adultness of her face, the sharpness and distinctness of her features, had faded, been erased, perhaps from so much sleep and stillness, so that she looked like a child of indeterminate gender that was somehow not young.

"They cut her hair short because it's easier to clean that way." He took in a deep breath, and without looking at Evelyn he said, quietly but with an edge of anger that she hadn't expected, "This is what you wanted to see, isn't it?" He turned and glared at her. "Damn it," he said, and Evelyn understood then that this was the fury he'd held back until now, the anger he'd been saving for her since last night. "You can see it, can't you? You can see that she's not going to wake up. You can see that. It's pretty damn clear, I'd say."

Evelyn sat quietly, waiting, hoping this would pass, and Russell reached out, snatched the small digital clock from the bedside table, and reset it to the correct time. She could see from the way he hit the plastic tabs that he was still angry, but when he set the clock back down, he did so gently and with great care. He let out a long sigh that became a moan, then bent over and began crying so softly that Evelyn could hear only the jagged little breaths he took in. She wanted to touch him, but stopped herself. After some time, he sat up and rubbed his eyes. "I shouldn't have said that," he said. "I'm tired. I'm worn out."

"It's all right." And then, after a moment, Evelyn asked, "How did it happen? You don't have to say if you don't want to. But I'd like to know."

He nodded and let out a humorless laugh. "It wasn't even a bad accident," he said. "Tessa was making a fuss in her carseat in the back, and Jenny took her seatbelt off. Just for a moment. You know, to fix whatever was wrong back there. Someone turning left ran a stop sign. Drove right through it. Jenny had been leaning into the backseat. Her body flew half the distance of the car. She hit the windshield. Nothing happened to Tessa and me. We didn't get a scratch. We had an old car with no air bag. An old Volvo. A tank, you know. We'd decided on that car. All those stories about kids dying from air bags scared us. Scared me, I should say. Of course, if we'd had a car with air bags, a normal car, Jenny wouldn't be here now." He looked at Evelyn and smiled a little. "I've always been overly cautious, even before all this. Even as a kid. I've always been a worrier. Jenny never thought twice about taking small risks, reasonable risks. I used to hate it when we'd go to the coast, to Lake Michigan for a weekend.

She liked to swim out a little ways—out where it was deep. She was a strong swimmer, but that worried me." He shook his head. "She'd even do it because she knew it bothered me. I'd guess you know what I'm talking about."

Evelyn felt a hot rush of guilt.

"I know I'm difficult that way," he said. "I know I'm paranoid. It used to drive Jenny crazy, and I can see that I'm doing the same to you. And I'm sorry, but I can't help it." He shook his head. "I tell Tessa not to climb on the maple tree in our backyard, and as soon as I turn my head she does it. It's a good tree for climbing, with low limbs. She never climbs too high. Sometimes when I look out the kitchen window and see her doing it, I make myself look the other way. I make myself go do something to take my mind off it. But I can't just tell her to go ahead and climb it . . . because if something did happen . . . if she fell and I had told her she could do it . . ."

He made a fist. "I didn't like it when anyone in my car took a seatbelt off. Even for a moment. But I didn't stop Jenny from doing it that day. I didn't say anything. I try to convince myself that it wasn't her fault for doing something that any mother would have done. I try to convince myself that it had nothing to do with Tessa, with making a fuss, just being a kid. She was three then and doesn't remember any of this, thank God. I didn't see that bastard who ran the stop sign. I didn't see him until he'd hit us." He put his hands on his knees and took in a deep breath. "Anyway," he said, "this is her. This is Jenny."

The wedge of light in the room had retreated, but it was sunset and still bright in the distance. Evelyn took Russell's hand again, squeezing it firmly. "I'm sorry," she said, only now realizing she had never before offered her condolences. "I'm sorry that this ever happened to you."

He nodded, and Evelyn felt his hand tighten around hers.

A few days after returning home from the hospital, Evelyn answered the front door and greeted a fireman, his red SUV parked in her driveway, who held at his side what was left of her mountain bike, the front wheel bent, a handlebar splayed back, and the crank shaft smashed and dangling in its casing. "This would be yours," he said, smiling. "I'd say you were very lucky. We're glad to see that you're OK."

"My God," Evelyn said.

A week later her stitches were removed, and a week after that her plastic brace came off, and she was, as Russell had said she would be, as good as new.

In late June the heat came and the air was still and the afternoons were long and unrelentingly bright. On the banks of the Huron, mosquitoes, born in the sticky humidity, thrived and tormented Evelyn, who coated herself in bug dope to no avail and spent most of her energy fighting off these pests and scratching the welts they left on her arms. After an hour or two on the river, she and Russell would return to her place and, in the cooling half-dark of evening, make love. Fishing and sex had somehow been paired in their relationship, and when Russell was inside her she could still smell the scents of the river on him—the damp earth, the weeds and grasses. "I feel guilty," Russell confessed one evening after they had finished. "I feel guilty for wanting you so much."

Evelyn lay still beside him, naked in the warm air, and felt a familiar frustration at the fact that Russell had once again brought up his tragedy in the wake of their lovemaking. Yet when had Ed, her grumpy, taciturn ex-husband, who would nod, say yes, say everything was just fine when nothing was, who'd sit on a grudge for weeks or months at a time, ever come out and simply told her how he felt? And so she remained silent. She listened. "We didn't have much sex. Not in our last years. It wasn't that we didn't love each other. It was the opposite, really. We'd loved each other so much and for so long that we didn't have as much desire somehow. Of course, there was Tessa, too. She changed things. And earlier, when we had sex often, in high school and afterwards, it was . . ." He laughed, then started giggling in an infectious way that compelled Evelyn to laugh with him. "You know . . . awkward. Not very skilled. We'd never had sex before. Neither of us. It got better, but never this good, never this . . ." He paused. He searched for the word and discovered it suddenly. "Wonderful. So I feel guilty."

Evelyn didn't say it, but she felt it and wanted to say it. She was glad their sex was better. She was happy to have bested his sleeping wife in this way. She turned, kissed him, and offered her own confession. "I hate fishing. I wanted to like it. I wanted to fish with you because Jenny didn't."

He laughed. "That's fine. I'm happy fishing by myself."

For some weeks, Evelyn and Russell gave up biking and took long walks instead. They walked through the Old West Side, the houses quiet in the heat, or strolled through the university campus, mostly deserted save for a few summer students, who studied in the shade of trees, and gangs of bare-chested adolescent boys on skateboards and roller blades, who sped over the wide sidewalks.

"Do you think we're serious yet?" Russell asked one afternoon. They'd just sat down on a stone bench in front of the engineering building, where one such gang, shirtless and wearing helmets, performed increasingly dangerous stunts on the entryway stairs, at the top of which each boy would break into a sprint, leap to the hand railing, and ride—skates sideways—the metal bar, as a surfer might ride a wave, to the bottom. "Jesus," Russell said.

"Serious?" Evelyn said.

"I mean," he said, "should we be hopeful? Are we more than just dating?" They looked on as a boy lost his balance, landed butt-down on the rail, bounced off and fell to the concrete steps, from where he sprang to his feet and, rubbing his backside, climbed the stairs to try again.

"Nice butt plant, dude!" one of the boys shouted in mock admiration.

"They're made of rubber," Evelyn said. "You don't have to worry about them." And then she added, "I'm hopeful. I'm more than just dating, if you are. If you want me to be."

He looked away from the boys and at Evelyn. "I do."

In the weeks that followed, they ate plenty of meals together, dinners and lunches, breakfasts on Saturdays and brunches on Sundays. Occasionally, they met at Evelyn's house in the evenings, where she would prepare a meal for Russell and make love to him afterwards. More often, they ate with Tessa and Margaret, who remained distant and watchful, if not openly hostile. Evelyn could—and did—come over unannounced. She began gardening with Russell and Tessa while Margaret, whose knees were bad, sat on the porch and read. Evelyn attended Tessa's soccer games at ten on Saturday mornings in West Park and cheered with more enthusiasm than she'd thought herself capable of where sports were concerned. On the Fourth of July, she threw a party, inviting Heidi, Michael, and their boys, Dennis and Chad, to meet Russell and his family. They ate bratwurst that Russell barbecued in the backyard and Evelyn's favorite summer dish, a grilled vegetable and potato salad slathered in olive oil and balsamic vinegar. Heidi and Evelyn lifted glasses, toasting their latest and biggest success, the contract they had just signed with Detroit Edison. "To tracking your kilowatt use online and paying your electric bill in cyberspace," Heidi said. Later, they watched a distant fireworks display from Evelyn's porch and, despite Russell's hesitation and worry, set off a small number of fireworks in the street for Tessa and the boys.

One afternoon, Evelyn answered her front door and was surprised to see Margaret, dressed in shorts, a white shirt, and large white summer hat. When she took her hat off, she was sweating, and her expression was severe and businesslike. "I came to visit with you," she said, not sounding particularly friendly.

Evelyn poured two glasses of iced tea, and they sat on the screened-in porch where Margaret spoke of the summer day camp Tessa attended and the little girl's love for gardening with her father. After she'd finished her tea, Margaret sat up stiffly and said, "I came here to ask you something." Her fine, pointed features—her chin, her narrow nose, her deep-set eyes—gathered intensity.

"OK," Evelyn said.

"Russell has been different recently, different in a good way. He's a fearful person. I'm sure you know all about that by now."

Margaret looked at her then, pausing, so that Evelyn felt obliged to nod, to confirm that she did in fact know about this side of Russell.

"He has always been fearful, but what happened to Jenny made him even more so. Lately, he's been both happy and miserable. He's been"—she pursed her lips, searching for the word—"tumultuous. You know that your accident almost finished him. And he's stood up to me on several occasions. I've not been entirely approving of his frequent afternoon visits to your house. But he hasn't let me dissuade him. That's rare for Russell. I didn't like it at first. And it's still hard for me. I'll admit that. But I was wrong. It's been good for him. Evidently, you've been good for him."

Evelyn smiled. "I'm glad you think so."

But this concession seemed difficult for Margaret, who gave Evelyn only the slightest smile before continuing. "I have one more thing to add. I only want to say that I hope very much that you won't play with him. I understand that people do that these days. They're with someone for a while and then they're not. I have nothing against that, per se. But Russell needs more than that. And Tessa needs more than that."

Evelyn should have been angry at this old woman's nosiness, her extreme presumption, but she wasn't. It was clear to her that, if she were to become in some way a part of this family, she would not be the only "force," as Russell had called her, to contend with. "I don't intend to play with him. I want more than that, too."

"Well, then," Margaret said, and nodded approvingly.

On a Saturday morning at one of Tessa's soccer games, Russell told Evelyn that Jenny might be dying. They'd been walking beneath the giant maples that bordered the park, waiting for the second half to begin.

"Oh," Evelyn said, experiencing a physical sensation of relief, a lightening in her chest, at hearing him say so, and wishing she had felt something more appropriate.

"It's not the first time we've thought so," he explained. "Her kidneys seem to be failing. They're not sure why. Margaret and I made the decision not to interfere. The decision had nothing to do with you. We made it months ago."

Evelyn nodded. She was relieved to hear this, too.

"Of course, she might not die. She might keep living for years. And if she did, I wouldn't quite know what to do, should we . . . you and I . . . want more, want . . ." He stopped walking and faced her now. "To marry." Neither of them had brought up this possibility before, and Evelyn was so surprised, so blatantly happy, that she had to hold back a smile. "It might be that in a few years I would feel OK about filing for divorce. After all, that would just be a technicality. But I'm not sure I could do it."

In the distance, the girls were huddled on their separate sidelines and listening to their coaches. Evelyn took Russell's hand and said, even as she imagined him standing before a justice of the peace, nervous and very handsome in a tuxedo, "You don't need to do that. I'd understand. Besides, I've been married. I don't have to do that again anytime soon."

Russell shook his head, then looked up into the leafy canopy. "Oh, God," he said. "Sometimes I wish she'd just go. She'd just finally go. But I'm not sure what I could or couldn't do if she didn't." He looked down at Evelyn now. "Is that OK?"

She kissed him on the cheek. "It's going to have to be," she said, though in truth she felt the familiar anxiety rush through her that somehow, improbable though it might be, his sleeping wife might wake up, might step out of bed one day and take everything from Evelyn.

In the weeks since her accident, she'd left her wrecked bike in the garage and felt a shiver of dread whenever she saw it. Nonetheless, she hadn't expected her hesitation on the morning of her forty-fourth birthday when Russell knocked on her door with a new mountain bike, fire-truck red, beside him. "Happy birthday," he said. He handed her a jet-black helmet. "I've been missing our bike rides. I thought you might like to take a birthday jaunt. So long as you promise to look both ways before you cross the street."

Evelyn laughed, hoping he wouldn't notice her nervousness. "I promise."

Some minutes later, after Russell had pedaled out of the driveway and down the sidewalk, Evelyn froze on her bike. She gripped the hand brakes tightly, leaning forward and testing the feel of the seat beneath her, then closed her eyes, opened them again, and pushed off. The concrete rushed too suddenly beneath her, and the bike seemed unfamiliar and wobbly, a strange, dangerous thing, with nothing but air and pedals at her feet. She steadied herself and followed Russell through the neighborhoods, stopping when he stopped, crossing the streets just behind him. When they pulled onto Main Street, teeming with afternoon traffic, Evelyn felt her body tense, her arms and shoulders flex, each time a car whipped past her, each time the rush of air and furious sound threatened to topple her. She kept her eyes on the narrow shoulder of the road and tried not to imagine what would become of her should she swerve out too far. The worst could happen. Anything could happen. But it wouldn't, she told herself. And once they'd reached Huron River Way, quieter and less traveled, she took in deep, steadying breaths and began to enjoy the cool shade of trees, taking in the blue sky and feeling the warm air part for her as she sped forward. When she pulled alongside Russell, he lifted a hand with surprising calm from the handlebars and pointed at something out on the river that he wanted her to see.

Acknowledgments

I would like to express my gratitude to the Michigan Council for the Arts and Cultural Affairs for their generous financial support of this project. I am also grateful for the support of the English Department and the College of Liberal Arts at the University of Massachusetts-Boston. Many thanks to Sheilah Coleman, Joshua Henkin, Christopher Shainin, and Ian Reed Twiss, who read drafts of these stories and helped make this a better book; to Dr. Paul Sorum, who advised me on medical details; to Carol Stein, for the cover; to Alicka Pistik, my agent; to John Sarnecki and Mary-Catherine Harrison, for their enduring friendship; and to all the people at LSU Press who brought this book into being, especially Michael Giffith, a thorough, smart, and incredibly generous editor. Finally, I owe my greatest debt of gratitude to Eve, for her advice, her willingness to be my first and last reader, and her love.